WEST OF THE PECOS

WEST OF THE PECOS

PECOS

A Western Story

ZANE GREY

Skyhorse Publishing

First Skyhorse Publishing edition 2016 by arrangement with Golden West Literary Agency

Copyright © 1931 by Crowell Publishing Company
Copyright © 1937 by Zane Grey
Copyright © renewed 1959, 1965 by Romer Zane Grey, Loren Zane Grey, Betty Grey Grosso

Skyhorse Publishing books may be purchased in bulk at special discounts for sales promotion, corporate gifts, fund-raising, or educational purposes. Special editions can also be created to specifications. For details, contact the Special Sales Department, Skyhorse Publishing, 307 West 36th Street, 11th Floor, New York, NY 10018 or info@skyhorsepublishing.com.

Skyhorse® and Skyhorse Publishing® are registered trademarks of Skyhorse Publishing, Inc.®, a Delaware corporation.

Visit our website at www.skyhorsepublishing.com.

10 9 8 7 6 5 4 3 2 1

Library of Congress Cataloging-in-Publication Data is available on file.

Cover design by Brian Peterson

Print ISBN: 978-1-5107-0200-4
Ebook ISBN: 978-1-5107-0347-6

Printed in the United States of America

WEST OF THE PECOS

Chapter I

WHEN Templeton Lambeth's wife informed him that if God was good they might in due time expect the heir he had so passionately longed for, he grasped at this with the joy of a man whose fortunes were failing, and who believed that a son might revive his once cherished dream of a new and adventurous life on the wild Texas ranges west of the Pecos River.

That very momentous day he named the expected boy Terrill Lambeth, for a beloved brother. Their father had bequeathed to each a plantation; one in Louisiana, and the other in eastern Texas. Terrill had done well with his talents, while Templeton had failed.

The baby came and it was a girl. This disappointment was the second of Lambeth's life, and the greater. Lambeth never reconciled himself to what he considered a scurvy trick of fate. He decided to regard the child as he would a son, and to bring her up accordingly. He never changed the name Terrill. And though he could not help loving Terrill as a daughter, he exulted in her tomboy tendencies and her apparently natural preferences for the rougher and more virile pleasures and occupations. Of these he took full advantage.

Lambeth saw that Terrill had teachers and schooling beginning with her fifth year, but when she reached the age of ten he was proudest of the boyish accomplish-

ments he had fostered, especially her skill in horsemanship. Terrill could ride any four-footed animal on the
plantation.

Then came the Civil War. Lambeth, at that time in
his middle thirties, obtained an officer's commission,
and his brother, Terrill, enlisted as a private.

During this period of slow disintegration of the
South's prosperity Mrs. Lambeth had her innings with
Terrill. Always she had been under the dominance of
her husband, and could not stress the things she desired to see inculcated in her daughter. She belonged
to one of the old Southern families of French extrac-
tion, and after her marriage she had learned she had
not been Lambeth's first love. Pride and melancholy,
coupled with her gentle and retiring virtues, operated
against her opposing Lambeth in his peculiar way of
being happy by making Terrill's play as well as work
those of a boy. But during the long and devastating
war the mother made up greatly for those things she
feared Terrill had lacked. Before the end of the war,
when Terrill was fifteen, she died, leaving her a heritage
that not all the girl's passionate thirst for adventure
nor her father's influence could ever wholly eradicate.
Lambeth returned home a Colonel, destined to suffer
less grief at finding himself ruined as a planter, than
at the certainty of his brother's early demise. Terrill
had fallen victim to an incurable disease during the
war, and had been invalided home long before Lee's
surrender.

His wife's death and his ruin did not further em-
bitter Lambeth, inasmuch as these misfortunes left

the way unobstructed for tearing up root and setting out for the western frontier of Texas, where vast and unknown rangelands offered fortune to a man still young enough to work and fight.

Texas was a world in itself. Before the war Lambeth had hunted north as far as the Panhandle and west over the buffalo plains between the Arkansas and the Red Rivers. He had ideas about the future of the country. He was tired of cotton raising. Farther west he would roam to the land beyond the vague and wild Pecos, about which country alluring rumors had reached his ears.

Colonel Lambeth's first move upon arriving home was to free those slaves who still remained on his plantation despite the freedom for which the war had been waged. And the next, after selecting several favorite horses, a wagon and equipment, and a few possessions that would have been hard to part with, he put the plantation and everything on it under the hammer. Little indeed did he realize from this sale.

Then came news of his brother's death and with it a legacy sufficient to enable him to carry on. But Lambeth had had enough of a planter's ups and downs. The soil was poor and he had neither the desire nor the ability to try again. The West called. Texans impoverished by the war, and the riff-raff left over from the army, were spreading far and wide to the north and west, lured on by something magnetic and compelling.

Lambeth journeyed across the Mississippi, to return with sad and imperishable memories of his brother, and with the means to fulfill his old forlorn hope—to find and stock a ranch in the West.

Two of Lambeth's younger generation of slaves, out of the many who wanted to cleave to him, he listened to, appreciative of what their help would mean on such a hazardous enterprise as he was undertaking.

"But, Sambo, you're a free man now," argued Lambeth.

"Yes, suh, I sho knows I'se emancipated. But, Kuhnel, I don' know what to do with it."

This was a problem Sambo shared with the other slaves. He had been sold to the Lambeth plantation from the Texas plains, and was a stalwart, sober negro. Lambeth had taken Sambo on his latest buffalo hunts, finding in him a most willing and capable hand. Moreover he was one of the few really good negro vaqueros. It was Sambo who had taught Terrill to stick like a burr on a horse and to throw a lasso. And he had always been devoted to the girl. This last fact decided Lambeth.

"Very well, Sambo, I'll take you. But what about Mauree?" And Lambeth indicated the handsome negress who accompanied Sambo.

"Well, Kuhnel, we done got married when you was away. Mauree's a-devilin' me to go along wid you. There ain't no better cook than Mauree, suh." Sambo's tone was wheedling.

Lambeth settled with this couple, but turned a deaf ear to the other loyal negroes.

The morning of their departure, Terrill walked along the old road between the canal and the grove of stately moss-curtained oaks that surrounded the worn and weathered Colonial mansion.

It was early spring. The air was full of the sweet, fragrant languor of the South; mockingbirds were singing, full-throated and melodious; meadow larks and swamp blackbirds sang their farewell to the South for that season; the sky was blue and the sun shone warm; dewdrops like diamonds sparkled on the grass.

Beyond the great lawn a line of dilapidated old cottages faced the road, vacant-eyed and melancholy. From only a few rose the thin columns of blue smoke that denoted habitation. The happy, dancing, singing slaves were gone, and their whitewashed homes were falling to ruin. Terrill had known them all her life. It made her sad to say good-by to them, yet she was deeply glad that it was so and that slaves were no longer slaves. Four years of war had been unintelligible to Terrill. She wanted to forget that and all of the suffering and the bitterness.

When she returned from this, her last walk along the beloved old canal with its water-lily pads floating on the still surface, she found the horses in the yard, and Sambo carrying out her little brass-bound French trunk.

"Missy Rill, I done my best," said Sambo, as he shoved the trunk into the heavily laden canvas-covered wagon.

"Sambo, what're you sneakin' in on me heah?" demanded Lambeth, his sharp dark eyes taking in the situation.

"Missy's trunk, suh."

"Rill, what's in it?" queried her father.

"All my little treasures. So few, Dad! My jewelry, laces, pictures, books—and my clothes."

"Dresses, you mean? Rill, you'll not need them out where we're goin'," he replied, his gaze approving of her as she stood there in boy's garb, her trousers in her boots, her curls hidden under the wide-brimmed, soft hat.

"Never?" she asked, wistfully.

"I reckon never," he returned, gruffly. "After we leave heah you're the same as a real son to me. . . . Rill, a girl would be a handicap, not to speak of risk to herself. Beyond Santone it's wild country."

"Dad, I'd shore rather be a boy, and I will be. But it troubles me, now I face it, for really I—I'm a girl."

"You can go to your Aunt Lambeth," responded her father, sternly.

"Oh, Dad! . . . You know I love only you—and I'm crazy to go West. . . . To ride and ride! To see the buffalo, the plains, and that lonely Pecos country you tell me aboot! That will be glorious. . . . But this mawnin', Dad, I'm sorrowful at leavin' home."

"Rill, I am, too," replied Lambeth, with tears in his eyes. "Daughter, if we stayed heah we'd always be sad. And poor, too!—But there we'll take fresh root in new soil. We'll forget the past. We'll work. Everything will be new, strange, wonderful. . . . Why, Rill, if what I heah is true we'll have to fight Mexican hoss thieves and Comanche Indians!"

"Oh, it thrills me, Dad," cried Terrill. "Frightens

me! Makes cold chills creep up my back! But I'd not have it otherwise."

And so they rode away from the gray, dim mansion, out under the huge live oaks with their long streamers of Spanish moss swaying in the breeze, and into the yellow road that stretched away along the green canal.

Sambo headed the six free horses in the right direction and rode after them; Mauree drove the big wagon with its strong team of speckled whites. Terrill came on behind, mounted on her black thoroughbred, Dixie. Her father was long in catching up. But Terrill did not look back.

When, however, a mile down the road they reached the outskirts of the hamlet where Terrill's mother was buried, she looked back until her tear-blurred eyes could no longer distinguish objects. The day before she had taken her leave of her mother's grave, a rending experience which she could not endure twice.

All that endless day memories of the happy and grievous past possessed Terrill as she rode.

Chapter II

LAMBETH traveled leisurely. He meant to make this long-wished-for journey an education. Most of his life he had lived in that small part of Texas which adjoined Louisiana, and partook of its physical and traditional aspects. Now he wanted to find the real Texas—the Texas that had fallen at the Alamo and that in the end had conquered Santa Ana, and was now reaching north and west, an empire in the making.

To that end he traveled leisurely, halting at the occasional hamlets, making acquaintances on the way. Sometimes when sunset overtook his little cavalcade on the march he would camp where they were, usually near grass and water. Terrill grew to love this. Sambo made her bed in the wagon under the canvas, where she felt snug, and safe from prying eyes. To wear boy's clothes had once been fun for Terrill; now it augmented a consciousness that she was not what she pretended to be, and that sooner or later she would be found out. Otherwise as days and leagues lengthened between her and the old home she began keenly to live this adventure.

They stayed only one night in Austin, arriving after nightfall and departing at dawn. Terrill did not have much opportunity to see the city, but she did not like it. New Orleans had been the only large place she had

8

visited, and it, with its quaint streets and houses, its French atmosphere, had been very attractive to her.

From Austin to San Antonio the road was a highway, a stage line, and a thoroughfare for travelers going south and west, and Terrill found it tremendously interesting. So long as she could be astride Dixie and her contact with people confined to the rôle of a looker-on, she was happy. To ride through the long days and at night to creep into her snug bed in the wagon brought her an ever-growing joy. She could have gone on this way forever.

When they arrived at San Antonio, however, Terrill seemed plunged into a bewildering, bustling world, noisy, raw, strange, repellent to her, and yet strangely stirring. If only she really were a boy! How anyone could take her for a boy seemed incredible. Her masculine garb concealed the feminine contours of her form, almost to her satisfaction, but her face discouraged her terribly. At the hotel where they stayed Terrill regarded herself in the mirror with great disapproval. Her sunny curls, her violet eyes, above all her smooth girlish skin—these features that had been the joy of her mother, and which somehow in the past had not been distasteful to Terrill—now accorded her increasing embarrassment, not to say alarm. She must do something about it. Nevertheless, reflection relieved her, inasmuch as it made clear there could be no particular annoyance while they were traveling. She would never see the same people twice.

She had to remain in her room, next to her father's, unless she was accompanied by him or Sambo. Lambeth was tremendously keen on the track of something, and he went everywhere; but he took Terrill along with him whenever she wanted to go. Or he would send her to a store with Sambo. This pleased Terrill, for she had money to spend, and that was a luxury vastly pleasant. Only Sambo was disconcerting. Boy's boots and pants did not change his adored young mistress to him.

"Sambo, stop callin' me Miss Rill," protested Terrill. "Call me Master Rill."

"I sho will, Missy Rill, when I thinks aboot it. But you is what you is an' you can't nebber be what you ain't."

One morning, accompanied by Sambo, she went farther down the main street than usual. The horsemen and wagons and the stage-coaches accorded Terrill an increasing delight. They smacked of the wild, vast open Texas land, about which she had heard so much.

A little store attracted her, but she did not go in the first time she passed it because it stood next to a noisy saloon, in front of which shaggy, dusty saddled horses gave evidence of riders within. But finally Terrill yielded to temptation and entered the store, very soon to forget all about Sambo. When she had indulged her fancy to the extent of compunction, and had started out, she suddenly remembered him. He was nowhere to be seen. Then loud voices outside augmented anxiety to alarm. She ran out. Sambo was not waiting for her.

Terrill started hurriedly down the street, aware that several men were moving violently just ahead of her.

As she got even with the door of the saloon it swung open and a man, backing out, collided with her, sending her sprawling. Her packages flew out of her hands. Terrill indignantly gathered herself together, and recovering her belongings, stood up, more resentful than alarmed. But suddenly she froze in her tracks.

The man had a gun in each hand, which he held low down, pointing into the wide open door. All the noise had ceased. Terrill saw men inside, one of whom was squirming on the floor.

"Reckon thet'll be aboot all," announced the man with the guns, in a cold voice. "Next time you deal crooked cairds it shore won't be to Pecos Smith."

He backed by Terrill. "Kid, untie my hoss. . . . Thet bay. An' lead him heah," he ordered.

Terrill obeyed clumsily. Sheathing one of the guns the man retreated until he bumped into his horse. He had a young clear-cut cold profile, set and ruthless. From the high curb he mounted his horse in a single step.

"Smith, we'll know next time you happen along," called a rough voice from the saloon. Then the door swung shut.

"What you shakin' aboot, boy?" queried Smith, in a cool, drawling voice, suggestive of humor.

"I—I don't know, sir," faltered Terrill, letting go the bridle. This was her closest contact with one of these tawny stalwart Texans. And this one had eyes too terrible for her to look into. A smile softened the set of his lean hard face, but did not change those light piercing eyes.

"Wal, I only shot his ear off," drawled Smith. "It stuck out like a jack rabbit's. . . . Much obliged, sonny. I reckon I'll be goin'."

Whereupon he rode off at a canter. Terrill watched the lithe erect figure with mingled sensations. Then she stepped back upon the pavement. At this juncture Sambo appeared. Terrill ran to meet him.

"Oh, Sambo!—I was so frightened," she cried, in relief. "Let's hurry. . . . Where did you go?"

"I'se done scared myself," replied the negro. "I was waitin' by dat do when one of dese wild Texans rode up an' got off. He seen me an' he sed, 'Niggah, move away from mah vecinnity.' An' I sho moved. He got into a fight in here, an' when he come backin' out wid dem big guns I was scared wuss."

"Santone," which was what its inhabitants called San Antonio, appeared crowded with Texans and hordes of other men. Terrill took the Texans to be the rangy, dusty-booted youths, tight-lipped, still-faced, gray-eyed young giants, and the older men of loftier stature who surely were the fathers of the boys. Terrill was suddenly crestfallen when she became aware that she had several times been interested at sight of handsome young men. And this Pecos Smith had strangely thrilled her. Despite the terror and revulsion he had roused, his memory haunted her.

The Mexicans, the teamsters, the soldiers, the endless hurrying, colorful throng of men, gave Terrill a vague and wonderful impression. These were men of the open, and according to her father they had come from everywhere. Buffalo-hunters on their way out to the plains to catch the buffalo herds on their spring migration north; horse-dealers and cattlemen in from the ranches; idle, picturesque Mexicans with their *serapes*, their tight-legged flared-bottom trousers, their high-peaked sombreros; here and there a hard-eyed, watching man whom Lambeth designated as a Texas Ranger; riders on lean, shaggy, wild horses; tall men with guns in their belts; black-coated, black-hatted gamblers, cold-faced and usually handsome; and last, though by far not least, a stream of ragged, broken, often drunken men, long-haired, unshaven, hard and wretched, whose wolfish eyes Terrill did not want to meet. These, according to Lambeth, were the riffraff left of the army, sacrificed to a lost cause. He also remarked emphatically that he desired to put such men and such reminders far behind him.

"Rill, I've an hour now," said her father, on their third day at San Antonio. "Reckon I won't let you miss the Alamo. As long as Texas exists the Alamo will be sacred. Every boy should stand once on that bloody altar of heroism and country."

Terrill knew the story as well as any Texas boy. She tripped along beside her father, whose strides covered a good deal of ground. And soon they were on the threshold of the historic edifice. Lambeth had been there before. A distant relative of his had fallen in that battle. He took Terrill around and showed her where and how the besiegers had been repelled so long and with such deadly loss.

"Santa Ana had four thousand Mexican soldiers under him," explained Lambeth. "They surprised the

Americans by charging before daylight. But twice they were repulsed with terrific loss, and it looked as if the greasers would retreat. But Santa Ana drove them to another attack. They scaled the walls, and finally gained the top, from which they poured down a murderous fire. Then the Alamo doors were forced and a breach opened in the south wall. Hell broke loose. . . . In this room heah Bowie, who was ill, was murdered on his bed. . . . Over heah Travis died on his cannon. . . . And heah Davy Crockett went down with a ring of daid aboot him. . . . Rill, I could ask no more glory than that for my son. . . . The Texans perished to a man. One hundred and eighty-two of them. They killed sixteen hundred of Santa Ana's soldiers. Such were Texans of that day."

"Oh, how splendid!" cried Terrill. "But it horrifies me. I can see them fighting. . . . It must be in our blood, Dad."

"Yeah. . . . Never forget the Alamo, Rill. Never forget this heritage to Texans. We Southerners lost the Civil War, but we can never lose the glory of freein' Texas from Spanish rule."

Pensive and roused by turns, Terrill went back uptown with her father. Later that day she experienced a different kind of stimulation—something intimate and exciting. Lambeth took her to the large outfitting store, where he purchased a black Mexican saddle with *tapadores*, a silver-mounted bridle and spurs, *riata*, gauntlets, bandanas, and a sombrero so huge that when Terrill donned it she felt under a heavy cloud.

"Now you will be a vaquero," said Lambeth, proudly.

Terrill observed that he bought guns and ammunition, though he had brought along his English arms; also knives, belts, axes, a derringer for her, and in fact so many things that Terrill had her doubts that the wagon would carry them all. But she was to learn, presently, that he had acquired another and larger wagon which Sambo was to drive with two teams.

"Rill, I may as well tell you now," announced her father, "that I've given up the plan of followin' the stage road. Too many travelers, not healthy to meet west of Santone! We'll start out with some buffalo-hunters I've met and travel with them for a while. You'll get to hunt buffalo with me. We'll see the country."

Two days later Terrill rode out with a fair-sized cavalcade, there being six wagons besides her father's, and eight men, none of whom, however, were mounted. They were experienced buffalo-hunters, knew the country, and hunted buffalo for meat and hides. Much to Terrill's relief, there was not a young man in the party.

They traveled in a northwesterly direction, along a stream where beautiful pecan trees lined the banks. These Texans were hard drivers. When sunset came the first day they must have made thirty miles. Sambo with his heavy wagon did not get in until after dark, a fact that had worried Lambeth.

The hunters took good-natured notice of Terrill, but she was sure none of them suspected her secret. This night she had courage to sit back at the edge of the camp-fire circle, and listen. They were a merry lot, mostly ranchers and horse-raisers. One of them had been a Texas Ranger, and he told bloody tales which made Terrill's flesh creep. Another of the group, a stockman from the Brazos River, talked a good deal about the L'lano Estacado and the Comanche Indians. On a former hunt he, with comrade hunters, had been camping along the Red River, and had narrowly missed losing their scalps.

"Them Comanches air shore gettin' bad," he said, shaking a shaggy head. "An' it's this heah buffalo-huntin' thet's rilin' them. Some day Texas will have to whip off not only the Comanches, but the Arapahoes, the Kiowas, the Cheyennes, mebbe all the Plains Injuns."

"Wal, I reckon we're too early an' too fer south fer the Comanches at this time of year," remarked another. "Buffalo herds comin' up from the Rio Grande won't be as far as the Red River."

"We'll strike them this side of Colorado," replied the red-faced hunter. "Which is a darn good thing, fer thet river ain't no slouch to cross. Our friend Lambeth heah would have hell."

"No, he could haid the Colorado. Fair to middlin' road. But I don't know the country west."

Terrill might indeed have been a boy, considering the sensations aroused in her by this casual talk of hostile Indians, the Staked Plains, dangerous rivers, stampeding buffalo, and the like. But sometimes the lamentable fact that she was a girl forced itself upon her when she lay in bed unable to sleep, prey to feminine emotions that she could never dispel, yet all the while tingling with the wonder and zest of her existence.

Several days later, Terrill, riding with Sambo, somewhat behind the other wagons, imagined she heard something unusual.

"Listen, Sambo," she whispered, turning her ear to the south. Had she only imagined that she heard something?

"I doan heah nuffin'," replied the black.

"Maybe I was wrong. . . . No! There it comes again."

"Lud, Massa Rill, I sho hopes yo doan heah somethin' like thunder."

"That's just it, Sambo. . . . Rumble of low thunder. Listen!"

"I doan heah it yet. Mebbe storm down dat way."

"Sambo, it cain't be ordinary thunder," cried Terrill, excitedly. "It doesn't stop. It keeps right on. . . . It's getting louder."

"By gar! I heahs it now, Massa Rill," returned the negro. "I knows what dat is. Dar's de buffalo! Dat's de main herd, sho as I'se born."

"Main herd!—Oh, that hunter Hudkins was wrong, then. He said the main herd was not due yet."

"Dey's comin' an' dey's runnin', Massa Rill."

The rumble had grown appreciably louder, more consistent and deeper, with a menacing note. Lambeth and the saddle-horses had vanished in a dusty haze. Terrill thought she noted a quickening in the lope of the buffalo passing, closer pressing together of the lines, a gradual narrowing of the space around the wagons.

"Oh, Sambo, is it a stampede?" cried Terrill, suddenly seized by fright. "What has become of Dad? What will we do?"

"I dunno, Missy. I'se heahed a stampede, but I nebber was in one. Dis is gittin' bad. It sho is. We'se gotta be movin'."

Sambo ran and turned Mauree's team in the direction the buffalo were moving. Then he yelled for Terrill to get off her horse and climb into Mauree's wagon.

"What'll I do with Dixie?" screamed Terrill, as she dismounted.

"Lead him so long's yu can," yelled Sambo, and ran for his wagon.

Terrill thought she would have to mount Dixie again to catch up with Mauree. But she made the wagon, and vaulting high she got on, still hanging to the bridle. Fortunately it was long. Dixie loped behind, coming close so that Terrill could almost reach him. Then she saw Sambo's team gaining at a gallop. He did not pull them to accommodate Mauree's gait until at the heels of Dixie.

Then fearfully Terrill gazed from one side to the other. The streams of buffalo had closed in solid and were now scarcely a hundred yards from the wagons. The black and tawny beasts appeared to bob up and down in unison. Dust rolled up yellow and thick, obscuring farther view. Behind, the gap was filling up with a sea of lifting hoofs and shaggy heads. It was thrilling to Terrill, though her heart came up in her throat. The rumble had become a trampling roar. She saw that Sambo's idea was to keep his big wagon be-

hind Mauree's smaller one, and try to run with the
beasts, hoping they would continue to split behind it.
But how long could the horses keep that gait up, even
if they did not bolt and leave the wagons to be crushed?
Terrill had heard of whole caravans being flattened out
and trodden into the plain. Dixie's ears were up, his
eyes wild. But for Terrill's presence right close, holding his bridle, he would have run away.

Soon Terrill became aware that the teams were no
longer keeping up with the buffalo. That lumbering
lope had increased to a gallop, and the space between
the closing lines of buffalo had narrowed to half what
it had been. Terrill saw with distended eyes those
shaggy walls converging. There was no gap behind
Sambo's wagon—only a dense, gaining, hairy mass.
Sambo's eyes rolled till the whites stood out. He was
yelling to his horses, but Terrill could not hear a word.

The trampling roar seemed engulfed in deafening
thunder. The black bobbing sea of backs swallowed
up the open ground till Terrill could have tossed her
sombrero upon the shaggy humps. She saw no more
flying legs and hoofs. When she realized that the increased pace, the change from a tame lope to a wild
gallop, the hurtling of the blind horde, meant a stampede and that she and the two negroes were in the
midst of it, she grew cold and sick with terror. They
would be lost, smashed to a pulp. She shut her eyes to
pray, but she could not keep them shut.

Next she discovered that Mauree's team had bolted.
The wagon kept abreast of the beasts. It swayed and
jolted, almost throwing Terrill out. Dixie had to run

to keep up. Sambo's team came on grandly, tongues out, eyes like fire, still under control. Then Terrill saw the negro turn to shoot back at the charging buffalo. The red flame of the gun appeared to burst right in the faces of the maddened beasts. They thundered forward, apparently about to swarm over the wagon.

Clamped with horror, hanging on to the jolting wagon, Terrill saw the buffalo close in alongside the very wheels. A shroud of dust lifted, choking and half blinding her. Sambo blurred in her sight, though she saw the red spurt of his gun. She heard no more. Her eyes seemed stopped. She was an atom in a maelstrom. The stench of the beasts clogged her nostrils. A terrible sense of being carried along in a flood possessed her. The horses, the wagons, were keeping pace with the stampede. Dixie leaped frantically, sometimes narrowly missing the wagon. Just outside the wheels, rubbing them, swept huge, hairy, horned monsters that surely kept him running straight.

The agony of suspense was insupportable. Terrill knew she soon would leap out under the rolling hoofs. It could not last much longer. The horses would fall or fail, and then——. Sambo's gun burned red through the dust. Again the wall on each side moved ahead, faster, and appeared to draw away. Little by little the space widened. Terrill turned to gaze ahead. The herd had split. Dimly she saw an X-shaped space splitting, widening away from a high gray object.

Terrill lost the clearness of her faculties then and seemed clutched between appalling despair and hope. But surely the wagon slowed, careened, almost upset.

Then it stopped and Terrill closed her eyes on the verge of collapse.

But nothing happened. There was no crash—no pounding of her flesh. And again she could hear. Her ears registered once more the fearful trampling roar. She felt the wagon shaking under her. Then she opened her eyes. The wagon stood on a slant. Mauree had driven into the lea of a rocky knoll. Sambo's team, in a lather of froth and dust, heaved beside her, while Sambo, on foot, was holding Dixie. To Terrill's left the black woolly mass swept on. To the right she could not see for the knoll. But she sensed that the obstruction had split the herd and saved them. Terrill fell back spent and blind in her overwhelming reaction.

The roar rolled on, diminishing to thunder, then gradually lessening. The ground ceased to shake. In an hour the stampede was again a low rumble in the distance.

"De good Lawd was wif us, Missy Rill," said Sambo, leading Dixie to her. Then he mounted to the seat of his wagon and calling to Mauree he drove back through the settling dust along the great trail. It was long, however, before Terrill got into the saddle again. At last the dust all blew away, to disclose Lambeth far ahead with the horses.

Chapter III

THE Colorado River from the far eastern ridge top
resembled a green snake with a shining line down
the center of its back, crawling over rolling, yellow
plains. In this terrain ragged black streaks and spots,
and great patches stood out clearly in the morning sunlight. Only a few were visible on the north side of the
river; southward from the very banks these significant
and striking contrasts to the yellow and gray of plain
extended as far as the eye could see, dimming in the
purple obscurity of the horizon.

These black patches were buffalo. There were thousands in the scattered head of the herd, and in that
plain-wide mass far to the south there were millions.
The annual spring migration north was well on its
way.

The hunters yelled lustily. Lambeth rode back to
speak to Terrill, his black eyes shining. He seemed a
changed man. Already sun and wind and action had begun to warm out the havoc in his face.

"Rill, they're heah," he called, exultantly. "What
do you think of that sight?"

"Glorious!" replied Terrill, under her breath. She
was riding beside Sambo on the wagon seat. Dixie had
fallen lame, and Terrill, after riding two of the harder-

gaited horses, had been glad of a reprieve from the daily saddle.

"Missy Rill, yo sho will kill yo' first buffalo today," declared the negro.

"Sambo, I'm not crazy aboot firing that Henry rifle again," laughed Terrill.

"Yo didn't hold it tight," explained Sambo. "Mighty nigh kick yo flat."

Despite a downhill pull the wagons did not reach the Colorado until late in the afternoon. Hudkins, the leader of the expedition, chose a wooded bend in the river for a camp site, where a cleared spot and pole uprights showed that it had been used before. The leaves on the trees were half grown, the grass was green, flowers on long stems nodded gracefully, and under the bank the river murmured softly.

"Wal, you fellars fix camp while I go after a buffalo rump," ordered Hudkins, and strode off with what Terrill had heard him call his needle gun. She wondered what that meant, because the gun was almost as big as a cannon.

Terrill sat on the wagon seat and watched the men. This arriving at a new camp and getting settled had a growing attraction for her. Even if this life in the open had held no appeal for her, she would still gladly have accepted it because of the change it wrought in her father's health and spirits. How resolutely had he turned his back upon ruin and grief! He was not rugged, yet he did his share of the work. Sambo, however, was the one who had changed most. On the plantation he had not seemed different from the other negroes, except when on horseback. Here he appeared to be in his element and the laziness of a cotton-picker had departed. He wore boots and overalls. There was a gun belted around his lean hips. When he swung an ax and carried the heavy picks his splendid physique showed to advantage. He whistled as he worked, and like Mauree had fallen happily into this new way of life.

Presently Terrill's father came to her, carrying the Henry rifle.

"Rill, from now on you pack this on your hoss, in the wagon, by your bed, and everywhere."

"But, Dad, I'm afraid of the darned thing," expostulated Terrill.

Colonel Lambeth laughed, but he was inexorable. "Rill, farther west we'll hit the badlands. Indians, outlaws, bandits, Mexicans! And we may have to fight for our lives. Red Turner has been across the Pecos. He told me today what a wild country it was. Cattle by the thousand and just beginnin' to be worth somethin'. . . . So come out and practice a little. Stuff a towel inside your shirt aboot where the gun kicks your shoulder."

Terrill accompanied Lambeth down to the river bank, where he directed Terrill how to load, hold, aim, and fire the big Henry. Terrill had to grit her teeth, nevertheless there was a zest in the thing her father insisted upon—that she fill the boots of a son for him. Five shots from a rest she fired, squeezing the rifle with all her might. The first shot was not so terrible, after all, but the bullet flew wide of the target. She did better on the second and third. And the last two she hit the black across the river, to her father's sober satisfaction. How seriously he took all this! It was no game to him.

"Sambo will clean the rifle for you," he said. "But that you should learn also. Familiarize yourself with the gun. Get used to handlin' it. Aim often at things without shootin'. You can learn to shoot as well that way without wastin' too many bullets."

Hudkins returned with the hump of a buffalo, from which were cut the steaks these hunters praised so much. Lambeth appeared as greedy as any of them. They made merry. Some one produced a jug of liquor which went the rounds. For a moment Terrill's heart stood still. She feared her father might ask her to take a drink. But he did not overstep the bounds of reason in his obsession to see in Terrill a son.

"Sonny, how you like rump steak?" asked Hudkins, merrily, of Terrill.

"It's got a kind of wild flavor," replied Terrill. "But I certainly like it."

She went to bed early, tired out from the jolting she had undergone on the high wagon seat. There were sundry places on her anatomy sore to the touch. And soon slumber claimed her. Some time in the night she awoke, an unusual thing for her. A noise had disturbed her rest. But the camp was dark and silent. A low rustle of leaves and a tinkle of water could scarcely have been guilty. Then from across the river a howl that curdled her blood. She sat up quivering in every muscle, and her first thought was that the dreaded Comanches were upon them. The howl rose again, somehow different. It seemed like the bay of a hound, only infinitely deeper, wilder, stranger, with a fierce, mournful note. Answers came from above camp, and then a chorus of chirping, shrieking barks. These sounds she at once associated with the wolves and coyotes that the hunters said followed the buffalo in packs. So Terrill lay back in relief and listened. It was long, however, before she stopped shivering and fell asleep again.

After all, Sambo and not her father took Terrill out to see the buffalo and perhaps shoot one. Lambeth had gone with the hunters.

"Missy Rill ——"

"Say Master Rill, you pestifercatin' nigger," interrupted Terrill, only half in fun.

"Sho I done forgot," replied Sambo, contritely. "Wal, Massa Rill, tain't goin' be no trick atall fo' yo' to kill a buffalo. An' it'll sho tickle the Kuhnel."

No boy could have been any more eager than Terrill, nor half so scared. She trotted along beside the striding negro, packing the heavy rifle, all eyes and ears. She saw birds and rabbits, and presently had her first view of wild turkeys and deer. The surprise to Terrill was their exceeding tameness. Then she heard the boom of guns far over the ridge of grassy ground. Sambo said the hunters were at it and that Terrill would soon see buffalo at close range.

Suddenly Sambo dragged her into the cover of the trees and along the edge of the woods to a log. This appeared to be at a bend of the river from where Terrill could discern a slope rising gradually to the high bank.

"Bunch a-comin', Massa Rill," said Sambo, examining his rifle.

"I heah slopping in the water," replied Terrill, excitedly.

"Sho. Det's some buffs. Dey'se wadin' across an'll come out on det sandbar."

Suddenly a shaggy, elephantine beast hove in sight directly in front of Terrill. Her tongue clove to the roof of her mouth. It was an enormous bull. Another climbed out of the shallow water, and then dozens of woolly, hump-backed buffalo swarmed over the dry sandbar. Some were black, some were tawny. Terrill thought she saw little ones in behind the others. Terrill heard them pant. She heard them rub together. She smelled them.

"Rest yo' gun heah, Miss Rill," whispered Sambo. "Hol' tight an' aim low."

"But—but it's like murdering cows," protested Terrill.

"Sho is. But it'll please yo' Dad."

"Won't they r-run o-over us?"

"Naw, Missy, dey won't run atall. Don't be afeared. We kin hide heah. . . . 'Member how. Hol' tight an' aim low."

Terrill seemed monstrously divided between two emotions. The stronger forced her down over her rifle, made her squeeze it tight, squint along the barrel, and align the sight generally on that wide, shaggy, moving mass, and pull the trigger. The recoil threw her to her knees and the smoke blinded her. Then Sambo's gun boomed.

"Oh, I hope I missed!" cried Terrill.

"Yo' sho didn't, Miss Rill. . . . Look! Dat bull tryin' climb. He's shooted through. . . . Dar he goes down, Missy Rill . . . he's sho a-rollin'. . . . Now he's kickin'. Ain't yo' gonna look, gal?"

Terrill wanted to look, but she could not. She let her rifle balance on the log on which she sank down, rubbing her shoulder, fighting her fears.

"Daid! . . . 'Em both daid. We sho is de hunters, Massa Rill, we sho is! Dat tickle yo' Dad 'most to death."

"Where are—the others?" gasped Terrill, fearfully.

"Dey's mozied round de bend. Look Massa Rill. . . . Dat big bull closest to us is yo's. Ain't he sho black an' shiny? Dar's yo' buffalo robe, Missy, an' we is gonna skin it off right now."

"We is—not," retorted Terrill, still shakily, though now she had the courage to peep over the log. There, scarcely a hundred steps away, lay a huge, black buffalo flat on the sand, motionless. Beyond and to the left was another. Terrill experienced a wild thrill, instantly checked by a pang.

"Yo' gonna help me skin off dat buffalo robe of yo's?" queried the negro.

"Skin the—poor creature!" cried Terrill. "No, indeedee, I'm not. It was awful enough to—kill it."

"Please yo'self, Missy. But I done tell, yo' whar yo's gwine yo'll soon git over squackishness at daid things an' hair an' blood," replied Sambo, philosophically.

Then bidding Terrill wait there, he made for the buffalo. She watched long enough to see him draw a bright blade and drop to his knees. Then she backed out of sight of that sandbar.

The grove seemed dreamy and silent. Presently Terrill found a grassy seat, and reclining there in the sun-flecked shade, with sweet fragrance all around and pale-blue flowers peeping up at her from the green, she felt the slow receding of excitement and fear and nausea. That buffalo was the first creature she had ever wittingly killed in all her life. She sensed the truth in Sambo's practical words, but not yet could she bear to dwell upon it. After all, she was not a man and she never would be a man.

Birds and squirrels and rabbits soon trusted her. Finding in her nothing to fear, they came close and pleased her with their soft-hued beauty and saucy barking and nibbling at the grass. She was distracted from these, however, by a rustling of brush, a queer sound like put-put, put, put, put. Then she heard a gobble. Wild turkeys near! This would be an event. And presently she espied a huge gobbler, bronzed and flecked, with a purple beard and red comb. How stately he strutted! Then he stopped under a tree to scratch in the leaves and grass. Other turkeys appeared, some smaller, sleeker, with subdued colors and wild bearing. These were the hens. They came close to Terrill, eyed her with curiosity, and passed on, put-put, put, put, put. Terrill went back to lesser attractions, vaguely content. She was sorry when Sambo disrupted the spell, as he crashed along the edge of the brush, bowed under a heavy burden.

"Massa Rill, whar yo' is?" he called.

Terrill hurried up, and securing her rifle ran out to join him.

"Aw, dar yo' is. I done feared the Comanches had got yo'. . . . Heah's yo' robe, Missy. Look dar."

The heavy, black mass thumped on the ground. Sambo laid aside his rifle and spread the magnificent buffalo hide out on the grass. Terrill could not believe her eyes.

"Dey don't come any finer," he declared. "Now, Missy, yo' take my gun, so I kin pack dis dog-gone heavy hide to camp. Den I'll fetch in de meat."

Soon they reached camp, having been gone only a few hours. Mauree was still alone. When Sambo exhibited the hide and extolled Terrill's prowess the negress rolled the whites of her handsome eyes.

"Fer de land's sake! Yo' done dat, Rill? I sho is s'prised. I sho is! An' I sho is sorry—dat no-good niggah husband of mind done make a killer out of yo'."

About mid-afternoon several of the hunters returned to hitch up the wagons and drive back to fetch the proceeds of the hunt. At sunset Lambeth rode in, covered with dust and lather. His horse was spent. Hands and face were begrimed. He yelled for water. Presently, after he had washed, he espied the great buffalo hide which Sambo had carefully stretched where it must command instant attention.

"You hoss-ridin' nigger!" he exclaimed. "Been huntin' yourself."

Yas, suh. Yas, Kuhnel, I ben. Ain' dat a mighty fine hide?"

"Best I ever saw," declared Lambeth, smoothing the glossy fur. "Biggest I ever saw, too. . . . Sambo, see heah. You give it to me."

"I'se powerful sorry, Kuhnel," replied Sambo, shaking his kinky head. "But I done cain't do it."

"Reckon you gave it to Rill?"

Sambo shook his head solemnly.

"No, sah. I didn't. Missy Rill killed de buffalo dat wore dat hide. Jest one shot, Kuhnel. Plumped over de biggest bull in de herd."

"*Terrill!*"

"Yes, Dad," replied Terrill, coming out from her hiding-place.

"Is this heah nigger lyin' to me? Did you shoot a buffalo?"

"Yes, Daddy," she returned, nonchalantly. "Aboot like murderin' a cow, I'd say. I don't think much of buffalo-huntin'."

Lambeth whooped and gave Terrill a tremendous hug. When the other hunters returned he proudly acclaimed Rill's achievement, which indeed immediately took precedence over many and eventful deeds of the day. Nineteen buffalo, selected for their hides, had been killed by the party, all, in fact, that could be skinned and cut up and hauled in that day. They could not leave the meat out on the prairie for the wolves to haggle. Lambeth had accounted for three of the slain beasts, and appeared elated. He loved the chase and had never indulged it as now appeared possible. If the camp had been a merry one before, it was this night a circus for Terrill. The hunters had too many drinks from the jug, perhaps, but they were funny. They stretched and pegged buffalo hides until midnight.

"A hunter's life for me!" sang Hudkins. "Too bad one more day will load us up. They shore come too easy."

On the morning of the third day after this successful start the hunters were packed and ready to return to San Antonio. Lambeth's horses were headed west from the Colorado. Here was the parting of the ways for the hunters and the pioneers. For Lambeth the real journey began from this camp.

"Stick to your direction an' don't git off. Four days . . . eighty miles to San Saba River," advised Red Turner. "Then haid west an' keep yore eye peeled."

Many were the gay and kindly good-bys directed at Terrill, one of which, from the old Texan, Hudkins, she thought she would never forget.

"Good-by, sonny. Hang on to thet rifle an' yore curly hair."

Chapter IV

THOUGH Lambeth had struck away from the Colorado River he did not get rid of the buffalo. During that day the caravan was frequently held up by strings of the great, shaggy beasts. They grazed as they traveled. When the horses and wagons approached a bunch they would swerve ahead or behind, at a lope, and then drop back to feeding again. But when a large number barred the way there was nothing to do save halt and wait until they had passed.

A hundred times buffalo were within easy rifle range and showed less concern at sight of the travelers than the travelers did of them. They were not wild. The inroads of desultory hunting showed no effect whatever.

The horses grew accustomed to the great beasts and ceased to shy or balk. Dixie was the only one that stuck up his ears at every new straggling line. Sambo almost went to sleep over the reins. Lambeth rode out in front, ever watchful, at last a scout in reality. Terrill rode Dixie for some hours, then returned to the wagon seat beside Sambo.

It was while she was on the wagon that the largest contingent of buffalo met them. "We'se a-gwine to get corralled," observed Sambo. "An' if dat Kuhnel doan' be keerful he'll lose us."

"Sambo, is there still danger?" asked Terrill, anxiously, as she surveyed the straggling lines, with a black mass behind. "They are so tame now."

"Wal, I reckon we doan' need to worry. De main herd is back an' south."

"Golly! If this isn't the main herd, what must that be like?"

"Black as fur as eye kin see. . . . Dar! Dat is jes' what I sed. Yo' Dad is bein' cut off."

Lambeth, with the saddle horses, was far in the lead, and a line of buffalo intervened between him and the wagons. Then another line swerved back of the wagons, and presently Terrill saw they were surrounded. The belt of black, bobbing backs between her and Lambeth broadened until it was half a mile across. Sambo got off to step back and assure Mauree that there was no danger. Terrill, however, could scarcely accept that. Still her fears gradually subsided as nothing happened except a continual passing of buffalo to the fore and rear. The herd split a couple of hundred paces below the wagons and the two streams flowed by. Terrill could not help shuddering at the prospect of a stampede. But the gentle trampling roar went on uneventfully. Dust filled the air and a strong odor prevailed.

It took an hour for this branch of the herd to pass. Sambo drove on. When the dust blew away Lambeth was seen waiting with the horses, and the plain ahead appeared clear. Behind and to the south rolled the slow dust cloud, soon settling so that the stringy, black horde once more showed distinct against the gray.

Thereafter only occasional lines of buffalo were crossed, until at last, toward sunset, the herd appeared to have been passed. The undulating prairie appeared the same in every direction, except that there was a gradual uplift to the west. Lambeth disappeared over a ridge, and when the wagon topped it Terrill saw a willow-bordered swale where he had elected to make camp that night.

Twilight was stealing over the land when Sambo hauled up beside the willows where Lambeth was hobbling the horses. Terrill sat a moment longer on the seat. The perils of the day were past. Coyotes were barking at the far end of the swale. A melancholy solitude enfolded the place. Behind Terrill the weeks seemed years. They were dimming old associations. She sighed for them, yet she welcomed the future eagerly. What work and life lay ahead for her! Terrill leaped off the wagon, conscious of a subtle break as of something that had come between her and the old house. It was time she set brain and hand to help her father in the great task he had undertaken.

The ring of Sambo's ax in the gray dawn was Terrill's signal to arise and begin the momentous day. Sambo rolled his ox eyes at her. "Now what fur is yo' up so early, Miss Rill?"

"To work, Sambo. To help my Dad be a pioneer. To become a vaquero. . . . Nigger, never you Missy Rill me again. I'm a man!"

"Yo' is! Wal, dat am funny. How is yo' come aboot bein' a man?"

Terrill was abashed at the approach of her father, who had heard. His eyes took on a dark flash, burning out a sadness that had gloomed there. The kiss he gave Terrill then seemed singular in that it held an element of finality. He never kissed her again.

The rosy sunrise found them on their way, headed toward the purple horizon. There was no road. Lambeth led a zigzag course across the prairie, keeping to the best levels, heading ravines and creek bottoms.

Summer had come to the range. The bleached grama grass rose out of a carpet of green. Flowers bloomed in sheltered places. Deer trooped in the creek bottoms, and there was a varied life everywhere in the vicinity of water.

That day the vastness of Texas and the meaning of loneliness grew fixed in Terrill's heart forever. On all sides waved the prairie, on and on, in an endless solitude. The wild animals, the hawks and ravens, the black clouds of passenger pigeons that coursed by, the faint, dark lines behind in the Colorado valley, —all these only accentuated the solitude.

Hour after hour the wagon wheels left tracks in the rich soil, and the purple beckoning distance seemed ever the same. Terrill rode Dixie, drove Sambo's wagon, and she even walked, but nothing changed the eternal monotony of the Texas plains. She forgot the Comanches and other perils about which she had heard. And at times she caught a stealing vacancy of mind that had entranced her, for how long she could not tell. It was a strange and beautiful thing.

But for the most part she watched and listened and felt.

The next day was like the one before, and then Terrill lost track of days. She could recall only events such as a rain that drenched her to the skin, and what fun it was to dry in the sun, and a hard wind which blew in their faces all one day, and the doubtful crossing of a sand-barred river that Lambeth was sure was the Llano, which Red Turner had claimed was a tributary to the Colorado, not many days south of the San Saba.

On the north side of the Llano they had crossed a road that ran east and west. Lambeth vacillated long here. It troubled him. A road led somewhere. But he had at length pushed on toward the San Saba.

Dry camps alternated with those at which water and grass were abundant. At night, round the camp fire, Lambeth and Sambo would discuss the growing problem. As they climbed out of the vast valley the springs and creeks grew scarcer. It would soon be imperative to follow rivers and roads, and that meant a greater risk than they had been incurring. The Comanches lived up on the Staked Plains, and the Kiowas farther north, and the Jicarillo Apaches west.

"Yas, suh," agreed Sambo, in relation to an unavoidable peril. "'Mos' a matter of luck, Kuhnel. But Texas done be as big as de whole Yankeeland."

It was July when they struck the San Saba, a fine river watering a beautiful country Lambeth did not want to leave. Pressing on on the left bank, they came to a crossing. This was the road Red Turner had in-

formed Lambeth he would find. There were wheel
tracks in it. He followed that road for days, and at
last, where the forking of creeks with the San Saba
indicated the headwaters, he sighted cattle on the
plain.

They camped near a ranch that sunset. Lambeth
made the acquaintance of the settler before night.
His name was Hetcoff and he hailed from Missouri.
He had neighbors, but they were few and far between.
Their cattle had been unmolested, but it was hard to
hide horses from the marauding Comanches. Lambeth was advised to pick his range somewhere along
the San Saba. It had possibilities. At Menardsville,
a day's ride west, there was a junction of roads and
that point would be thickly settled some day. The
Staked Plains to the north was a barren plateau,
known only to the savages, and decidedly to be
avoided by white men. A road staked out by the
Spaniards across its sandy wastes had been the death
of many a settler. Hetcoff knew little of the Pecos
country, but the name Pecos itself had a sinister
significance.

Terrill was excited at the prospect of entering a
town again. But Menardsville was disappointing, as
it consisted of but a few adobe houses surrounded by
ranges. A Texan named Bartlett maintained a post
there, freighting supplies at infrequent intervals. He
was also in the cattle business, which at that time had
only a prospective future. Cattle were plentiful and
cheap.

Lambeth camped at Menardsville for a week, resting, buying supplies, mending harnesses, gaining information. When he left there he had both wagons loaded to capacity—a fine haul for Comanches, Bartlett averred.

Terrill still occupied the smaller canvas-covered wagon, but she had less room and comfort. She had ceased to suffer from sun and wind, and had become hard and strong. She did not lose weight because she was growing all the time. Increased height and a widening of her frame favored her disguise. Often she gazed in rueful wonder at her hands, still shapely, but hardening from work, growing callous of palm and a deep gold tan on the back. At intervals she cut her rebellious curly locks, though never very short. And she was troubled at the thinning of her cheeks and coarsening of her skin, which she had once desired; at the look in the dark blue eyes which watched her gravely from the little mirror.

West of Menardsville the road Lambeth chose to travel headed northwest over an increasingly difficult country, barren and fertile in patches. Settlers had drifted into this region, and a few ranches established before the war were accumulating more cattle than they took the trouble to brand.

Lambeth decided to buy cattle enough to make the nucleus of a herd. Wakefield, a rancher who did not know how many long-horn cattle he owned, sold Lambeth what he wanted at his own price, and to boot lent him a couple of vaqueros. He advised against the Pecos country. "Best of cattle ranges," he said;

"but wild, hard, an' lonely, shore to be a hotbed of rustlers some day."

Terrill sustained a peculiar feeling at her first close sight of a Texas long-horn steer. The enormously wide-spreading, bow-shaped horns had inspired the name of this Mexican breed, and they quite dwarfed the other characteristics of the animal. Terrill was destined to learn the true nature of this famous Texas stock. All in a single day she became a vaquero.

At every ranch Lambeth added to his herd; and after every night stand some of them eluded the guards and departed for home. Nevertheless, the herd grew, and the labors of driving a number of long-horns increased in proportion. Necessarily this slowed down their daily travel to less than a fourth of what it had been.

The end of August found Lambeth's wagon train and cattle drive encroaching upon the bad lands of west Texas. They rimmed the southern edge of *L'lano Estacado*, a treeless, waterless, sandy region faintly and fascinatingly indicative of its impassable and destructive nature.

They encountered a wandering, prospective settler and saved his life. He had come across the arid plateau from the Panhandle, how or where he could not explain. He was glad to throw in with Lambeth and help drive that growing herd. For now Lambeth's steers, leisurely driven and as carefully looked after as was possible, had begun to pick up cattle along the way. Lambeth could not prevent this. He had no brand of his own. He could not pick out from his herd all stock he had paid for and all that had joined it of their own accord. So he became an innocent rustler, something which Wakefield had seriously warned him against; and had then removed the sting of his words by a laughing statement that all ranchers, at some stage or other of their careers, appropriated cattle not their own.

The two borrowed vaqueros had to work so hard that Terrill seldom came in direct contact with them. The Mexican was a sloe-eyed, swarthy rider no longer young, silent and taciturn, with whom conversation, let alone friendliness, was difficult. The white vaquero was a typical Texan who had been reared on the plains. He was rough and uncouth, yet likable and admirable to Terrill. She learned much from watching these two men. At the last ranch Lambeth had added a boy to the caravan, whose duty it was to drive the large wagon while Sambo helped with the herd. There was never a day dawned that Terrill did not expect to see the last of the herd. But they drove on and on into the west, always finding grass at the end of a day's travel, and seldom missing water. The frequent rains, summer storms they were, favored travel over this increasingly arid land.

September came. At least that was how Terrill calculated. And with it cooler nights and dawn with a nip in the air. Terrill often stood hours of the night guarding the herd with her father. These were wonderful hours. The Mexican vaquero sometimes sang to the herd, strange, wild Spanish songs of the range.

While the cattle rested and slept, the guards took
their turns of four hours on and four off, Sambo and
Steve, the white vaquero alternating with Lambeth
and the Mexican. Terrill did her share, which, however, had so far been only guarding. As luck would
have it, nothing stampeded the long-horns.

For days on end dim blue hills had led Terrill's
gaze on to dimmer and bluer mountains, like ghosts
above the hazy horizon. Steve said those mountains
lay across the Pecos, that they must be the Guada-
loupes. The blue hills, however, were the brakes of
the Pecos.

The white-and-yellow plain undulated on to meet
these rising uplands. And the naked slope of the
Staked Plains imperceptibly receded. Lambeth had
been most fortunate in finding stream beds to follow.
He grazed the herd along only a dozen miles a day,
gradually slowing up as the harder country intervened.

October! Lambeth's caravan was lost in a forlorn
and desolate country. They had no landmarks to
travel by—no direction except west. And half the time
that was impossible to follow, owing to the character
of the country.

The blue hills they had sighted from a distance
were the rock-and-ridge region through which the
Pecos cut its solitary way. Lambeth had been told to
strike the river wherever he could and then to travel
west to Horsehead Crossing, a ford that had been used
by the Spaniards a hundred years before.

When the situation began to be very serious they

stumbled upon the Flat Rock Water Holes, and were thus accorded another reprieve. Two dry camps brought them to Wild China Water Holes. From there the dim road faded among the rocks. But the Mexican vaquero, upon whom had evolved the responsibility of getting them through, had his direction, and led on with confidence.

Grass grew plentifully over the scaly ridges, but so scattered in little patches that stock had to range far to get enough. That further slowed the caravan. Nevertheless, Lambeth pushed on with relentless optimism. He had a vision and it could not be clouded. He cheered on his hands by promise of reward, and performed miracles of labor for a man who had been a Southern planter. The adventure could not recall his youth, for that was irretrievably past, but it rehabilitated his strength and energy.

As for Terrill, the seven months in the open had transformed her physically. She was at home in the saddle or on the wagon seat. The long days under the blazing sun, or facing the whipping wind with its dust and sand, rain and chill, the lonely night watch when the wolves mourned and the coyotes wailed, the hard rides over stony ridges to head refractory old longhorns—these all grew to be part of the day to Terrill Lambeth.

Again the Mexican lost his way. Washes to cross, sandy and dragging, cattle that must graze, ravines deepening to gorges, which had to be headed, all these confused the guide. Lambeth preferred to corrall the stock at night in one of the gorges or a bowl between two ridges. Ridge tops were less favorable places.

They drove two days without water, except enough for the horses. The cattle began to suffer. They grew harder to hold. The riders had little rest and no sleep. Next day they dropped down over a ridge into a well-defined trail coming up from the south. Rain had almost obliterated hoof tracks which might have been so very old.

Lambeth wanted to turn south. The vaquero shook his head. "Mucho bad, Señor. Ver seco. Water mañana. Rio Pecos," he said, and pointed north.

But the following night found them in a precarious predicament. Two canteens of water left! The horses were in bad shape. Cattle had fallen along the wayside. Another hot day without rain or water would spell the doom of the stock. And that meant horrible toil and suffering, probably death, for the travelers.

Terrill remembered her prayers that night and her mother's face came to her in a dream.

Lambeth had the caravan on the move at break of day, hoping to find water before the sun got high.

The road penetrated deeper into this wilderness of stone and cactus, greasewood and gray earth. Still there was always grass. The stock now, however, no longer grazed.

Notwithstanding the dangerous situation, Lambeth's luck seemed not wholly to have departed. Before the sun grew hot, clouds rolled up to obscure it. The riders, grasping at straws, mercilessly drove the cattle on.

A gloomy canopy overhead fitted the strange, wild

country, which every mile appeared to take on more of its peculiar characteristics.

Terrill, driving the smaller wagon, noticed a developing uneasiness in the long column of cattle. They had been plodding along wearily, heads down, tongues out, almost spent. Suddenly a spirit seemed to run through the whole herd. Here and there a cow bawled. They quickened from a crawl to a trot. The Mexican and the other vaquero, far in front, were not succeeding in holding them back. Apparently they were not trying. They waved wildly back to Sambo and Lambeth, who had the rear positions. Something had gone wrong, Terrill feared. How would this terrible drive end?

Then the cattle, as if actuated by a single spirit, stampeded in a cloud of dust and disappeared. Lambeth rode on with drooping head. Sambo approached him as if to offer consolation for the loss.

It was a downgrade there. Terrill had to hold in the team, that had also become imbued with some quickening sense. Ahead where the dust cloud hung, a rugged line of rocks and ridges met the gloomy sky. Terrill could not see far. Where had the cattle gone? What had frightened them? They were gone, and hope was, too. It was over, the suspense of the endless weeks of driving longhorns. A sterner task now confronted her father—to save the horses and their own lives.

Terrill was plunged into an abyss of despair. Somehow she had kept up, believing her prayers would be answered. But now she succumbed. Theirs would be the fate of so many who had wandered off into that Godforsaken wilderness, lured on by the dream of the pioneer. It would have been better to meet a quick and fighting death at the hands of Comanches.

Terrill had caught up with her father and Sambo when she saw the Mexican turn in his saddle to cup his hands and yell. But she could not understand. She did not need to understand his words, however, to realize that some new peril impended. Then several strange riders appeared out of an arroyo. At first Terrill feared they were Indians, so dark, lean, wild were their horses.

It was only when the leader advanced alone that Terrill made out they were white men. But how sinister! The leader was suspicious. He had no rifle over his pommel. The vaquero, riding beside Lambeth, halted his horse.

"Massa, dat's a rustler, if I ebber seen one," said Sambo. "We'se held up, we sho is."

The rider approached to halt some paces from the wagons. Suddenly, with a violent start, Terrill recognized him. Pecos Smith! The young Texan who had backed out of the saloon in San Antonio with a gun in each hand!

"Who air you an' what you doin' heah?" he queried, curtly, his piercing eyes taking in all of the travelers, to go back to Lambeth.

"My name's Lambeth. We're lost. An' my cattle have stampeded," replied Lambeth.

"Where was you goin' when you got lost?"

"Horsehaid Crossin' of the Pecos."

"Wal, you're way off yore direction. Horsehaid is east from heah."

"We were told to travel north whether we lost the road or not."

Evidently the rider had his doubts about this outfit. Finally he called to Sambo: "Niggah, you get down an' come heah."

Sambo obeyed precipitately.

"Where'd I ever see you?"

"I dunno, sir, but I'se sho seen you," replied Sambo.

"Santone, wasn't it?"

"Yas, sir. I was standin' in front of a saloon an' you told me to move along."

"Reckon I remember you," returned the rider, and then directed his attention to Lambeth. "But thet don't prove nothin'. Lambeth, you may be all right. But this vaquero is not. I know him. How'd you come by him?"

Lambeth explained how the Mexican had been lent to him for the trip across the Pecos. And he added, stiffly: "I'm Colonel Templeton Lambeth. What are you takin' me for?"

"Howdy, Pecos Smith!" spoke up Terrill, feeling at this moment that she might well ease the situation.

"Wal! . . . An' who're you?" exclaimed the rider, amazed, as he bent eyes that bored upon her.

"He is my father."

"Ahuh. An' how'd you know me?"

"I was the—the kid you knocked over that day in Santone—when you came out of the saloon. . . . You made me fetch your horse. . . . And you said you'd only shot the man's ear off—that it stuck out like a jack rabbit's."

"Wal, I'll be dog-goned!" ejaculated the rider. "I

remember, but you're shore changed a lot, boy." Then he turned to Lambeth. "We've been trailin' a rustler outfit up from the Rio Grande. Reckoned mebbe they'd run across somebody with wagons. Sorry to annoy you, Colonel. Turn yore wagons an' I'll lead you to the crossin'."

"Is it far?" asked Lambeth, anxiously.

"Wal, it's far enough, considerin' yore hosses. I reckon you'll just aboot make it."

The ensuing drive, short though it might have been, proved to Terrill that if they had not been led out of this maze of hot draws and ridges they would have been irrevocably lost. As it was, the weary horses were barely goaded to the gap in a summit of gray bluff. The rider sat his horse, waiting for the caravan to come up.

"*Rio Pecos!*" he called, and pointed down.

The riders galloped forward at his call. Terrill, with a wild start and a sob of thanksgiving, urged the team ahead. Sambo dismounted and turned back to wave at Terrill. She had all she could do to pull the horses up beside the riders.

"De good Lawd am delibbered us," said Sambo, and hurried back to meet Mauree.

"Rill—he has led us—to the river!" exclaimed Lambeth, with deep emotion. "Look! Heah is Horsehaid Crossin'—of the Pecos. And look there—the cattle!"

Terrill gazed down from a height. Just on the moment pale sunlight filtered through the drab clouds, to shine upon a winding silver river that formed a bend like the shape of a horse's head. It flowed out of gray and green wilderness, and probably came through a gap in the distant stone bluff.

The foremost cattle had reached the water. It had been the scent of water that had stampeded them. Sand bars gleamed white.

Terrill caught her breath. The joy of deliverance had momentarily blinded her to something that struck her like a blow, but which she could not yet grasp. She stared at her father, at the other riders. Pecos Smith was riding by. "Adios an' good luck!" he called, and galloped away. Sambo's deep voice pealed from behind, where he was rejoicing with his wife.

All along this trail, surely once a traveled road, lay skulls and bones of animals. Horses, cattle—a line of bones! From a rock stuck up the ghastly skull and weirdly long horns of a Texas steer—fit guidepost for that crossing. The place was desolate, gray, and lonely, an utter solitude, uninhabited even by beasts of the hills or fowls of the air. It stretched away to infinitude. In the east rose a pale streak—possibly the slope of *L'lano Estacado*.

But it was to the west that Terrill forced her gaze. West of the Pecos! How, for what seemed a lifetime, had she lived on those words, with an added word— home! Could home have any place in this strange and terrific prospect?

The river changed its course with Horsehead Crossing, but soon veered back to its main trend southward. It dominated that savagely monotonous and magnificent scene. Miles were nothing in this endless expanse. The green and the gray along the river were but delusions. Back to the west and south mounted the naked ridges, noble and austere by reason of their tremendous size and reach, and between them gloomed the purple gorges, mysterious, forlorn, seemingly inaccessible for beast or man. No grassy pasturelands such as had existed in Terrill's hopeful dreams! All that was not gray stone, gray earth, were mere specks of cactus, of greasewood on the boundless slopes.

Terrill's heart sank. After all, she thought bitterly, she was only a girl. She had loved the open rangeland of Texas, over which she had ridden nearly a thousand miles, but could she ever do aught but hate this deceitful desert? She had loved the river bottoms of the Red, the Sabine, the Brazos, the Colorado, and the San Saba. They had openness, color, life, beauty. But this Rio Pecos, for all its pale silver gleam, its borders of white and green, seemed cold, treacherous, aloof, winding its desolate way down into the desolate unknown.

"Oh, Dad!" cried Terrill, voicing her first surrender. "Take me back! . . . This dreadful Pecos can never be home!"

Chapter V

TO THE cowhands at Healds' ranch he called himself Pecos Smith. They were not long in discovering that he was the best horseman, the best shot, the best roper that had ever ridden up out of Southwest Texas. But that was about all they ever learned about his past.

Pecos had come up the river with a trail driver named McKeever, who had a contract to deliver cattle at Santa Fé, New Mexico. The Spanish towns of Santa Fé, Taos, Las Vegas, and Albuquerque furnished a growing market for beef. The Government forts added largely to this demand. Cattlemen, believing in future protection against the marauding bands of Indians, had followed the more adventurous settlers into southern New Mexico and western Texas. Most of the cattle at this period came from the Rio Grande.

McKeever, on his return, stopped at Healds' minus one of his rangy vaqueros, and it was observed that that rider was Smith.

"We left Smith behind at Santa Fé," explained the trail driver. "He pecosed another man an', like he always does after a shootin', he got drunk. We couldn't wait fer him. But I reckon he'll be along soon."

"Quarrelsome cowhand, this Smith?" asked Bill Heald, one of the brother ranchers.

"Not atall. He's aboot the best-natured boy you'd want to meet," returned McKeever. "But he gets picked at, seems like, or else he's everlastin' bustin' into somebody's trouble. An' he's shore hell with a gun."

That was Smith's introduction to the Healds. Several days after that he dropped in at the ranch, a clean-cut, smiling, devil-may-care Texas boy of the old stock. Bill Heald took a fancy to him, and being in need of riders offered him a job.

"Wal, I'll shore take ye up," drawled Smith. "Mac won't like it. But he was ornery up there at Santa Fé. Cussed me powerful."

"McKeever told me you shot a man," rejoined Heald, slowly, watching the rider. "In fact, he said *another* man."

"Damn Mac's pictures, anyhow," complained the rider, annoyed. "He's always talkin' aboot me."

Heald decided it would be wiser to waive personal inquiries, despite the curiosity Smith aroused. Heald's experienced eye, however, took in certain details about this rider that prompted one more query. "Ever work for a Mexican?"

"Yeah. Don Felipe Gonzales," admitted Smith, readily. "My father was killed in the war an' my family busted up. Don Felipe was an old acquaintance of ours. So I went across the Rio Grande an' rode his range four or five years. I'm not shore how many. Anyway, till I got chased back over the river."

Further than that Smith never vouchsafed information about himself, to the Healds or any of the hands.

Upon close scrutiny of Pecos Smith, Heald decided

that his appearance belied the boyishness that seemed to be born of his careless, free insouciance. His age must have been between twenty and twenty-five years, which was not very young for a range rider in Texas. He was just above medium height, not so lean and rangy as most horsemen, having wide shoulders and muscular round limbs. He struck Heald as a remarkably able horseman, which opinion was soon more than verified. All the leather trappings about Smith and his horse were ragged and shiny from use, particularly the gun holster which hung low on his left thigh and the saddle sheath. The ivory handle of his gun was yellow with age. What metal showed, and this was also true of his rifle, shone with the bright, almost white luster of worn, polished steel. His saddle, bridle, and spurs, also his black sombrero, were of Spanish make, decorated with silver; and if they had not been so old might have made a thief out of many a vaquero.

"Smith, you're on," declared Bill Heald, finally, having been unaccountably slow in decision, for him. "Thet's a grand hoss you're forkin'. If he ain't Arabian I'll eat him. Have a care for him. What with this outfit an' the Comanches you'll have hell keepin' him."

"Wal, Cinco cain't be caught in a race, anyhow," drawled the rider, patting the tired and dusty horse. "Heald, I'm shore thankin' you for the job."

"Not atall. We're short-handed. An' you strike me right. But, Smith, if you've got thet queer hand-itch fer a gun, won't you doctor it with axle grease or somethin'?"

"Never no more, boss. I'm a sick hombre. Red lik-

ker an' me air on the oots," drawled the rider, his
flashing smile answering the other's levity.

"Then you're set heah," concluded Bill Heald.

It chanced that Heald's sister, Mary, had watched
this interview from the door, unobserved. She was only
sixteen, and with the brothers had been made an orphan not so long ago. She was the pride of their eyes
as well as the disturber of their peace.

"Oh, Billy!" she exclaimed, her black eyes shining
roguishly. "That's the handsomest rider I've seen since
I came West."

"Thunder an' blazes!" ejaculated Heald. "If I'd
seen thet I'd never hev hired him. . . . Mary, if you
make eyes at him ranchin' will shore stop heah."

The next time Heald saw Smith he remembered
Mary's tribute and took keener note of the stranger.
Smith was not an unusual type for a Texan, though he
appeared to have Texas characteristics magnified.
Many Texans were sandy-haired or tow-headed, and
possessed either blue or gray eyes. This rider had flaxen
hair and he wore it so long that it curled from under
his sombrero. His face was like a bronze mask, except
when he talked or smiled, and then it lightened. In profile it was sharply cut, cold as stone, singularly more
handsome than the full face. His eyes assumed dominance over all other features, being a strange-flecked,
pale gray, of exceeding power of penetration. His lips,
in repose, were sternly chiseled, almost bitter, but as
they were mostly open in gay, careless talk or flashing
a smile over white teeth, this last feature was seldom
noticed.

The *remudo* filed in that night, enlivening the ranch again, and next day Bill Heald asked his brother what he thought of the new cowhand.

"Strikes me fine. Likable cuss, I'll gamble," replied John Heald. "Real Texas stuff in thet fellar."

"Mary has fallen in love with him already."

"O Lord! What'll we do, Bill? Send her back to Auntie Heald?"

"Hell no! She stays if she puts the outfit up a tree. Mebbe this Pecos hombre can win her."

"I don't know aboot thet," replied John, soberly. "Mary's tryin' an' thet's no joke. I want her to settle out heah an' marry some good fellar. But this Pecos has a gun record, Bill. Did you know thet?"

"McKeever told me Smith had killed another man," admitted the elder brother, thoughtfully.

"Sandy told me more than thet," went on John, impressively. "Sandy says he sneaked a peep at this Pecos fellar's gun. It had six notches on the handle an' one of them was cut fresh."

"Six. . . . I reckoned it might be more. Let's not borrow trouble, John. Anyway, it's a shootin' country an' we might be most damn glad to have thet kind of a Texan among us."

"Shore. An' it ain't likely Mary will capitulate to a blood-spiller. She's squeamish for a Heald. But she might flirt with the fellar. Mary's the dod-blastedest flirt I ever seen."

"Flirtin' might be as bad as a real case," rejoined Bill. "What concerns me is the effect thet'd have on our outfit. You know, John, every last man Jack of them thinks he's goin' to wed with Mary."

Pecos Smith gave opportunity for various discussion among the brothers and their cowhands. It was a lonesome country, and strangers, that were not to be avoided, were few and far between. Their opinions, however, fell far wide of the mark, except as they had to do with Smith as a vaquero. The horse Cinco lived up to his looks and his rider's pride. Pecos was a whole outfit in himself. He never knew when work was done. His riding and roping might have been that of the famous vaquero, Rodiriquez. Every cowhand in the outfit had his sombrero full of bullet holes, proofs of Pecos' marksmanship. Pecos was most obliging and he could not resist any kind of a bet. He seldom missed a sombrero tossed into the air, and as often as not he put two bullets through it before it dropped. He would never let anyone handle his gun, which shared with Cinco in his affections. Pecos proved to be a round peg fitting snugly into a round hole. Riders were scarce, cattle growing plentiful, likewise rustlers, and always the horse-stealing Comanches.

Long before McKeever drove north again with a herd of steers Pecos had won the regard of the X Bar outfit, which was run by an adjoining rancher, as well as that of the H H outfit, belonging to the Healds.

The singular thing about Pecos, remarkable in view of the universal esteem in which he was held, was that he avoided contact with people, save the riders with whom he worked or those of the neighboring ranch. Mary Heald gave a party one night to which all the people in that part of the country were invited. Somebody had to be out with the cattle on that particular night, and Pecos took the job for another rider. Mary Heald was furious with him, and snubbed him on the following day when he happened to run into her at the corrals.

"Wal, I just cain't please the ladies, nohow," he drawled to Sandy McClain.

"Huh! Say, you mysterious cuss—you could have 'em eatin' out of your hand if you'd give 'em a chance."

"Sandy, yore what them Colorado chaps call loco."

"Am I? What's thet?"

"Wal, it's a kind of weed thet hosses eat an' go off their haids."

"Pecos, air you hitched to some gurl?—Married, I mean?"

"Me?—Santa Maria!"

"Air you a woman-hater then? Had yore heart broke? . . . Honest, Pecos, yore laughin' an whistlin' an' makin' fun don't fool this heah chicken none. You're a sad hombre."

"No, Sandy, my heart's shore not broke yet, but doggone me, it wouldn't take much."

Bill Heald and his brother satisfied themselves finally as to Pecos' peculiar aloofness.

"First off I figured Pecos was one of them Texas-Ranger-dodgin' hombres," said Bill. "But I've changed my mind. Thet fellar never did a shady thing in his life. He comes of a good family, you can tell thet, an' he's had trouble."

"Bill, I agree with you. More'n thet I'd say if there

was a sheriff or a ranger huntin' Pecos he'd never dodge him. I'd shore hate to be the sheriff that tried to arrest him, provided it was an even break."

"He fooled us aboot Mary, didn't he? Darn good lesson fer thet little lady. Only I hope she doesn't fall daid in love with Pecos."

"Wal, if she did it wouldn't last. . . . No, Pecos is just one of them driftin', fascinatin' vaqueros. I've met as many as I have fingers. Texas is the only country thet could produce such a breed."

McKeever, on his return from Santa Fé spent a night at the Heald ranch and not only inquired about his lost vaquero, but wanted to see him. Pecos was not to be located.

"Reckon he likes it hyar an' wants to hang aboot," concluded the trail driver, with a sly look at Mary, which made her blush flamingly.

"I'm shore nobody hyar wants him hangin' aboot," she retorted, her chin tilting.

"My loss is your gain, folks," returned McKeever, resignedly. "They don't come any finer than Smith."

If there were any doubts at the H H ranch as to the status of Pecos Smith, that recommendation definitely dispersed them.

The time came when Pecos Smith justified the prefix to his name, if he had not already done so. Like an Indian, it was second nature for him to remember any trail, any thicket, any creek bottom, or canyon that he had ever seen. His brain instinctively photographed places.

The Rio Pecos from Castle Gap Canyon to the New Mexico border became his intimate possession. The Healds did not know whether they were running twenty thousand head of stock or thirty thousand. Pecos Smith had a more accurate estimate of their cattle than anyone, and his reports of unbranded calves and yearlings and steers hiding in the thickets of the creek bottoms or the brakes of the Pecos ran into the thousands.

Bill Heald took this with a grain of salt, while his brother pondered over it seriously. Like all ranchers of the period, they were careless branders. That was to say they did not have the hands nor the time to comb the range for unbranded stock. Cattle had begun to demand a price and the future looked promising. But money was scarce. Texas was in her first stage of recovery after the ruin left by the war. The Healds were doing about all that was possible for them.

Rustlers appeared on the Pecos range. The long-horns had come originally from south of the Rio Grande; so had the cattle thieves. Nowhere had there ever been such wholesale and tremendous thefts of cattle as along the Mexican border. That was one reason why Texans like the Healds had moved to isolated ranges.

But up to this period the X Bar, the H H, and other outfits had not suffered much from rustling. At least they had not been aware of it. Every rancher lost stock, the same as he appropriated a little that really did not belong to him. There had not been, however, any appreciable inroads upon the herds.

It was through the trail driver, McKeever, that the Healds found the opportunity they had planned and waited for, and this was a considerable market for their product. McKeever bought cattle from them in large numbers and drove them to the Spanish settlements in New Mexico and the Government headquarters. Extensive military operations against the Indians were already under way. Rumors of railroads through New Mexico and Texas were rife. Altogether the Healds looked forward to huge markets, to advancing prices, and trail herds of their own.

To this end Pecos Smith was promoted to be their outside man. He accepted the job with reluctance, and upon being asked why he was not keen about it he replied rather evasively that it held too much responsibility. His duty was to ride all over the country, to the farthest outlying ranges, not only to keep track of the Heald cattle, but to gauge general conditions, study the methods of other ranchers, and watch their round-ups. Thus Pecos Smith added to his already wide knowledge of the country.

Upon his return from one of these trips, in the autumn of his second year's service to the Healds, he ran into the inevitable trouble that had always hounded his trail.

Pecos had ridden into the ranch early in the morning, and after cleaning up was enjoying a much-needed rest and a smoke when Sandy McClain came hurrying over from the ranch-house. Pecos divined there was something up before Sandy drew near enough to distinguish his features. He could tell by that hurried yet suspensive stride. So that when Sandy arrived at the porch of the cabin, his hazel eyes full of fire and his lips hard, Pecos cursed under his breath.

"Pecos, thar's shore—hell to pay," declared Sandy.

"Who's payin' it?" queried Pecos, in his cool, lazy drawl.

"Nobody yit, but you'll have to. An' I'm gittin' this off my chest first. If it comes to a fight I'm with you."

"Thanks, Sandy, I shore appreciate thet. But usually I can tend to my own fights. Suppose you tell me aboot what's up?"

"You know thet Sawtell, foreman fer Beckman?" rushed on Sandy.

"Shore. I was at Marber's Crossin' not two months ago," replied Pecos, his boots coming down from a bench. "They had a round-up. I was there, you bet, an' I stayed, in spite of the cold shoulder from Sawtell."

"Pecos, it ain't so good. Sawtell is hyar, with three of his outfit. An' he's been hittin' the bottle, Pecos. He's loud an' nasty."

"What's it all aboot?"

"I didn't heah. But I can guess. Bill is all upset, an' madder'n hell under his hat, as I could see. He sent me to fetch you."

Pecos sat silent a moment with slowly contracting brows. His eyes were downcast. Presently he drew his gun, and flipping it open he extracted an extra cartridge from his vest pocket and inserted it in the one empty chamber. Then he arose to his feet, sheathing the gun. Without another word he strode off toward the ranch-house, with Sandy beside him, talking wildly.

Presently Pecos espied four saddled horses standing, bridles down, across the open space in front of the house. He sheered a little to the left so that he would not go abruptly around the corner.

"Keep out of this, Sandy," he ordered.

"But they're four to one, Pecos," expostulated Sandy. "An' thet red-faced Sawtell doesn't talk like he savvied you. I've got a hunch, Pecos. It won't do no harm to let them see you got a pard."

Pecos answered with a gesture that needed no speech. Sandy sheered widely to the right. Pecos heard a loud voice. Next moment he came into the open, where he had a clear view. Mary Heald was the first person he saw.

"Go in the house," Bill Heald ordered her.

"Oh, your grandmother!" retorted Mary. She was flushed and excited, and upon espying Pecos gave a violent start.

"Bill! . . . Hyar he is," she called.

Pecos took in the prospect. Sawtell, a tall cattleman wearing a bandana as red as his face, stood out before three cowhands whose posture was not easy. Bill Heald, turning from Mary, called to his brother: "This ain't no mix fer her. Drag her inside."

"Let her stay. Mebbe she'll hyar somethin'," declared John.

"I *did* hyar somethin' and it's a confounded lie," flashed Mary, hotly.

Upon seeing Pecos approaching, Bill Heald showed a subtle change of manner.

"Sawtell, hyar's Pecos now, to speak fer himself. We think you're on a wrong track. An' if you'll listen to reason, you'll go mighty slow."

"Hell!—Air you threatenin' me, Bill Heald?" returned the visitor, harshly.

"Not atall. I'm just advisin' you."

"Wal, I don't need any advice. I was ridin' these ranges long before you."

"Shore. But you don't know Pecos Smith."

"Pecos! Whar'd he git thet handle?"

"I don't know. He had it when he come."

Pecos halted some paces out.

"Boss, what's up heah?"

"I'm ashamed to tell you, Pecos, an' I swear I'd never done it if I could have persuaded Sawtell to ride off."

"Thanks, Heald. . . . Get back an' leave this to me."

Bill promptly acted upon that suggestion, and it was equally noticeable that the three cowhands behind Sawtell moved out of line with him.

Pecos eyed the cattleman and read him through. There would be no equivocation here. The matter had been settled in Sawtell's mind before he arrived at Healds' ranch, and he had fortified it with drink.

"You know me, Smith?" demanded Sawtell. He was loud, authoritative, but not of the braggart breed.

"I haven't the honor, Señor," replied Pecos, coldly. "When I called on you at Marber's Crossin' not long

since you didn't give me the chance. An' I reckoned I
didn't miss much."

"Wal, you might have missed hyarin' aboot the
maverick-brandin' thet's goin' on."

"No. I didn't have to heah thet."

Bill Heald could not keep out of the colloquy.

"Pecos reported to me. The H H is losin' a dribble
of mavericks."

"Is thet so?" sneered Sawtell. He was ugly and
could not be conciliated.

"See hyar, Sawtell," retorted Heald, sharply, at
last out of patience. "You come shore set to make
trouble. An' by Gawd, you're liable to run into more'n
you bargained fer."

"Air you defendin' maverick-brandin'?" demanded
Sawtell, sarcastically.

"Boss, would you mind leavin' this deal to me?"
interposed Pecos.

"All right, Sawtell. You're makin' your own bed.
I've no more to say," concluded Heald, and he backed
away.

Pecos made two strides which brought him within
ten feet of the irate cattleman. Everyone present except Sawtell must have sensed the singular, cold
menace of the vaquero. Only the false stimulus of
whisky could have blinded a matured Texan to imminent peril. And at that Sawtell seemed confronted
with an obstructing thought.

"Sawtell, you gave me a cold shoulder up at Marber's Crossin'."

"You bet I did."

"If it hadn't been fer my boss, I'd have called you then, in yore own back yard. I took thet as an insult."

"Wal, you took it proper. An' if it hadn't been fer the Healds hyar I'd run you off my ranch."

That was definite and it settled all but the conclusion of this meeting, which the cattleman was evidently too obtuse or bull-headed to sense. One of his men made a movement as if to intercede, but was restrained by a second. They edged nervously to one side, as if wary to get out of line with Pecos' piercing eyes. But they would have had to dissolve in thin air to accomplish that.

Pecos' silence, his strained intensity, the suspense of the moment penetrated Sawtell's befogged brain. But it was too late.

"Mr. Pecos Smith," Sawtell blustered, "you know them X Bar cowhands, Curt Williams an' Wess Adams?"

"Reckon I do."

"They rode fer thet greaser Felipe, down on the Big Bend."

"So did I."

"Wal, thet ain't any recommend fer them or you."

"Beggars cain't be choosers. I had to ride to live. . . . Yore beatin' aboot the bush. Come on!"

"I had Williams an' Adams fired off the X Bar."

"No news to me."

"They was seen brandin' mavericks on my range."

"Sawtell, it's not beyond the bounds of reason thet them mavericks wasn't yore'n," replied Pecos, coldly.

"No, it ain't. But I'm choosin' to claim them."

"Thet's yore affair. Tolerable unhealthy, I'd say—
on the Pecos."

Sawtell's hurried speech apparently augmented his
anger, but did not relieve the cramping effect of Pecos'
front.

"I'm down hyar to have you fired off the H H,"
shouted the cattleman.

"Cain't be done. I quit."

"Ahuh. When?"

"Aboot two minutes ago."

"You're a slick hombre, Mr. Smith," retorted Sawtell, exasperated to derision. "Wal, then, I'll drive
you off the Pecos range."

Pecos made a singular movement, too swift to discern, though it left him as if in the act of leaping.
From his whole being suddenly emanated terrible
suspense.

"You —— idiot! Drive *me* off the Pecos? . . .
What's all yore gab aboot?"

Sawtell had again gone too far. There was no retreat. The red of his face receded in a marked line,
leaving it a leaden gray.

"You was thick with them maverick-branders."

"Who accuses me?" cried Pecos, piercingly.

Sawtell let out an incoherent roar—rage at himself
as well as at Pecos—at the realization that he had
misjudged his man. His arm moved stiffly. His hand
jerked at his gun.

The single, whipping throw of Pecos' gun dis-
charged it. Sawtell's body lost its vibrant tension. It
slumped. His head dropped forward. Then he swayed.

Pecos leaped like a tiger past the falling man to face the cowhands, his gun high, quivering to flash down with the force that would fire it.

"Any of you back him up?" he yelled, stridently.

"Smith, it weren't our mistake," hoarsely replied the one who would have importuned Sawtell. "Honest to Gawd—we wanted him—to go slow."

Pecos waved them off, and watched them go hurriedly toward their horses. When he turned, Bill Heald was kneeling beside Sawtell. Sandy was running over and John Heald was trying to drag the white-faced girl away.

"Daid! . . . Shot through the heart! . . . Pecos, this is shore bad bizness," ejaculated Bill.

"You heah him!" Pecos' voice cracked like steel on ice.

"Shore. But my Gawd, man, I didn't expect you to kill him," returned Heald, suddenly rising.

"You believe ——"

"No, Pecos! Not fer a second," protested Heald, hastily, lifting a hand. "An' thet's straight. John an' I think you're as clean an' fine as they come. McKeever swore by you. This damn fool Sawtell must have been drunk. I *told* him. . . . Pecos, don't hold any of it against the H H."

Pecos lowered the gun, but he kept up his pacing to and fro, his strange eyes pivoting like the oscillations of a compass needle. All his cold poise was gone. He had the lunge, the standing hair, the savageness of a wild animal. Sandy approached him, to halt in hesitation.

"Pecos, you had to bore him," he ejaculated. "You jest had to. We'll all stick up fer you. Sawtell brought it on himself."

One of the retreating cowhands, now mounted on their horses, called to Heald: "We'll send a wagon back fer him."

"All right. Make it pronto," Heald replied.

Pecos sheathed his gun, and with that motion appeared to sag. He ceased his cat-like stride. Freckles no one had ever seen stood out on his clammy face. His hair was wet. He stooped to pick up his sombrero, which had fallen when he leaped to confront Sawtell's men.

"Bill, didn't I tell you not to give me thet outside job?" he queried.

"You shore did, Pecos. I'm sorry. But I don't see what difference thet could have made."

"I seen too much, Bill. An' I tried to—wal, never mind aboot thet. . . . I'm shore thankin' you an' John fer keepin' me heah so long an' fer defendin' me to thet white-livered liar."

His implication must have been clear to Heald. At least he looked as if he had grasped at the truth—Pecos had come upon these roistering cowhands at some shady deal. He had tried to show them the error of their ways and had kept his mouth shut about it.

"Pecos, listen hyar. Sawtell must have had a showdown on Williams an' Adams. He was aimin' to bluff you into squealin'—shore he didn't know you."

"You heah somethin' aboot Curt an' Wess?"

"Yes. More'n once, an' I have my doubts, Pecos."

The vaquero threw up his hands. "—— the fools!"

At this juncture Mary Heald broke away from her brother and ran out to confront Pecos. She was still white, sick, trembling, but she was brave.

"Pecos, I know you're not a thief," she burst out.

His somber face lightened beautifully.

"Wal, Miss Mary, thet's shore good fer me to heah. . . . I've no home, no family, no friends, an' when I go out on the long trail again, it'll be good to remember you an' yore brothers believed in me."

"We do, Pecos. Oh, we do," she replied, brokenly. "Don't say you've no friends—no home. . . . Do not leave us, Pecos."

"I cain't stay. It might do yore brothers harm. Those cowhands will tell how Bill stuck up fer me. An' they'll add to it. If I stayed on ——"

"Mary, he's right," interposed Bill. "Much as I regret it, Pecos will have to leave the H H."

"Shore. An' I may as wal have the game as the blame," added Pecos, bitterly.

"Don't say thet, boy," entreated Heald who heard in this resignation the spirit and the hopelessness that had sent so many fine Texas boys down the wrong trail. It was cruel, because in that great state, depleted by wars and overrun with ruined boys and men, there seemed so slight a line of demarcation between the right trail and the wrong.

"Oh, you wild vaquero!" burst out Mary, passionately. "That is wrong—to yourself—to us . . . . to *me*! . . . Pecos, you're such a—a wonderful boy. Don't let the horror of—of killin' another man drive you to—to

. . . He deserved it. He was mean. I—I could have shot him myself. . . . Bill—John—say somethin' ——"

The girl failed of utterance there. She had much excuse for agitation, but neither her youth nor the shock of seeing a man killed could wholly account for all she betrayed.

"Pecos, I reckon you'd better stay on," said Bill, huskily. "I'll ride up to Marber's an' prove your innocence—explain how Sawtell was drunk an' forced this shootin'."

"No. Bill, you cain't do thet," returned Pecos. "I've riled up bad blood before an' I shore don't want to do it heah."

"Pecos!" whispered the girl.

The vaquero turned to her in a realizing amazement that almost hid his gratitude. "Miss Mary, I shore thank you. . . . An' I promise you—thet if *anythin'* can make me go straight from now on—it'll be you—yore faith—yore goodness. Adios."

He reached as if to take her hand, drew back, and wheeled away. Sandy McClain ran to stride beside him.

"Adios, Pecos!" called the girl. "Go straight—an' come—back—some—day."

Chapter VI

BUT it developed quickly that neither the sweet memory of Mary Heald, nor the scorn Pecos Smith had for rustlers, nor the promise he had given could keep him straight.

Branding mavericks was not a crime in Texas at that early stage of cattle-raising. All ranchers did it more or less, without being absolutely sure that the calves belonged to them. There could be no positive identification, unless the calf accompanied a branded cow. And if a calf or a yearling or a two-year-old did not get the mark of one outfit, it would eventually find that of another.

But in his heart Pecos Smith knew that he had slipped, for the first time in his range life. Bitterly he regarded it as being shoved, rather than having slipped. Nevertheless, what could he do? The X Bar made the excuse that they did not require an extra hand; so did another outfit below the New Mexico line. Pecos' good sense urged him to work south and take up with McKeever again, or some other cattleman west of the Pecos, or even Don Felipe. But his pride and his bitter conviction that there was a step on his trail set his face the other way. He made up his mind to throw in with Curt Williams and Wess Adams, who were indeed trafficking in unbranded mavericks. There was no

law against it. There was no obstacle, except that of
a gun; and bold maneuvers like Sawtell's were the
exception rather than the rule. Pecos argued that if
he stuck to the branding of mavericks, and collected a
herd of his own, or saved his share of the money he
would not long need to do questionable work that was
offensive to him.

Williams and Adams had not vouchsafed any information as to their market, except that it was unfailing. Pecos did not care to know. There were ranchers in New Mexico buying stock and asking no
questions. There were Government buyers dealing
directly with rustlers. The stage was almost set for a
great cattle business in the Southwest. Pecos sensed it
so well that he thought it a pity he had not already a
sizable herd of his own to start with.

Wherefore he trailed the two X Bar cowhands
down into the Pecos brakes and joined them.

This couple had a string of horses and a pack outfit.
Strengthened by Pecos, they made a formidable band.
Pecos knew where to locate more unbranded stock than
any cowhand in Texas. The thicketed canyons were
full of cattle, many of them that had never felt an
iron. The operations of Williams and Adams were too
loose to satisfy Pecos. He tightened them. These two
riders were on their way to becoming rustlers very
shortly. Pecos did not think he could afford to train
with them very long. Still, he had to take risks.

"Listen, you footloose hombres," he said. "I can
round up thousands of unbranded stock south of hyar.

Hard work an' lots of time, but shore an' we cain't get in trouble."

"We'll take 'em as they come," replied Wess Adams, a craggy faced young rider, dissolute and forceful.

"Pecos has some good idees, Wess," interposed Williams, who was more amenable and less reckless. "So we gotta compromise."

"If you must work out these brakes—which is shore pore judgment—it'd be best to throw together a bunch of say a hundred haid or less, an' drive them to yore buyers once a month."

"A hundred haid an' once a month? Bah!" blurted Adams.

"I'm sidin' with Pecos," said Williams, thoughtfully. "An' then it ain't so damn safe."

"Wal, when it gits hot for us we'll change tactics," rejoined Pecos. "We'll clap on another brand thet nobody ever saw, an' throw the stock out on the range. None of the ranchers will know thet brand is ours. Later when the brands are old we can round up an' drive a big herd without much risk."

"Wess, it's a good idee," ventured Williams. Adams at length gave in with bad grace.

The trio set to work. They did their roping and branding alone; at least Pecos did, and he accounted for as many as both his comrades. In a few days they had a mixed herd of over five score. Williams and Adams started north with this bunch, expecting to drive twenty-five miles a day, which would get them to their market in less than a week. Pecos remained in camp and went on with his riding, roping and branding. He regretted that he had not been able to go into this game alone. However, that required horses and outfit and especially a market, unless he could afford to wait and watch his herd grow. He liked the lonely life and came to love the Rio Pecos. It was now a refuge.

His comrades returned in due course, and Pecos found himself the richer for something in excess of two hundred dollars, more money than he had ever possessed at one time in his life. His exuberance was short-lived; this money had been earned, but not by honest toil and sweat.

In far less than a month Wess Adams had prevailed upon Williams to make another drive north, with all the stock they and Pecos had burned brands on. Pecos entered strong objection, but in vain. He deliberated just which of two courses to pursue—the first, to pick a quarrel with Adams and shoot him, the second, to let his partners go on their perilous way without further resistance. Pecos found the latter more to his liking. He needed to resist this strange tendency to resort to his gun, and if he could keep strict watch in their absence, prepared for anything, so that if they were trailed back, as seemed most likely, he need not be caught. On the other hand, he reasoned that if they never returned, well and good; he would take the outfit and move to a wilder country farther south on the Pecos.

But Adams and Williams came back. They were hard riders, cunning and resourceful, driving mostly at night, and they must have had allies somewhere along the trail. Thus for Pecos the situation remained the same, except that he had another and a larger roll of greenbacks.

From late summer, through autumn and winter, those two indefatigable riders made ten drives to their market in New Mexico. Towards spring they grew bolder, as was inevitable for such characters and as a result of such success. Moreover, Adams returned smelling of strong drink. Therefore, when sometime in April, the two did not return from their drive on time, Pecos was not surprised. Nor was he worried or grieved. He had decided this drive was to be the last for him, under any circumstances.

Pecos had so much money that he did not dare count it; assuredly enough to start him with a ranch of his own somewhere. The Pecos near its junction with the Rio Grande took his fancy, but that had long been the seat of Mexican depredations, and he had had enough to do with Mexicans. He indulged in long cogitations about this future venture. He had been clever to allow Williams and Adams to make the cattle drives to their market—which, after all, was their own wish; nevertheless Pecos felt that he might be implicated, too, when these two riders had gone to the end of their tether. In that case he had only to lie low in hiding for a year or so to be forgotten. Texas was too enormous, too wild, too swiftly changing on its course to empire, for a few unbranded mavericks to be remembered. There were a thousand real rustlers to be contended with before considering that. Sometimes Pecos had his doubts as to the latest status of his comrades. What a slight step it was from branding mavericks to burning brands! Yet therein lay the actual dishonesty. When mavericks grew scarce, as they certainly were decreasing in number down the river as far as Pecos had ridden, Williams and Adams might be expected to resort to burning out of brands.

A week or more beyond the date Pecos had set as the latest for the return of his two partners, he became certain some untoward circumstance had befallen them. They might have been caught; they might have sold this last bunch of stock and departed for other fields, without the formality of returning to give Pecos his share of the proceeds. Adams would have done it, but Williams seemed hardly that kind of a man.

Anyway Pecos moved his camp, choosing a wild and almost inaccessible retreat some miles below. He packed most of the fast diminishing supplies, and he left the pack-horses there with Cinco. A dense thicket choked the mouth of the little side canyon, where it opened on the Pecos, and back of it there were water and grass in abundance. It could not be entered from the mouth, owing to the matted underbrush, and as there were no cattle or horse tracks leading into it there was little danger of pursuers bothering with the place. Pecos had no concern about its being discovered from above.

From here he went forth every day, carrying his rifle and a pocket full of ammunition, to make a slow, cautious way back to the old camp. When his comrades returned it would be time enough to explain his action to them.

On the fourth morning after Pecos had left the old camp, and the eleventh since his partners had been overdue, he sighted a bunch of Indians on the east bank of the river. He had only a glimpse of lean wild forms and ragged mustangs crossing a brake back from the high bank, but that was enough for Pecos Smith. His persistent and unerring watchfulness had at last earned its reward. With the arrival of spring Kiowas or Comanches might be expected to ride down off the Staked Plains to make a raid anywhere in West Texas.

Pecos deliberated awhile. These savages might be on their way upriver, returning from a raid. There was an Indian trail across on that side. The camp that the three maverick hunters had chosen was in a low-walled canyon, well hidden from the west side of the Pecos, but exposed to the other. If Williams and Adams had returned it would almost surely have been the night before, in which case their horses and camp-fire smoke would betray them to the Indians.

Keeping well out of sight, Pecos made his way toward the old camp. He had traveled more than two miles when his sharp eye detected movement and color at the mouth of a ravine on the eastern bank. A band of mounted Indians, that he made sure were Comanches, rode out of the ravine and into the river. A lone string of half naked savages! He counted eighteen. The river was shallow there and could be forded at this stage of the water. Pecos watched them with hard eyes. More than once he had nearly lost his scalp to these painted devils. They crossed without difficulty and disappeared.

Half a mile up the river opened the canyon in which lay the camp Pecos was approaching. He knew that horses could not be ridden up that far. There was a brake, however, between the impassable bank and where the Indians had crossed. Perhaps they would pass up that. At any rate, they were bent upon mischief.

Pecos retraced his steps to a brake where he could get up out of the river bottom. Once out of the ravine, he took to the rocks and brush, making fast time until he got into the vicinity of the gorge he expected the Comanches to work up, when he proceeded very warily. But they had not passed that way. This meant that their procedure must almost certainly be directed against the old camp.

This point was not now far distant, and it appeared certain that Pecos could arrive there ahead of the Comanches, if he chose to risk traversing rather open ground. His first impulse was to risk anything to warn his comrades, provided they had arrived. Sober reason, however, gave him pause. He could warn them as well from the rim of the canyon wall, and be in a much more advantageous position to help them ward off the impending attack.

Nevertheless the moments became fraught with uncertainty. Pecos hoped his comrades had not returned, but he had a queer intuitive conviction that they had. Adams would be sleeping off the effects of liquor and a long ride; Williams was certainly not a wary man around camp, at least this camp in the brakes of the Pecos.

Something not only held Pecos from hurried action,

but forced him to make slow detours under cover. Once near the south wall of the canyon he would be secure, as it was exceedingly broken.

As he neared its vicinity he thought he heard a distant neigh of a horse. He waited in suspense. The morning was quite advanced, clear and bright, not a cloud in the sky, with the sun burning the herald of summer near at hand. Buzzards sailed high above the camp. These uncanny birds always annoyed Pecos. A sarcastic enemy had once told Pecos that he would be food for buzzards some day. The enemy had verified that presagement for himself, but Pecos had never forgotten. Buzzards had a strange prescience of death and carrion soon to be visited upon a certain locality. Bees hummed by Pecos as he crouched among the rocks, listening. Presently he went on, eyes and ears strained.

But it was his nose that gave first and sure proof of his sagacity. Smoke! "I shore smell smoke," he whispered.

That meant Williams and Adams were back. The fact shot a cold sense of tragedy through Pecos, which he could not explain on the score of imminent peril. He could not understand it, but it felt so. No more could he have explained his feeling about the buzzards. Three men under cover could stand off a larger force of Indians than this one Pecos had seen crossing the river.

At last Pecos gained the canyon, but some distance above camp, and round a bend. He had to work down along the broken rim among thick thorned bushes and gray sage, the treacherous dagger-spiked *lechuguilla* and the maze of broken rocks.

He soon got out of breath, not being accustomed to long climbs out of his saddle, and this going was very rough. Panting and sweating, he thought it best to rest a little. He imagined he might need the clearest of faculties and all his breath before so very long.

Still back and down from the ragged rim-wall he made his way, not at all sure of where he should peep over in to the canyon. Presently he espied a column of blue smoke lazily rising. He had passed the camp. That was all right, for it placed him between his comrades and the sneaking Comanches.

Pecos got down on his knees and one hand, to crawl toward the rim. He had not proceeded far when he was brought stockstill by a horrid scream abruptly cut off. Cold sweat now broke out over the hot sweat. "What'n hell? Was thet a hoss or a man?" he whispered low. Then his sensitive ear caught loud angry voices. Whatever was going on down below, the Comanches had not yet made their presence known. Wherefore Pecos made short work of the remaining distance to the rim, coming out in a niche of the wall, covered by brush. He could not be seen; he could get away swiftly; and pursuit was impossible within a reasonable time.

Pecos raised himself to peep down, the voices guiding him. His eyes nearly popped out at sight of four men holding Adams on a horse. He was cursing, bellowing, entreating. They had a lasso round his neck, with an end thrown up over the branch of a tree.

This led Pecos' startled gaze to something dark and moving. It jerked. A man hung by his neck. Williams! He was kicking in a horribly grotesque manner. His distorted face, eyes distended, mouth wide, tongue out, was in plain sight across the canyon.

An instant of paralyzed staring was long enough for Pecos, Adams and Williams had been surprised by cattlemen, who were meting out the law to rustlers. They were hanging them. Pecos had heard of that summary justice coming to the Texas range. His blood froze, only to gush again in a bursting fire. No cattlemen would ever put a noose over his head.

All five men were shouting, but Adams' voice could be heard above the others. Pecos grasped that the coward was trying to beg off or buy his freedom. What a fool! He did not know Texans!

Suddenly Pecos had a lightning-swift realization of his complicity in this tragedy. He was an ally of Adams, though he had never liked or trusted the man. But he had thrown in with them, he had helped them brand mavericks; he had shared their ill-gotten spoils. He did not consider himself a rustler. But it was monstrously evident that these cowmen regarded Adams and Williams as rustlers.

This, then, was the inevitable climax Pecos had dreaded. He had killed Sawtell because he had been unjustly accused. But if he killed here, in defense of the comrades who had been outlawed by the range, he would be an outlaw himself.

Pecos made his choice instantly. His code left him

no alternative. He cocked and raised his rifle, deadly sure of saving Adams' life.

"*Stretch hemp!*" yelled the leader, in a stentorian voice. And he heaved on the rope, while two of his men wheeled from the victim to assist.

Even as Pecos swerved the rifle to align its sights with this leader, Adams was jerked half out of the saddle.

Then from below Pecos, and to his right, boomed a buffalo gun. The leader of that hanging squad uttered a hoarse cry. Dropping the rope, he staggered, arms spread wide to fall into the grass.

Before Adams had sunk back into the saddle a roar of heavy rifles followed the first report, accompanied by the hideous war cry of Comanches.

Pecos went stiff in every muscle. He lowered his rifle, his gaze riveted on the terrible scene opposite. Another cattleman fell. The horse leaped up, throwing Adams off. It plunged down, to kick with all four hoofs in the air, suddenly to sag quiet. Adams had been crippled. Still with the noose around his neck he tried to crawl. The rope, which had been over a branch, caught up in the tree. While Adams frantically pulled to free it he received more bullets and slid face forward. The third cattleman leaped behind the tree. And the fourth was brought down before he could reach shelter behind the rocks. But he was not killed. With a broken leg at least, he flopped behind the fallen horse.

Puffs of blue smoke rose from behind the tree.

Pecos saw the man behind the horse slide a rifle out of its saddle-sheath to level it and fire.

Pecos crawled out of the niche to a point where he could see below. Fortune favored him, as it ruled disaster to the Comanches. Pecos watched them slipping, sliding, gliding, down among the rocks, into the thicket that fringed that side of the canyon. They filled the air with their wild cries of hate and exultance. Emboldened by the success of their surprise attack, they were charging. Still they kept shooting as fast as they could reload, and the din of the heavy rifles was so loud that Pecos could scarcely hear the rapid fire from the two cattlemen.

At this juncture Pecos grimly entered the engagement. He could not be seen and his lighter calibre rifle scarcely heard. The last line of the gliding Comanches appeared scarcely fifty feet below him. When Pecos drew a quick bead on a naked red back he pulled the trigger, then looked for another Indian. He fired seven shots in less than two minutes.

While he reloaded he saw the front line of savages spread to left and right. At least six of these, in their thirst for blood charged out of the thicket. Pecos discerned arrows flying like glints of light through the air, some to stick in the carcass of the horse, others in the tree.

Suddenly the cattleman who had been firing from behind the tree lunged into sight with an arrow through his middle. Evidently a cunning redskin far to the right had been able to hit him. One after an-

other, he killed the three foremost charging Comanches. The others turned tail to flee.

Here Pecos got into action again, killing the Indian
nearest him. But it was a blunder, for the other two,
out in the open, discovered him, and fled along the
edge of the thicket, screeching like demons. The remaining four or five flashed here and there among the
rocks, in open patches in the brush. Pecos connected
with another, but he was sure not fatally.

Suddenly the yelling ceased. Pecos saw that the
attack had been turned into a rout. No doubt the
Comanches supposed reinforcements had arrived. No
sign, no sound! The canyon had become appallingly
silent. Looking across, Pecos was in time to see the
cattleman who had come out from behind the tree sink
to his knees. His smoking gun dropped, and his hands
pressed round the arrowshaft in his abdomen. He fell
forward, which action could only have driven the arrow deeper. Pecos veered his searching gaze to the
crippled man behind the horse. He could not be seen.
But the rifle had slid over on this side of the horse—
a significant and ominous sign. Then on the instant,
proving the brevity of that fatal fight, Williams
kicked his last in the hanging noose.

Chapter VII

THERE was no fear that the remaining few Comanches would return. Nevertheless, Pecos got back up on the level rim and ran down to the wall that dropped off into the river. Several hundred yards below he espied them in great haste driving their ponies into the water. Presently Pecos made out five riders, one of whom was holding a sixth Indian, badly crippled, on his mount.

The range was too far for accurate shooting, nevertheless Pecos thought that while hurrying their retreat he might hit one. So from behind his covert he fired seven more shots. The bullets all fell short of a few feet, sending up white splashes, but they were almost as effective as if they had found their mark. The Comanches raced madly across the river, to disappear in a brake in the bank.

Reloading, Pecos retraced his steps to a point above camp where he could get down over the wall. He had satisfied himself fully that there were no crippled Indians, so he hurried to the scene of the hanging.

It was ghastlier than any Pecos had ever heard of, tragic and common as were fights in Texas. The swinging Williams, black in the face; the dead horse full of arrows; the cattleman lying on his face, with a bloody barb protruding far from his back—these were the details which lent most sinister and grisly aspect.

"All daid!" muttered Pecos. Then the choking rattle of blood in a man's throat informed Pecos that he was wrong. Not Adams, not the brained man behind the horse—it was the fellow with the arrow through his middle.

Pecos made haste to turn him over on his side. He was a stranger to Pecos, a man of middle age, apparently not a Texan, and he was alive, conscious, but dying. He called incoherently for water. Pecos rushed to the packs that he had stowed away under the wall, and seizing a vessel he dashed to fill it at the spring.

A moment later while Pecos held the man's head so he could drink it became more pitifully evident that he was mortally hurt.

"They're gone," he said, huskily.

"Shore. I saw the last of them crossin' the river."

"Comanche hell-hounds. . . . How many'd we do fer?"

"Eleven, I reckon, an' one crippled."

"You all alone?"

"Yes. I had the drop on them, as I was back up on the rocks."

"Wal, they spoiled our necktie party—an' you spoiled their game. . . . Reckon it—was fair. . . . Air my outfit all daid?"

"Yes, an' I'm afraid yore a gonner, too."

"Thet's a safe bet. . . . Gimme another drink?"

"Any message you want sent?" queried Pecos, presently.

"None, onless you happen to—meet this Pecos Smith," replied the other, his pale blue eyes steady on Pecos.

"Wal, thet's likely, as I happen to be Smith."

"I reckoned so. . . . But was you burnin' brands with Williams an Adams?"

"No! . . . So thet's what you was hangin' them fer. . . . They double-crossed me. The deal I made with them was maverick-brandin'."

"Wal, they shore been cheatin' you. The Heald boys spoke well of you, Smith. It's Breen Sawtell, brother of Beckman's foreman who you shot at Healds'—he's the fellar who's got it in fer you."

"Breen Sawtell? . . . Shore don't know him. What's he look like?"

"Daid ringer fer his brother. . . . An' see hyar, Pecos Smith, as I'm aboot to cash, it won't hurt me none to tell you somethin'. As I got it Breen Sawtell was stealin' his own brother's stock. Thet's why he put him on your trail, as he has—of others. . . . Want another—drink."

"Ahuh. An' why'd he pick on me?" returned Pecos, after he had given the failing man the last of the water.

"Wal, they do say Breen had a look in at Healds'—fer the gurl, you know—until you rode along."

"Bill never told me thet," exclaimed Pecos, aghast.

"Wal, it's true. . . . Smith, things air—gettin' sort of dark—an' I'm cold."

"It's kinda tough—to croak hyar, with an Indian arrow in yore gizzard," declared Pecos, feelingly.

"All in—the day's—ride," panted the dying man. "Gawd—I'm glad—thet burnin's over."

"Yeah, it's aboot all over."

"Smith, you strike me—as bein' too—good a fellar —fer rustlers like them—X Bar cowhands."

"If I'm a rustler, they made me one," declared Pecos, with passion.

"Wal, they're daid—an' nobody can hyar aboot this. . . . Chuck the game—Smith," gasped the other.

Pecos had a poignant cry on his lips, but it never left them. The cattleman's last conscious look was unforgettable, in that it changed from one of kindness to the stranger he had pursued, to a somber divination of his own lonely end. Then his senses failed, and a moment later he quivered with a cough and lay still. He had ceased to breathe.

Pecos got up to contemplate the scene. And his mind worked fast. These four cattlemen would eventually be trailed. The thing for Pecos to do was to leave everything precisely as he saw it then. Shrewd trackers might suspect the presence of an outside hand in this massacre, especially if they were keen enough to figure on the Comanches shot from the canyon wall; nevertheless Pecos considered it wisest to leave all the bodies as they lay.

There was nothing on them that he wanted, except the money he knew he would find on Adams and Williams. This he secured, in the latter's case by untying the rope and letting him down. On second thought, however, Pecos took Adams' gun, a box of ammunition, and a sack of fresh food supplies, all of which, with his rifle, made a pretty heavy burden to carry down to his own camp.

By resting frequently he made the three miles in somewhat less than two hours, which time brought the day to about noon.

Pecos decided to pack at once and strike south. A hundred miles down the Pecos would put him in another world, so far as Breen Sawtell and his ilk were concerned. He thought of Don Felipe, of McKeever, both of whom he wished to avoid, for very different reasons. Still, if he happened to encounter the trail driver it would be of no great moment, except that Pecos preferred to be unseen by anyone who knew him for a long time.

There was not a single settlement until Eagle's Nest, just above where the Pecos River joined the Rio Grande. That probably would have grown, in the years since Pecos had ridden north.

Saddling Cinco and packing the other horse were soon accomplished. What to do with all the money he had Pecos was at a loss to decide. He could not carry it all on his person, as it made too much bulk and would certainly be observed if he encountered any riders. Finally he selected out of the dozen rolls of bills all those of large denomination, and these he stowed away in deep pockets. The rest he secreted in the lining of his heavy coat, which he tied back of his saddle. Handling this money made Pecos sweat from sheer excitement. He could not persuade himself that he came by it in strict honesty, though he certainly had not stolen it. The facts narrowed down to this—some

Texas ranchers had collectively lost a good many head
of stock and he had amassed a small fortune.

Never had Pecos set out on a long ride with faculties more keenly alert. As soon as he had placed a score
of miles between him and the camp of dead men he
would breathe freer and look only ahead.

That night he camped across from Alkali Lake, a
place on the east bank which he knew less well than the
west side of the Pecos.

Adobe Wells, to which another day's travel brought
him, was also on the opposite side of the river. Likewise
Frazier's Crossing, which he was careful to pass at
night, and Dapper's Bend and Red Bluffs, were to be
feared more from the eastern shore. Another ten-hour
ride gained Castle Gap Canyon, within striking distance of the most notable, dangerous, yet solitary point
on the Rio Pecos, no less than the old ford of the Spaniards—Horsehead Crossing.

Much as Pecos loved lonesome places, he could not
abide this haunted ford. He would not even camp
there, but pushed on into the wilderness of twisted,
swelling, greasewood-spotted ridges and the shallow ravines that ran between. Canyons were few along this
somber reach of the Pecos, there being only at long
intervals a break in the lofty walls. At times Pecos
could see the opposite side of the canyon, with its high
rim wall, and part of the shaggy-brushed and rock-
ribbed slope; at other times the road curved far west of
the river.

"Tough country on hosses an' cattle, Cinco," said
Pecos. "But the grass is heah, an' the water is there.

Nothin' on earth to keep a rancher from gettin' rich, 'cept hard work, greasers, an' redskins."

These were handicaps which Pecos discovered, two days later, had not deterred a rancher or ranchers from throwing cattle onto that rocky range. He did not see many cows or steers at one given point, but in the aggregate, after a day's ride, they amounted to a surprisingly large number. Not so surprising, but certainly more significant to Pecos was the fact that he saw few calves.

Of ranchers, however, there was no sign. Cowhands probably had to ride fifty miles or more to round up these cattle. Pecos did not envy them the job on that desolate range. But the farther he rode south, finding, if anything, an increase in cattle tracks, the more it was driven home to him that somewhere along these reaches of the Pecos, there was an ideal location for his own cherished plan to materialize. Still, he was not far enough south, though he calculated he had come somewhere near a hundred miles. The trails and roads, however, had been devious. Pecos pushed on. He must not forget another thing, that he should lie low for months before starting in the ranching game. And in the ensuing days he was to recognize that the road on which he traveled south was not the trail on which he had come north.

Therefore when he rode out of a great depression to higher ground to espy the red adobe and gray stone shacks of Eagle's Nest, half hidden by green trees, and the gigantic bluff of the Rio Grande beyond, he was neither surprised nor sorry. Perhaps it was just as well, or better: something unforeseen always guided his solitary steps.

There did not appear, at a moment's glance, any appreciable change in Eagle's Nest; still, as he drew near he made out a number of adobe houses that he did not remember, and lastly a new gray structure, apparently a frame one, alongside the low flat stone and adobe post run by Dale Shevlin.

It was not an hour for the inhabitants, especially the Mexicans, to be stirring. Pecos espied a wagon far down the wide street, and there were half a dozen sleepy horses distributed from the corner of Shevlin's place past the new gray house.

Pecos got off in the shade of some trees, and tying his horses looked around for some one to question. Shevlin would scarcely remember him, and he was not likely to encounter Felipe there. Nevertheless, Pecos did not want to be recognized. There were difficulties, however, that stood in the way of his desires. He had about run out of food supplies and he was hungry; moreover, he could not avoid towns and people forever. It was here that his temper had to be encountered.

Finally he sat down in the shade. To all outward appearance Eagle's Nest was having a siesta. Presently Pecos espied a Mexican far down the street toward the Rio Grande, which flowed under the big bluff just back of the town. Then he became aware of voices in Shevlin's place. There were two doors, one opening into the post, the other into the saloon but Pecos could not tell from which the voices came. Several men were talking, evidently all at once. Pecos was amused. Men were a queer lot, always squabbling, particularly in the neighborhood of red liquor.

A moment later several persons emerged from the post, the foremost of whom was a barefooted boy who ran out into the street, gazing back over his shoulder. He did not appear exactly scared, but he certainly was excited.

Pecos accosted him. "Say, sonny, what's goin' on aboot heah?"

This did scare the youngster, as he had not observed the vaquero. He was about to bolt when Pecos' friendly smile disarmed him.

"Aw, I—never seen you."

"No wonder, son. You shore was lookin' hard back there. What's goin' on in Dale Shevlin' place?"

"He ain't there no more."

"Wal, you don't say? What's become of Dale?"

"Somebody knifed him in the back."

"Too bad. Dale was a white man. Did he have any family?"

"Yes, but Don Felipe drove them off. He runs both store an' saloon now."

"Aho. He does? Wal, thet's news. . . . Is Don Felipe heah now?"

"No, sir. He stays a good deal in Rockfort, where they say he sells cattle to Chisholm trail drivers."

"Who runs these places?"

"Man from New Orleans. Frenchy, we call him. His name is Conrad Brasee. He has two Mexicans workin'

for him, an' a white bartender. Don't know his name.
He just got to Eagle's Nest."

"Come heah, Johnny," said Pecos, persuasively.
"I'm a rider, a Texan, an' shore yore friend. Fact is
I've got a dollar thet's burnin' a hole in my vest pocket.
You want it?"

"Betcha," retorted the lad, with wide-open eyes, approaching with diminishing reluctance.

"There. Now tell me some more. I'm restin' an'
darned lonesome. It's good to listen to some news,"
went on Pecos. "So Don Felipe's doin' things around
Eagle's Nest? He must be a greaser, or a Mexican
shore."

"He's more white than Mex. But he's a greaser, all
right," replied the boy, his shrewd gray eyes, belonging
unmistakably to the breed of Texans who hated anything Mexican, seeking Pecos' with subtle meaning.

"How's the Don stand in Eagle's Nest?"

"Mister, he 'most runs it. But nobody likes him.
Why, he's killed seven men, three of them white."

"Holy smoke! He's a bad hombre," declared Pecos,
in assumed wonder. As a matter of fact he was surprised, because Felipe, when Pecos left him, had a
record of only four killings, just one of whom had been
reputed to be a white man, and that a foreigner. "So
Don Felipe is sellin' cattle to Chisholm trail drivers.
What's become of McKeever? He used to drive up
heah."

"He made his last trip 'most a year ago. My dad
says McKeever is drivin' up the Chisholm trail now."

"Ah, I see. Cattle driftin' south from heah. . . .
Don Felipe's ranch is down the Pecos, isn't it?"

"Yes, sir. Devil's River. But his vaqueros are rakin'
the brakes farther up than Eagle's Nest."

"Does yore dad say whether Felipe's vaqueros are
brandin' mavericks—or burnin' brands?" inquired
Pecos, casually.

The lad hesitated at that, which was significant
enough for Pecos.

"I—I— He never said," at length the lad faltered. "For goodness' sake, Mister, don't get the
idee ——"

"Son, I was just thinkin' out loud. Forget thet. . . .
Any other cattleman workin' the river near heah?"

"Yes, sir. Hails from New Mexico. Calls himself
Sawtell. Funny name."

A slight vibration, like a shooting spark, ran along
Pecos' nerves. Sawtell! He had once had a presenti-
ment that he was not through with that name. Certainly his questioning of the lad had not been idle, but
it had scarcely been more than curiosity. He desired to
avoid Don Felipe rather than be thrown across his
path again. His queries, however, had led somewhere.
Pecos grew soundly interested, and delved in his mind.

"Who's the big darky over there?" he asked, to
keep the lad talking. "Is he drunk?"

"Oh no, sir! Thet's Sambo, a good nigger if there
ever was one. He came hyar as vaquero to Kurnel Lambeth, who was killed a year or so ago."

"Lambeth. Wal! . . . I've heahed of him. . . .

Wal, what's the nigger look so down aboot, if he isn't drunk?"

"It's because Brasee shet Terrill up—'cause he didn't have no money to pay what was owin'. That was yestiddy. Sambo got hyar this mawnin'. He cain't do nothin'. He wasn't packin' no gun. They throwed him oot fer makin' such a fuss aboot Terrill."

"Who's Terrill?"

"This Terrill is the finest young feller who ever come to Eagle's Nest. But he ain't hyar often. Once a month, mebbe. He's the son of thet Kurnel Lambeth, an' now boss of the nigger. They have a ranch somewhere up the Pecos; Dad says Lambeth was rich in cattle a couple of years ago. But he wouldn't sell at six dollars a haid. An' now most of his cattle are gone. An' they're so poor they cain't pay fer grub."

"Cattle gone. Seems like I've heahed such words before. Gone where, son?"

The boy laughed. "You're west of the Pecos, Señor."

"So I am! I shore 'most forgot," drawled Pecos. "Wal, heah's another peso."

"Oh sir, thank you. I—I never had so much money. You must be orful rich. . . . Oh, if you are—pay Terrill's bill an' get him oot!"

"Out of where? There's no jail heah."

"Yes there is—or what Brasee calls his jail. It's a red 'dobe back of the post. The bartender throws drunken greasers in there, too. Terrill is shet in with one now."

"Wal, this is gettin' warm, boy. Is this Brasee a sheriff, too?"

"Naw, sheriff nothin'. He plays at it. There ain't no law west of the Pecos, Señor. You jest bet Brasee never fools with a Texan."

"Ahuh. I savvy. Wal, I'll go over an' get your friend Terrill out," drawled Pecos, as he arose.

The lad gave him a wondering, grateful look, and bounded away, proving in his flight that whatever the issue might have been before, it was not something to lend wings to his feet.

Pecos sauntered across toward the downcast negro. Things happened to Pecos in every conceivable way. He never learned a lesson. At every turn he encountered selfishness, crookedness, greed, brutality, bloodshed, and murder. Wherever one of these attributes flourished there was some boy or man or woman suffering loss or pain or bereavement.

Pecos Smith had known negro slaves as worthy as any white man, though he had the Southerner's contempt for most of the black trash. This man, Sambo, had the build of a vaquero, and Pecos remembered him. His boots and spurs gave further proof to Pecos. Negro vaqueros were so rare that they were remarkable. If Pecos needed anything more than recognition to heighten his ever-ready sympathy, here it was.

"Howdy, Sambo! What's it all aboot?" he queried, kindly.

The negro started violently out of his dull misery and rolled his dark eyes at Pecos from head to foot, lingering a moment at the gun sheath so prominent and low on Pecos's left thigh.

"Yas, suh. I'se Sambo, suh. What yo say, suh?"

"A lad told me you were in trouble."

"Gawd, suh, I is, I is. Turrible trubble. . . . But 'scuse me, Mister, who yo' is? Don' I know yo'?"

"Wal, Sambo, I might be a friend in need," replied Pecos, putting a hand on the negro's shoulder. As he did so the Mexican and white man whom he had observed emerging from the post went back in rather precipitately.

"Man, yo' lend me dat gun an' I'll believe yose a friend," declared the negro, suddenly flaring.

"What'll you do, Sambo?"

"I'll kill dat cussed Brasee, sho as yore borned."

"But thet'll get you into more trouble, Sambo. . . . Come over away from thet door. . . . Now don't be afraid to talk. Tell me your story, quick an' straight."

Thus admonished, the negro seemed to collect his wits. "You ought to remember me, suh. I'se Sambo, vaquero fo' Kuhnel Lambeth, dat yo' found lost up on the Crossin'. We're frum east Texas an' we come out heah 'mos' five years ago. We druv in a herd of cattle an' two years ago we had 'mos' ten thousand haid. . . . Marse Lambeth no sell when he ought. De rustlers done found us, suh, an' dey—or sumbody killed him. Now we's pore. . . . Marse Lambeth's b-boy, Massa Terrill, rid ovah heah yes'day alone. We never knowed till dis mawnin'. I rid my hawse 'mos' to deff. But Brasee hit me over de haid wid something. He got Massa Rill shet up in thet 'dobe shack wid a greaser. . . . Lemme dat gun, man, an' I show yo'."

"Hold yore hosses, Sambo. . . . What'd Brasee shet up young Terrill for?"

"He swears fo' money det Kuhnel Lambeth owes. But dat's only a 'scuse, stranger. Det —— —— Don Felipe an' his pardner, Breen Sawtell, air behin' it. Dey was upriver—dey was gonna drive Marse Lambeth out. But dey couldn', an' Ah sho suspec's dat outfit made way wif de Kuhnel. My woman Mauree knows, suh. It come to her in a dream. . . . Dey stole mos' of our stock, suh, an' now it's Massa Rill they'se after."

"Wal, Sambo, come with me," replied Pecos, quietly, as he wheeled back toward the door of the post. In any case he had meant to buy young Lambeth's freedom, and he had asked for the negro's story just for verification. All at once the thing had assumed proportions, and that complex spirit of his had extracted stern purpose out of what had seemed trivial.

Pecos entered the store. It had been enlarged since his last visit to Eagle's Nest. A more complete stock of merchandise filled shelves and cluttered up the place so that there was scarcely room to move about. A Mexican made pretense of work, but the side slant of his beady black eyes told Pecos what he was interested in. Behind a counter stood a man in his shirt sleeves. He was fat and pale, and his dark thin hair fell over his brow, almost to his large, ghoulish eyes. For the rest he had a long, sharp nose, a small mouth, and a peaked chin with a dimple in the middle.

For years one of Pecos Smith's essential habits had

been to look at men, to gauge them in one lightning-swift glance. The fact that he had been able to do so in some instances accounted for the fact that he was still alive.

"Howdy. Air you Brasee?" drawled Pecos.

Chapter VIII

THIS new keeper of Eagle's Nest's only store looked to Pecos more like a New Orleans creole gambler than anything else.

"Yes, I'm Brasee. What you want?" he returned, in a voice with a slight accent, which, however, did not hint of negro taint.

"Wal, I'm sort of close to the Lambeth family," announced Pecos, coldly. "Not exactly a blood relation. Just come from east Texas. An' I'm some concerned to hear the Colonel is daid an' young Terrill is shet up in a shed of yourn. How aboot thet last, Brasee?"

"That's none of your business."

"Shore it is, Mister Brasee," went on Pecos, softly. This man no more knew Texans of Pecos' stripe than he would have been able to contend with them. Pecos' careless, easy manner misled him. "I come a long way to see young Terrill. He must be growed to quite a boy by now. An' I want to see him."

"You can't see him."

"What right had you to shet him up in a shed with a drunken greaser?"

Brasee gazed hard at Pecos, unable to meet him on common ground. There was something about Pecos that obstructed his will, but he did not know it. He had not long been west of the Pecos.

"Matter of owin' yu money, Sambo heah says," went on Pecos, indicating the glaring negro.

"Yes, Lambeth owes for the winter's supplies."

"How much?"

"No matter, Señor."

"It matters a hell of a lot," retorted Pecos, subtly changing. "If yore a sheriff or a Texas Ranger, show yore badge."

This Brasee did not attempt to do, as Pecos had known very well he would not.

"Ahuh. Playin' the law, eh? I've seen thet done before in Texas. But it shore doesn't make for long life. . . . How much does this boy owe?"

"Two hundred—ten dollars," replied Brasee, swallowing hard.

Pecos counted out that amount from a generous roll of bills and pitched it to Brasee. He had not failed to catch the greedy glitter in this man's hungry eyes; nor had Pecos missed other significant things. Dale Shevlin's place had degenerated into a questionable den. There was another man listening, perhaps watching, just inside the half-closed door that opened into the saloon.

"Write out a receipt," said Pecos as he reached behind to grasp the first thing available to throw. It happened to be a sack of salt, at least ten pounds in weight. Quick as a flash Pecos flung it at the door. Then followed three distinct sounds—the bang of the bag striking the door, then a solid thump of the violently moved door colliding with something soft, and lastly a sodden slump of that something on the floor. The door, having swung wide, disclosed a man struggling to a sitting posture, one hand fumbling at his bloody, flattened nose.

"Say, yu," demanded Pecos. "How'n hell do I know what yu was listenin' for behind thet door? . . . What kind of a den air yu runnin', Brasse?"

Brasee rolled up the scattered bills with hands not perfectly steady. Then, using a pencil, he scribbled something on a piece of paper.

"There's your receipt, Señor. But I'm holding young Lambeth till Felipe comes."

"Yu jest think yu air. Say, how do yu know I'm not a Texas Ranger?"

"Rangers don't come west of the Pecos," snapped Brasee, but he was wholly uncomfortable and uncertain.

"Wal, anythin' can happen west of the Pecos. An' thet's a hunch," flashed the vaquero. "Sambo, grab thet ax an' come with me."

Pecos backed out of the store. Contempt for such men as Felipe gathered around him did not make Pecos careless. Sambo had preceded him.

"I knowed it, boss, I sho knowed it," declared the negro, rolling his eyes.

"What'd you know, Sambo?"

"Dat Brasee wus yaller clean to his gizzard. But I sho kept my eye on de greaser. I'd 'a' busted him."

"Wal, I was watchin' him, too. Thet's a low-down outfit, Sambo. They cain't last hyar. . . . Show me this calaboose where they stuck yore young Lambeth."

Some little distance back of the store stood a new

adobe hut, small and square, with a wooden door fastened by a chain and padlock. Pecos walked around the structure, wondering where any air could get in. Sambo banged on the door.

"Massa Rill, is yo' dar?" he called, his voice thick and rich.

"Oh, Sambo! . . . If you don't—get me out—I'll soon be daid," came a plaintive reply.

"Tell him to stand aside from the door. We've got to break it in," directed Pecos.

"Git away f'om dat do', honey, 'cause I'se a-gwine to busticate it."

Pecos rather expected some interference from Brasee, possibly a shot from the back of the store. But there was no sign from that direction that anyone was interested in Sambo's lusty blows with the ax. The powerful negro soon sent the door crashing in.

"Whar yo' is, Massa Rill?" he shouted, breathing like a huge bellows.

Pecos expected to recognize a boy he tried to remember, but he saw a slender, well-formed youth stagger out into the sunlight. He wore a ragged gray coat and overalls and top boots, all of which were covered with dirt and grass. His battered black sombrero was pulled well down, shading big, deep eyes of a hue Pecos could not discern, and a tanned, clean-cut face. The sombrero, however, showed a tuft of glossy hair through a hole in its crown, and also straggling locks from under the brim. Pecos thought Sambo could be excused for his anxiety over this fine-looking youth.

"Sambo, I almost—smothered," gasped young Lambeth.

"Whar's det greaser dey done throwed in wid yo'?"

"He was let out this mawnin', still drunk."

Then Lambeth espied Pecos and gave a slight start. Pecos felt those strange, big eyes sweep over him, back again to his face, to fasten there a moment, and then revert to Sambo.

"Massa Rill, yo' have to thank dis heah gennelman fo' gettin' yo' out," said the negro, warmly.

"Oh, thank you, sir," said the boy, staring strangely at Pecos. There was deep gratitude in his voice, although his demeanor was shy.

"Massa Rill, it was dis way. I nebber discubbered yo' had left home till dis mawnin'," spoke up Sambo. "Den I rid some. I sho did. But dat Brasee banged me ovah my haid an' throwed me out. I wus plannin' to kill him when dis old friend of ours come up. 'Pears yo' little friend Bobby tole him 'boot us. An' he sed he'd get yo' out, Massa Rill. So we goes in. An' det yaller Brasee sho tuk water. Yo' bill is paid at de sto' an' you see how we busticated dis do' heah."

"Paid! . . . Sambo, did you pay it?"

"Me? laws amassy! No, Massa Rill, it was him."

Pecos stood listening and watching with an amused smile at the eloquent Sambo and the excited youth. How little it took sometimes to make people happy! But when Lambeth wheeled suddenly with face flushed and eyes alight, Pecos quite lost his sense of the casualness of the moment. Somehow there was a significance in the occasion for which Pecos was unable to account.

"Pecos Smith! . . . I remember you. How very—
good of you—sir!" exclaimed young Lambeth, extending his hand. It felt small and nervous to Pecos', but
it nevertheless was hard and strong. I am Terrill Lambeth. . . . You remember me?"

"Wal, I reckon I do—now," replied Pecos.

"Please tell me where you are staying—where I can
find you. Else how can I ever repay the debt?"

"Wal, I reckon you needn't worry none aboot thet."

"But I shall. . . . You have befriended us both.
Please tell me your address?"

"'Most the same, Lambeth. . . . Pecos Smith,
Texas, west of the Pecos," he drawled.

"Oh, you're not serious," laughed Lambeth.

"Massa Rill, he sho looks Texas an' talks Pecos," interposed Sambo, with a huge grin.

"Indeed yes," replied Terrill. "Sambo, I rode my
pinto pony in here yesterday. Left him in front of the
store. Bobby might have him."

They walked across the wide street, with Pecos in
advance. Presently, emerging from behind the post, he
espied his horses as he had left them.

"Lambeth, I'd like to talk somethin' over with yu,"
said Pecos, presently. "We can set down over heah in
the shade. How aboot it?"

"I'll be glad to," replied the youth. "Sambo, you run
over to Bobby's. See if he's got my pony. . . . I'm
starved and very thirsty."

An idea had taken root in Pecos' mind—one that refused several attempts to dislodge it. The boy Bobby,
the negro Sambo, and recognition of young Lambeth

had each in succession given it impetus. An opportunity knocked at Pecos' door.

"Wal, it's shore nice heah," began Pecos, when they had found shady seats on the grass not far from Pecos' horses. "Thet boy yu call Bobby told me things an' so did yore nigger. I'm plumb curious, Lambeth, an' I'd like to ask yu a few questions."

"Fire away. People do get curious aboot me. I don't wonder. Only I'm mum as an oyster. But you're shore different—and I'll tell you anything I—I can."

"Yu from eastern Texas?"

"Yes. We lived on a plantation near the Louisiana line. The war ruined my dad. . . . Mother died before he came home. There was nothing left. Dad decided to go west. When we were aboot ready to start my uncle died—he had been in the war, too—and left Dad some money. But we started west, anyhow. Dad had freed our slaves. Sambo and his wife, Mauree, refused to leave us. . . . We had a canvas-covered wagon and eight horses. I rode and I drove and I rode for eight months—all the way across Texas. Toward the end of that journey Dad picked up cattle. Texas longhorns!—You found us lost up the Pecos. After you guided us to Horsehead Crossing we drove the Pecos and worked down this side of the river, heading the brakes until Dad found a place that suited him. . . . There we started ranching. Two years ago we had around ten thousand haid. We were rich. But Dad wouldn't sell. Aboot that time we began to see our stock fade away. There were riders in the brakes. Dad made an enemy of a half-breed cattleman named Don Felipe.

Sambo was shot at twice. . . . Then . . . then . . .
Oh, it hurts so—to bring it back."

"Yore dad was killed," interposed Pecos, gently, as
the youth averted his face.

"Yes. . . . He was—murdered," went on Lambeth.
"Found with an arrow through his body. Felipe and
his vaqueros said it was the work of Comanches. But I
know better. Many times the Indians rode out on the
river bluff across from my home. They watched us.
They shot guns and arrows into the river. But bullets
and arrows could not reach halfway. The Indians could
not get across for miles above and below. They never
tried. So I *know* Comanches never killed my dad. . . .
From that time our fortunes fell. Felipe took on a
partner named Sawtell—a villain who had hounded
me. Sambo and I could not keep track of stock. You see
our range went twenty miles up river and more down.
And in low water our cattle crossed the river. There are
hundreds, maybe thousands of longhorns under the east
wall of the Pecos. They are mine. But how can I ever
get them? No doubt Felipe and Sawtell will get them
eventually. . . . Oh, Mister Smith, I've been cau-
tioned not to say that. Because I can prove nothing.
. . . But I've seen Felipe's vaqueros steal our cattle.
Brand-blotters! . . . Well, it's grown harder lately.
We had to have supplies. Dad had gone in debt for
them. And this last winter I had to. Brasee would not
take cattle in payment. . . . Last and worse—they've
waylaid me—tried to catch me alone. . . . Oh, I can't
tell you the half. . . . But yesterday this Brasee
dragged me—forced me into that stinking dungeon—

locked me in. . . . There, Mister Smith, have I anticipated all your questions?"

"Yu can call me Pecos," responded the vaquero, thoughtfully. "Wal, wal, it's a tough story, Terrill, 'most as tough as mine. But dog-gone! What I cain't understand is why, yu bein' shore old Texas stock, yu didn't kill this half-breed greaser an' his partner. Yu must be all of fifteen years old, ain't you?"

"Si, Señor," replied Terrill, with a little laugh. "I'm all of fifteen."

"Wal, thet's old enough to handle a gun."

"I can. I've shot buffalo, deer, wolves, panthers, javelin, mean old mossy-horns. But never a—a man. I might have, lately, if all our guns hadn't been stolen."

"Wal, Terrill, I'll shore have to kill Don Felipe an' Breen Sawtell fer yu," mused Pecos, softly, marveling that he had not long ago decided that this deed was decreed for him.

"Mister Smith! . . . *Pecos*, you can't be serious!" cried the youth.

"Never was so serious before. . . . Would yu want to heah somethin' aboot me?" drawled Pecos.

"Yes," whispered Lambeth, evidently overcome.

"An' will yu swear yu'll never tell what I tell yu?"

"I—I swear, Pecos," said Terrill, excitedly.

"Wal, yore not the only orphan in Texas. . . . I come of one of the old families, Terrill. But I never had much schoolin' or home influence. An' so I just growed up a vaquero. The years I spent in Mexico were good an' bad fer me. . . . Wal, I rode through heah first a few years ago, with thet trail driver, McKeever. An' last time, up at Santa Fé, I got reckless with my trigger finger again. Dog-gone it, there was always some hombre thet needed shootin'. . . . My last job was on the H H outfit up the river. An' I was almost happy. There was a girl I liked awful well, but never had the nerve to say so. An' the day I had to go . . . Wal, thet's not goin' to interest yu, an' maybe I was wrong. . . . Anyway, I got accused of rustlin' by one Sawtell, brother of this same Breen Sawtell thet's been houndin' yu. Course I had to kill him. Thet made me so sore I got to feelin' I might as well have the game as the blame. So I throwed in with two shady cowhands an' took to rustlin'."

Terrill gasped at that. The boy in his excitement pulled off the old sombrero to crumple it in his hands. Whereupon Pecos had his first clear view of the lad. He was surprisingly young and his clean, tanned cheeks bore not a vestige of downy beard. Indeed, he looked like a very pretty girl, notwithstanding the strong chin, the sad, almost stern lips. His eyes were large and a very dark blue, almost purple.

"Wal, it's my conscience that accuses me of rustlin'," went on Pecos, presently. "But as a matter of fact, Terrill, I wasn't no rustler. My game was brandin' mavericks, an' yu know thet's not crooked. Every cowman in Texas has done it. Only the drawback was thet I knowed damn well thet not one of those calves could be mine. There's the difference. A cowhand with a small herd grazin' aboot can brand a maverick with a kind of satisfaction. But shore I couldn't. . . . Wal,

thet went on all last winter. My pardners drove stock
to their market in New Mexico while I stayed in camp.
The last time they were trailed to our camp. Shore I
wasn't there. I happened to be watchin' a bunch of redskins thet were crossin' the river. To make it short,
when I sneaked back to camp, there was four cattlemen very busy with my pards. They'd already hanged
one an' had a rope on the other. They were haulin' him
up when hell busted loose right under me. The Comanches had sneaked up on the camp. There was a
pretty lively fight in which I took part from the hill-
side. When what was left of the Indians had run off I
found only one white man alive an' he was dyin'. He
told me my pards had been burnin' brands. Yu see, they
double-crossed me, for I never saw a haid of stock they
drove, except my mavericks. Thet deal made me a
rustler when I'm really not one atall. Do yu reckon I
am?"

"No, you're not a rustler—at heart," replied Terrill,
soberly. "Dad used to put our brand on mavericks. He
thought that was honest. So do I."

"Much obliged, boy. Thet shore makes me feel better, now it's off my conscience. An' I reckon I can hit
yu for a job."

"Job!" echoed Lambeth.

"Shore. I hate to brag. But there's nothin' I cain't do
with a rope. I'll bet I could find a thousand calves thet
yu never dreamed of in those brakes."

"You mean ride for me? Be my—my vaquero?"

"Yeah. I'm reckonin' yu need one," drawled Pecos,
pleased with the effect of his story and proposition.

"It would be—wonderful. . . . But I have no money."

"Wal, I'd trust yu."

"You'd *trust* me?"

"Shore, I would, if yu believed in me."

"What do you mean?"

"Thet I'm no thief. Thet I want to find a home in some lonely brake along the river, an' work, an' ferget a lot."

"I could believe that. If you tell me there will be no more cattlemen trailing you to hang you—I will believe you."

"Wal, Terrill, I'm not so dinged shore aboot thet. There's one man, an' he's this Breen Sawtell. The dyin' rancher told me Sawtell was stealin' his own brother's cattle. What aboot thet? An' it was he who sent thet brother down to have me fired an' run off the range. . . . So then this Breen Sawtell may turn up heah, like his brother did there. All of which doesn't mean anythin' to me, since I'm shore to kill him anyhow."

Pecos had been somewhat puzzled and nonplused over this Texas youth, and kept hoping he would overcome what seemed unusual agitations. Probably the soft-spoken lad had not recovered from the shock of his father's murder. Motherless, too—and he had lived alone with only a couple of negroes, harried by vaqueros and hounded by these crooked cattlemen. There was excuse for much. Besides, young Lambeth had not been brought up in the south and west of the wild Lone Star State.

"I hope you do kill Sawtell—and shore that Don

Felipe," suddenly burst out Terrill, after a long pause. His face turned pearl gray, and such a blaze of purple fire flashed upon Pecos that he was surprised out of the very change he had wished for.

"Then I get the job with yu?" retorted Pecos, responding to the other's fire.

"You shore do. I think I've found a—a friend as well as a vaquero. Heah's my hand."

It was minus the glove this time, and the little calloused palm, the supple fingers that closed like steel on Pecos', shot a warm and stirring current through his veins.

"So far as friend is concerned, I hope it works the other way round," replied Pecos. "An' if we get along good an' I build up yore herd of cattle an' buy a half interest in yore ranch—do yu think yu'd take me on as yore pardner?"

"Pecos, I think God . . . Well, never mind what I think," replied Lambeth, beginning with eloquent heat, and suddenly faltering. "But, yes, yes, I will take you."

Sambo's arrival, leading a pony with the lad Bobby astride, put an end to this most earnest colloquy.

"Heah yo is, Massa Rill," called out Sambo, happily. "Our luck has done changed."

"Take all this grub so I can git down," piped up Bobby.

The advent of the lively Bobby and the exuberant Sambo, together with the generous supply of food and drink they brought, effectually silenced Terrill and brought back the singular aloofness Pecos had sensed.

Still the lad could not be expected to be gay and voluble when he was half starved, with the means at hand to allay hunger and thirst. But there was something more.

Pecos shared a little of the food. He was thoughtful during this picnic and realized that he had made a profound and amazing decision. He could see no drawbacks. His mounting zeal had burned them away. He had not been caught burning brands. Williams and Adams were dead, as were all of the posse that had tracked them. He was free. What did a brawling cheat or two like Breen Sawtell matter to him? He was forewarned and forearmed. As for Don Felipe—the halfbreed was dangerous like a snake in the grass was dangerous. Both of these men failed to raise the tiniest clouds on Pecos' horizon.

For ten years Pecos had lived more or less in an atmosphere of strife. That was Texas. It had to grow worse before it ever could grow better. And this range west of the Pecos was bound to see stirring life as the cattle herds augmented. Ranchers and settlers would trail grass and water like wolves on a scent. Vaqueros would throng to the Pecos. And likewise the parasites of rangeland. Pecos had a vision of the future. He had had his one brief fling at outlaw life. No more! Let accusers flock in. No sheriff could put handcuffs on him, nor would any court in Texas uphold a sheriff who tried. A wonderful gladness flushed his veins. What a little incident could transform a career! He owed much to Bobby, to Sambo, and most to this strange orphaned lad, out of place there on the wild range. But for his plight Pecos might have gone on drifting. Somehow Terrill seemed a lovable lad. He needed a protector, a trainer, some one who could bring out the latent Texas qualities that must be in him. And Pecos felt eminently qualified for the position.

"Yo sho wuz starved," declared Sambo. "Whar yo put all dat grub?"

"I was hungry," admitted Terrill. "But I shore didn't eat it all, Sambo. Bobby was around. And so was Pecos, heah."

"Pecos? Thet's a funny handle fer a man," quoth Bobby. "Pecos means 'most anythin'. Hell an' killin' a man an' everythin' orful."

"Shore does, Bobby," drawled Pecos, fishing out another dollar. "Hyar's another peso."

"Aw! . . . I'm rich, Terrill, I'm rich! What's this one fer?" exulted Bobby.

"Wal, to keep mum aboot me bein' Pecos anythin' fer a while. Savvy?"

"Betcha I do," replied Bobby, his shrewd eyes bright. "I jest think you're wonderful."

"Folks, let's shake the dust of Eagle's Nest," suggested Pecos. "While we've been sittin' heah I've counted a dozen greasers snoopin' at us, along with Brasee an' his bartender. An' some white people down the street."

"Sambo, where's yore horse?" queried Lambeth.

"I dunno. Reckon he's eatin' his haid off out a ways."

"Wal, I ought to stock up on my supplies," said Pecos. "But I'm not crazy aboot buyin' from Brasee."

"We'll never deal with him again," spoke up Terrill, decidedly. "There's an army post upriver, aboot twenty miles from my home. Camp Lancaster. We seldom go there, because it's across the river and there were always Indians hanging around. But now it's preferable to Eagle's Nest."

"An' how far to yore ranch, Terrill?"

"Four hours, if we rustle along."

Pecos untied the halters of his horses and mounted. "Adios, Bobby. I won't forget yu."

"Aw, I'm sorry you're all goin', but gladder, too. Terrill, I'm 'most big enough to ride fer you."

"Some day, Bobby. Good-by."

Terrill got on the pony and led the way out of town, with the whistling negro following and Pecos bringing up the rear. Just before the road turned Pecos quickly glanced back. A crowd of people were standing before the store, with Brasee conspicuous among them.

Chapter IX

NOT many miles out of Eagle's Nest an unfrequented trail branched off the road toward the river. Here Sambo, who had found his horse and taken the lead, turned off into the brakes. And from that moment Pecos was lost.

No wheel had ever rolled along that trail, nor had a herd of cattle ever tramped its rocky, cactus-bordered course. At infrequent intervals cattle tracks crossed it, but no other trail for miles. Then a dim road intersected it from the west. Lambeth said this led down to Mortimer Spring.

For the most part Pecos rode down in washes and gulches, but occasionally he was up one of the snake-like, wandering ridges from which he could see afar. All the same was this wild Pecos country, bare grass spots alternating with scaly patches, greasewood and cactus contrasting with the gray of rocks, winding ridge and winding canyon all so monotonous and lonely, rolling endlessly down from the west to the river, rolling endlessly up toward the east, on and on, a vast wasteland apparently extending to infinitude. The course of the Pecos appeared only as a dark meandering line, its walls hidden, its presence sometimes mysteriously vanished.

Pecos was glad to have companions once again,

though he little availed himself of the opportunity to talk. Young Lambeth rode a fast-gaited mustang and was hard to keep up with. Most of the time he and Sambo were out of sight, hidden by rock corners or a descent into a gorge. And Pecos' pack-horse was tired.

About mid-afternoon Pecos espied the first bunch of cattle, wilder than deer—an old mossy-horn, a cow, two yearlings and a calf, for all he could tell un-branded. This encounter was in a shallow rock-bottomed gorge where clear water ran. From that point on cattle tracks increased markedly, and mixed stock showed on the ridges. At length Pecos made out a brand T L, and concluded that must belong to Lambeth. Thereafter he kept sharp lookout for cattle and brands, the latter of which, to his growing surprise, he saw but few.

No doubt Colonel Lambeth had been one of the loosest of branders. But how could any cattleman, even an old stager, with only one vaquero and a boy, expect to brand one tenth of the calves and yearlings that belonged to him? Conditions were changing and such ranching as that was of the past. With cattle demanding a price, with markets increasing, this vast range west of the Pecos would in time produce a million head. Pecos saw fortune in the future for this Lambeth lad and himself. Pecos possessed the money to buy, to replenish what had been left of Lambeth's stock; he knew how to raise cattle; he had the will, and particularly the nerve to stop extensive rustling.

Wherefore he rode this trail more nearly happy than he could recall.

At length, toward sunset, Sambo waited for Pecos in one of the shallow, rock-walled, rock-bedded draws. Evidently Lambeth had gone on. But Pecos failed to see where. There was no water, no sand or earth to mark tracks.

"Heah's whar we turns off," announced the negro. "Mos' deceivin' place."

"Wal, Sambo, I might have passed on heah myself," replied Pecos. "How far to the river?"

"Reckon not so fur as a crow flies. But we go round an' round aboot an' pilin' down an' down till yo sho t'ink it's miles."

The draw wound lazily down, turning back upon itself, keeping its narrow width, but heightening its rock walls. From an appreciable descent it fell off to jumps where the men had to dismount and lead the horses. It remained a gorge, however, never widening to the dignity of a canyon. Nevertheless, Pecos expected it to do so, for that was the nature of the brakes of the river. Down and down he went until the sky above appeared like a winding, blue stream. Water certainly poured down here in floods at certain seasons, but the bed of the gorge continued dry as a bleached bone in the sun. Gradually its dry fragrance failed, which fact came to Pecos' attention through the actions of the horses. They scented water. And presently Pecos smelled it, too, and felt in his face a warm, drowsy breath of air, moving, laden with sweet essence of greens and blossoms.

But Pecos was not prepared to turn a last corner suddenly and be confronted by a burst of golden sunlight and a blaze of open canyon.

"Heah yo is, boss," announced Sambo, with pride. "Dis is Massa Rill's ranch. An' it's sho de only purty place on dis ole Pecos ribber."

"Dog-gone!" ejaculated Pecos, and halted to revel.

The sun was setting behind him, far up over those rolling ranges, and it cast long rays of gold down across this canyon, to paint the gliding river and the huge, many-stepped wall of rock above. That wall appeared higher than any in view on this side of the river. It frowned forbiddingly, notwithstanding its front of glancing sunset hues.

"Up dar's whar de Comanches ride oot an' yell an' shoot at us," exclaimed Sambo, in his deep voice, pointing to the low center of the great cliff opposite. "But dey cain't reach us an' dey cain't git down."

"Dog-gone!" repeated Pecos, as he mopped his wet face.

From where Pecos stood the walls spread and curved on each side, lofty and perpendicular, craggy and impassable along the rims, rock-splintered and densely-thicketed at the bases, perhaps half a mile apart at the extreme width of the curve, and thereafter gradually closing to the mouth, which, however, was large enough to permit a lengthy view of the Pecos and the rugged wall opposite.

It was an oval canyon twice its breadth in length, remarkable in many ways, and strikingly so for a luxuriance of green. This charmed Pecos' eye, for he had never seen anything like it along this lonely, gray, walled river.

The center was an oval pasture inside an oval fringe of trees and cliffs. Horses dotted the green, and many cattle. The sunset had changed its gold for red, so that the eastern walls took on a rosy flush, while those nearer Pecos deepened their purple. In between, shafts of light slanted down across the canyon, rendering it ethereally lovely—a garden of fertile beauty lost in all that wilderness of gloomy, dismal, barren land.

"Dar's one big spring dat nebber goes dry," concluded Sambo, with importance. "It's so big it's a little ribber all by itself. So when de Pecos is low an' so full ob alkali dat de cattle cain't drink, why, dis water is pure as de good Lawd makes."

Sambo mounted again and rode down through the sections of broken cliff toward the canyon floor. And Pecos followed him, presently to emerge from the groves of willow and mesquite and blossoming brush to a trail that led on through the grass. A murmuring of many bees, buzzing and humming in the foliage mingled with a soft sound of an unseen, falling stream.

Here indeed Pecos rode by mossy-horns that were not wild. There were hundreds of cattle toward the lower end of the oval. This canyon alone, without the boundless ranges above, would support a rancher who was not ambitious to grow rich.

Meanwhile the sun set and with the fire and color changed to darkening gray, this isolated retreat returned to its true aspect as part of the hard Pecos country.

At length, just as twilight began to creep out of the larger canyon, gleaming cold on the steely Pecos, a cabin appeared on the edge of the fringe of trees that faced the river. It was fairly high on the bank and commanded a view across the river and down. A smaller cabin sat back and to one side.

"Heah we air an' I'se sho glad," sang out Sambo. "Mauree, yo unwelcomin', no-good woman, whar yo is?"

A negress, large of frame, comely of face, with a red bandana tied round her head, appeared in the doorway.

"So yo's back, yo lazy niggah," she ejaculated, rolling her eyes till the whites showed. "Yo sabed yo' life, man, fetchin' our Terrill home."

"Yas, I'se home, honey, thanks to dis gennelman," replied Sambo, happily. "Mauree, meet a real Texan, Mistah Pecos Smith."

"Wal, Mistah Smith, I'se sho happy to welcome yo," replied the negress. "Git down an' come in. Der's ham an' eggs an' milk—aplenty fo hungry men."

"Thanks, Mrs. Sambo," rejoined Pecos as he slid off his saddle. With swift, sure hands he untied his bulky coat from the cantle and slipped his rifle, to lay them upon the stone steps of the porch. Then he unsaddled Cinco while Sambo performed a like office for the pack-animal.

The cabin was long, with three doors opening out on the porch, and it had been crudely though strongly constructed of logs and poles, with sun-baked mud filling the chinks between. The several windows served equally for portholes. In the center it had a low-peaked roof, which shelved down to cover the porch. It did not, however, touch the side wall, thus leaving a considerable air space for the attic. When Pecos had deposited his saddle and pack on the porch he espied a bench upon which stood a wooden pail and an iron dipper, also a basin and soap, and above, hanging on pegs, clean, white towels. He laughed. When had he seen anything like this? The bucket was full of crystal water which proved to be as cold as ice and singularly free of taste. Pecos drank twice, verifying Sambo's claim for the water. Then he washed his hands and face, to feel a refreshment that equaled his enthusiasm. When he turned, Terrill stood bareheaded in the doorway.

"Pecos Smith," he said, shyly, "welcome to Lambeth Ranch."

"Terrill—our fortune's made!" he flashed, to express his appreciation of this welcome, and the opportunity a chance meeting had thrown to him.

"You think so? You like my lonely canyon?"

"Paradise! No man could have made me believe such a place could be found along the Pecos."

"Come in. Supper is ready. You wouldn't expect me to be hungry, after that lunch Bobby gave us. But I am."

"Wal, I wasn't particular hungry till Mrs. Sambo mentioned ham an' eggs. I shore fergot there were such things."

The interior was dark, like all log cabins, except in the neighborhood of the open fire. Evidently this large apartment was living-room and kitchen combined. A door at the end led into another room. Pecos sat down to a home-made table, upon which were a spotless white tablecloth, old silverware, and a supper the savory fragrance of which attested that it was good enough for a king.

Terrill had breeding, though he had not been used to company. If the situation was novel for Pecos, what must it have been for the lad? Here, more than at any other time since Terrill had been freed, that strange, rather aloof awkwardness, if not actual shyness, seemed noticeable to Pecos. It would not have been difficult for Pecos to burst into a hearty laugh and to slap the lad on the shoulder and ridicule him for such diffidence out on the west bank of the wildest river in Texas. But something inhibited Pecos. Lambeth must have had a sheltered childhood, a sad boyhood, and now he certainly was an orphaned youth. It would take time to get acquainted with him, and Pecos decided it would be worth some pains to keep much to himself and give familiarity time to grow. Vaqueros of his type were not usually rough and ready fellows, and Pecos was nothing if not quiet.

They did not exchange half a dozen words throughout the meal, to which Pecos did justice that assuredly flattered the cook.

"Wal, a few more suppers like thet an' I'll be spoiled," was Pecos' encomium.

"We have plenty to eat, even if we are poor," replied Terrill. "Raise 'most everything, I reckon. . . ."

"Wal, this has shore been an excitin' day, an' I'm sleepy. If yo don't mind I'd like to bunk up in thet hole under the roof. I'll get plenty of air there, and it's a good place for a lookout."

"That will be all right," the lad replied, quickly. "Sambo has been sleeping there since Dad was killed, so I wouldn't be afraid at night. Now he can go back to his cabin."

"Yeah. I shore hope my comin' will make things better all around."

"Oh, I know it will, Pecos," returned Lambeth. "I shore had some luck today, if never before."

"Thet reminds me. Yu 'pear far from starvin' hyar, yet yu had to take chances ridin' into Eagle's Nest for supplies. How aboot it?"

"Pecos, it wasn't food supplies that I went after, or I would have taken a pack-horse."

"I see. Wal, I'll turn in. Good-night."

"Wait. You said our fortune was made. . . . I cain't go to sleep if you don't explain."

Pecos laughed. "Yore a funny kid. Let me figure for yu. . . . This range is the best on the Pecos. What yu an' yore dad needed was a man who could ride this range. Sambo is a good nigger. But yu want a handy man with guns. He happens to have dropped in. Now takin' a ridiculous estimate, say yu have a thousand cows left. Thet number with the brandin' of mavericks will more than double this year. Thet means, say, twenty-five hundred haid. Followin' year five thousand haid. Third year ten thousand haid. Mind yu, we're allowin' for the brandin' of mavericks along this river as far up an' down as we can ride. Fourth year easy twenty thousand. An' so on. Wal, two-year-olds are sellin' now for six dollars a haid. Any Texan can see thet cattle-raisin' is goin' to save Texas. Prices will go up an' up. But suppose, for sake of bein' conservative, say prices go no higher. In four years we'll be worth way over a hundred thousand dollars. But I'd gamble it'll be double thet."

"*Pecos!*" cried Lambeth, his voice ringing high.

"Wal, don't Pecos me. Yu know thet Pecos means' most anythin'. I'm tellin' yu straight, Terrill. For ten years I've been layin' for this chance."

"Oh, thank God you—came in time!" exclaimed the lad, poignantly.

"See heah, lad, yore still upset. Let's talk no more tonight," replied Pecos, surprised into keen solicitude. Terrill stood against the stone chimney just out of the light of the freshly blazing sticks Sambo had put on. The shadow somehow heightened the effect of large dark eyes.

"I'm not upset. It's—it's just—I cain't tell you. . . . But I can tell you—that if Brasee had kept me shut up much longer—I'd have hanged myself."

"Aw, son, yore exaggeratin'," ejaculated Pecos. "Why, he wouldn't have dared. He was tryin' to scare you into borrowin' money."

"That's all you know," retorted the lad, with passion. "Brasee is only one of Don Felipe's hands. But he does terrible things. Not so long ago he held a *girl* prisoner in that 'dobe shack."

"A girl! . . . What the hell is wrong with the white men in Eagle's Nest?"

"She was—a—Mexican," replied Terrill, haltingly, and ended as if biting his tongue.

"Makes no difference," growled Pecos. "Reckon I'll have to inquire into thet."

Pecos went out and called: "Hey, Sambo, you big molasses. Come heah an' help me."

Sambo appeared, so promptly as to give rise to a suspicion that he had been listening. It certainly seemed natural under the circumstances.

"Yo climb up de ladder an' I'll fro up yore bed," suggested Sambo.

"Hand up my coat an' rifle first," replied Pecos as he ascended to the roof and knelt on the uneven pole floor. It was so dark Pecos could not see back into the loft.

"Yo fro my quilts down, Pecos."

Pecos felt around until he found a bed, which consisted of no more than several heavy quilts. He gave these a pitch into space. Sambo let out a smothered ejaculation and was evidently thrown off his balance. Pecos, peering down, found that this was the case. Sambo floundered around to extricate himself. His language and the commotion that he had created brought Mauree to the scene.

"Fo' de land's sake! Yo crazy black man, what yo doin'?"

"Go long wid yo, woman."

"Ex-cuse me, Sambo," called Pecos. "I reckoned yu was lookin'."

"Sho I wuz lookin', but it done no good. Yo is a real vaquero, Mars Pecos, yo sho is."

Presently Pecos had his bed spread in that dark loft and his preciously laden coat folded for a pillow. Before stretching his frame at length he gazed out in the direction of the river. He could not see well, though the pale, wide, winding bar under the black wall must be it. Above the bold rim blinked white stars, cold and austere in their message to him. By listening intently he caught a faint murmur of water chafing by reedy shore. An owl hooted on the canyon side of the river, to be answered from a distance. Cattle and horses were silent.

Pecos felt of the bundles of money in his coat. His conscience discovered a still small voice. Had he been wholly honest with young Lambeth? Angrily he cast the query aside. He had fought that out. He could look any man in the eye, with a hand on his gun, and swear that he was not a thief. Nevertheless, if he had so long lived the free, wild lawless life of a vaquero that his sense of right and wrong had suffered, now was the time to correct it. Whereupon he lay down and slept, an indication that his conscience was not too burdened.

Pecos did not awaken until rather late for him, which perhaps was owing to a sense of security. The sun was crossing the gap far down the river and the Rio Pecos appeared a path of glory.

Sambo came into sight below, his arms full of split fagots.

"Fine mawnin'," called out Pecos, pulling on his boots.

"Sho is. An' once more I'se glad to be alibe."

"Me too. . . . Where's our boss, Sambo?"

"Sho he's in de land ob Nod. Mauree she call him twice. But mos' always he's up early."

Pecos lay flat on the floor, with his head over the edge. The open door of the cabin was a little to his right. *"Hey, Terrill!"* he yelled.

"Yes—yes," came a quick, bewildered cry from the distant room.

"Pile out. The mawnin's broke. We gotta hang today on a peg an' all the days thet come after. . . . Ridin' the brakes, boy! Who could ask a happier lot?"

Pecos descended the ladder to begin the day himself, surprised at something that made him want to sing. He washed his face and hands, and brushed his tangled. hair, and felt of his stubby beard. Some day he might shave, if only for the comfort of a clean, smooth chin. There were gold and red ripples on the river, under a gentle wind. Ducks were winging flight upstream. Cattle spotted the green banks. Terrill's pinto mustang had come almost to the porch. Chickens were numerously manifest.

"Sambo, is there any other way in an' out of this canyon?" queried Pecos.

"They sho is. Yo can drive a wagon to the rim. It done ain't no shucks of a road, suh, but we've druv it many a time."

"Then we've got a wagon?"

"Sho—up thar on top. Harness, too, all nice hid in

de brush. Kuhnel Lambeth done bought dat wagon t'ree years ago."

"Did you ever drive it to Eagle's Nest?"

"Yas, suh. But dat's a long pull around. We can get to de fort in two days."

"Wal, we're shore startin' pronto."

A jingling step caused Pecos to turn. Terrill had come out in clothes much the worse for wear.

"Mawnin', Pecos. You scared me stiff."

"So yore up, lad? Wal, I was gettin' worried. If yore gonna trail with me, Terrill Lambeth, yore shore gonna rustle. . . . Do yu sleep in thet old sombrero?"

"Sometimes," replied Terrill, with a laugh.

"Yo-all come an' eat," called Mauree, from within.

Pecos followed him in. The living-room was full of sunlight now. Pecos, sitting at table, gazed from the flushed Terrill around upon the walls, at Mauree's crude cupboard, at the pots and pans on the coals, at the homemade furniture, the skins and horns over the rude mantel, at the old Henry rifles—and his mental reservation was that the Lambeths had the spirit of the pioneer, but not the resourcefulness.

"Pecos, I heahed you tell Sambo you were startin' pronto somewhere," said Terrill, his deep eyes glancing up fleetingly.

"What you think aboot it? We'll ride hossback. an' Sambo—an' his wife, too ——"

"Mauree has a pickaninny."

"Ump-um! Wal, she can shore take it, if she wants. We'll drive to thet fort—what'd yu call it—campin' along easy, an' load yore wagon till it sags."

"Pecos, you're the—the most amazing vaquero *I* ever heahed of. You filled my head with dreams last night. But this mawnin' I'm awake."

"Dog-gone, boy, yu do seem brighter. Not so pale. . . . Wal, what's wrong with my idee?"

"Nothing. It's just inspiring. Only I have no credit at Camp Lancaster, even if I—I dared go in debt again."

"Wal, yore pardner's got some money," drawled Pecos.

"You would lend it to me?"

"No. I'm investin' in yore ranch. I'll buy supplies, tools, guns, shells, cattle, hosses, any darn thing we need thet *can* be bought in this heah Gawd-forsaken country."

Terrill dropped his head, though not so quickly but that Pecos caught a glimpse of flaming cheeks.

"Terrill, don't take offense an' don't be uppish," added Pecos, in change of tone. "I want to help yu an' I know I cain't lose nothin'. Yu said yu trusted me, though I don't see how yu can on such short notice. Not west of the Pecos!"

"I do—trust you. But I—it's only that I'm overcome. It's too good to be true. Don't think me uppish or—or ungrateful. . . . I—I could scream. I could swear!"

"Wal, thet's fine. Come out with a good old Texas cuss-word."

"——— ———!" swore Terrill, valiantly. But the profanity did not ring true, so far as familiarity was concerned.

Sambo burst into a roar. "Haw! Haw! Haw! . . . My Lawd!—Wife, did yo heah dat?"

"I sho did an' I'se scandalized," declared Mauree, resentfully. "Terrill never wuz a cusser an' he ain't a-gonna begin now."

"Wal, I'm sorry, Mrs. Sambo," said Pecos. "But it shore did me good to heah him. . . . Now, son, yu get a pencil an' paper. Say, can yu write?"

"I'm not quite so ignorant as I look and sound," protested Terrill.

"Boy, listen to me. Yu gotta know when I'm in fun, which is shore most of the time, an' when I'm mad, which ain't often. I wasn't mad atall yesterday. . . . Now if yu've lived out heah five years an' yore fifteen altogether, how'n the devil did yu get much schoolin'?"

"Who said I was fifteen?"

"Reckon I did. Yu shore cain't be older?"

"I reckon I am, a little," returned Terrill, dryly. "But never mind my age. . . . Only, Señor Pecos Smith, I'm no child to tease. . . . Now I'll get pencil and paper."

"Wal, if yu balk at teasin' we'll dissolve partnership right heah an' now. What yu say?"

"I'm not a bit balky."

"Dog-gone! I'll bet yu are."

When it came to enumerating supplies and necessities for the ranch, Terrill showed a long-formed habit of economy. After he set his list down Pecos said: "Put an X an' a four after thet."

"X and a four?"

"Shore. Thet means multiply by four. . . . Heah,

Sambo, yu ought to know what yu've got an' what yu haven't. Answer my questions, an' yu, Terrill, write down what I say."

At the conclusion of this exercise, Sambo was jubilant and Terrill was awed. Pecos heard Sambo say to his wife: "Mauree, dat man take my bref. If he ain't crazy we'ze lookin' at hebben right dis minute."

Mauree elected to stay home with her pickaninny. "But yu, niggah, yu fetch me some stockin's an' shoes an' some clothes—an' if yu forgit my smokin' yu needn't come honeyin' around heah no mo.'"

What with climbing the gulch trail with saddle horses and team, and clambering over rocks and greasing the wagon and mending the harness, Sambo and Pecos were not ready to start until midday. Then Sambo drove off over rough ground where no sign of wheel tracks was visible. Terrill did not know the way, so he and Pecos followed behind the wagon.

"Boy, yu gotta pack a gun an' learn how to shoot it," advised Pecos.

"I told you I could shoot."

"Wal, take this an' show me," replied Pecos, handing over his gun—an action he had never done since that gun had become part of him. "Be careful. Yu have to thumb the hammer."

"Shoot from the horse?"

"Why, shore! If yu run into a bandit would yu git off polite an' plug him from the ground?"

"I did meet two bandits—and I ran for all I was worth."

"Wal, yore education is beginnin'. Hold the gun high with yore thumb on the hammer. Then throw it hard with a downward jerk. The motion will flip the hammer just as the gun reaches a level, an' it'll go off, yu bet. Yu gotta sort of guess instead of aimin'. Thet is at a man close to yu, but at some distance yu want to aim."

"Heah goes. If Spot hangs me in a tree it'll be on yore head," replied Terrill, and he threw the gun as directed, pointing it at a big rock. Bang! The mustang leaped straight up, almost unseating his rider. It took a moment to quiet him.

"Take your old gun," declared Terrill, returning it to Pecos. "It nearly kicked my arm off."

"Wal, yu hit the rock, anyhow, an' thet's fine. I'll let thet do till we git home."

Pecos was not long in discovering that Sambo kept to the ridge-tops, seldom crossing a wash. And the direction was away from the river. Once up on top, the horses made better time. They camped at the head of a ravine where water was to be had, having made, according to Sambo, more than fifteen miles. Soon after supper Terrill unrolled his bed in the wagon and crawled into it. Pecos talked to the negro for an hour, with the object of learning what Sambo knew about the country, cattle, rustlers, and all pertaining to the range.

Next day they struck into a road, well defined and lately used. It wound along the ridges, for the most part downhill, and late that evening they made camp on the west bank of the river. Pecos was relieved to hear a ripple of shallow water, denoting an easy ford on the morrow. Before the sky grew red next morning they were across and headed down a good road toward the military camp.

Chapter X

PECOS learned from an old army sergeant that Camp Lancaster was the post of the U.S A. Fourth Cavalry, who were operating against hostile Indians along the river; and at the present time were up somewhere on the Staked Plains.

It was an old post. Lieutenant N. F. Smith had camped there as early as 1849; and Lieutenant Michler in 1863, had traced out the road which Pecos had struck west of the river. There was a trading-post besides an army supply-store inside the old stone walls. The high chimneys made visible landmarks for miles around.

While Pecos helped Terrill and Sambo buy their extensive list, he did not let anything escape him. Indians lounged around on the stone steps and inside the stores, sullen, greasy, painted savages supposed to be peaceful. They were not Comanches, but all the same Pecos would not have trusted some of them out on the range.

According to the sergeant, the Comanches seldom raided below Horsehead Crossing. That ford, owing to the more frequent passing of the trail drivers, had become a favorite spot for the Indians to waylay and attack cattlemen driving herds up from lower Texas.

"Only last month a bunch of Comanches massacred

some cowhands at Horsehead," said the army man.
"Tolerable big bunch of cattle scattered all down the
river. The Pecos is treacherous an' many head of stock
mire down in quicksand or drown in floods. But there's
thousands of cattle in the brakes that no one will ever
claim."

Pecos did not linger at the fort after their purchases
had been packed in the wagon. He did not ask for an
escort back to the ford, but the sergeant sent three
troopers with him, jolly fellows who imparted much
information. They saw him and his companion safely
across the river, just before sunset. This was the last
water for a long stretch, but Pecos pushed on west
far into the night before halting for camp. Then he
staked the horses close, he and Sambo keeping alternate
guard. Their next camp was somewhere down on the
rocky slopes. And afternoon of the third day saw them
arriving safely on the rim above Lambeth Ranch. The
following day Pecos conceived the idea of letting the
supplies down over the cliff on lassos, a method which
saved much time and labor.

South of Lambeth Ranch was a range claimed by
Don Felipe before his association with Sawtell, after
which time they openly challenged any claim clear
down to Devil River. Several other cattlemen, according to Sambo, ran stock on both sides of the river. And
as cattle strayed far up and down the Pecos there was
a considerable mixing of brands, and always, for the
persistent vaqueros, an unfailing number of mavericks.

Pecos said cheerfully to Terrill and Sambo: "Every

time yu put a red-hot iron on a maverick we are six dollars richer right *then*."

They left the north brakes alone because even Felipe's vaqueros had not penetrated them, and confined their efforts to riding the river canyon, the intersecting brakes, and up these as far as the heads, where dense thickets never failed to yield calves and yearlings that had never smelled burned hair.

They rode together, or at least Pecos never allowed Terrill to get out of his sight, with the result that the average of brandings a day was small, in the neighborhood of six. This number, however, was eminently satisfactory to Pecos, and it elated Terrill so that the lad daily lost something of his reserve. Pecos, reviewing the situation, seemed to gather that Terrill apparently lost some kind of a fear of him. Pecos did not concern himself much about anything now except the amassing of a herd. He knew where to find mavericks, and many there were that Felipe's outfit had not sweat hard enough to find.

Summer came, hot and drowsy, with its storms. As a consequence work became harder on the men and easier on the horses. Lambeth owned less than a dozen horses, and these, with the two of Pecos', were not half enough to stand the grind.

Therefore a day here and there was given the horses to rest, during which time Pecos and his two followers worked on the ranch. There was no end of repairs, and when these were attended to, Pecos began improvements. He was indefatigable, and he made Sambo's red tongue hang out like that of a driven calf in the brakes.

Terrill turned out to be less hardy and enduring than he looked. Still, for a youth who had not reached his full growth and who had never experienced the grueling drill common to vaqueros, he won praise from Pecos. Terrill lost a little of the fullness of his cheeks and the graceful roundness of form that even the loose and ill-fitting clothes he wore failed to hide.

One still, scorching noon in August, after a hard morning's toil in pursuit of some wild three-year-old steers, they flung themselves down in a shady place on the banks of the river. Pecos was hot, and Sambo heaved and sweat like a horse, but it was Terrill who had suffered most from the exertion and heat. He had become expert with the rope under Pecos' tutelage and was mightily proud of it. He could run down, lasso, throw, and tie a calf in short order. But either Sambo or Pecos had to apply the branding-iron. Pecos often took the lad to task for his squeamishness, and finally Terrill, who was easy to exasperate, made a surprising and unanswerable retort. "Aw, burning hair and flesh stink!"

Pecos had gaped at the lad.

This particular day Terrill's face was as red as fire and as wet as if it had been plunged under water.

"You darned little fool!" ejaculated Pecos. "Why don't yu ride in yore shirt sleeves?"

"I haven't any heavy shirts like yours. Mine are thin stuff. Mauree made them for me. If I rode through the brush without my coat I'd be torn to pieces."

The coat Terrill referred to and which Pecos had complained of was a short jacket much too full for Terrill.

There was a flat rock along the bank and the current of the river swirled green and cool beside it. Terrill lay down to drink. Suddenly Pecos, possessed of one of his teasing moods, leaped down noiselessly, and with a quick action plunged Terrill's head clear under. Terrill nearly lunged into the river; then bounding erect, he burst out furiously: "Damn fool! . . . Pushing me in when I can't swim!"

"By gosh! Thet's an idee. Swim! We'll go in," shouted Pecos. "I was too durned lazy to think of it."

"No *we* won't," declared Terrill.

"Don't yu ever bathe, yu dirty boy?"

"Yes, but I'm not doing it today," retorted Terrill, resentfully.

"Come on, Terrill. I promise not to duck yu," rejoined Pecos, beginning to strip. By the time he had gotten his shirt off Terrill had disappeared under the trees. Pecos laughed, thinking he had offended the sensitive lad. He removed the rest of his clothes and had his swim.

"Sambo, why don't you come in? It's shore nice an' cool," called Pecos.

"Too much work. An' I'se had one baf dis summer. I fell in a hole."

When Pecos emerged to dress Terrill was not in sight, and did not return until fully half an hour later.

"Terrill, old pard, I'm sorry I ducked yu. Cain't yu

take a little fun? My Gawd! but yore a queer kind.
Not wantin' to go in swimmin' on a day like this!"

"I'd like it well enough, but I—I couldn't strip before yu and Sambo."

"Ahuh. So thet's it. . . . Terrill, I didn't savvy yu
was so modest. Heahafter Sambo an' I will go off an'
let yu take a swim."

This incident recalled certain things about Terrill
that had seemed peculiar to Pecos. Of late weeks, however, the boy had grown less aloof, and had become
so zealous in work, so evidently glad to be with Pecos,
so thoroughly promising in every way, that Pecos had
grown greatly attached to him. It was like bringing
up a boy who stayed boyish. There appeared to be
limits, however, that Pecos could not exceed; and an
altogether hopeless task to make a rough vaquero out
of Terrill.

Nevertheless, these convictions of Pecos' rather endeared Terrill the more to him, because of a sense of
guardianship, almost parental, that Terrill inspired.
The lad had lost his fear of being alone, and at times
he seemed almost happy. Naturally this drew Pecos
closer to him. And as the days slipped by, always full
of work in the open, these two grew insensibly the
closer.

Terrill could stand considerable teasing of certain
kinds. But one day, during a rest hour, Pecos had come
upon him lying flat on his stomach, so absorbed in
contemplation of some flowers—a habit of Terrill's—
that he did not hear Pecos' step. So that he was wholly
unprepared for Pecos' swoop down upon him, to

straddle his back and tickle him in the ribs with steel-like fingers. At first Pecos took the noise Terrill made and the amazing struggle he put up to be the natural outcome of extreme ticklishness. But presently it dawned upon Pecos that the boy was not laughing, or struggling in a sense of response to Pecos' fingers dug into his ribs. When Pecos got off, Terrill leaped up in a rage.

"If you ever do that again—I'll fire you!" cried Terrill.

"Fire me?" echoed Pecos, aghast.

"Yes, fire you! Have you no respect for a—a fellow's person? I told you once before it drives me crazy to be tickled."

"Shore I remember now, Dog-gone it, Terrill, cain't I treat yu as I would any other boy?"

"You bet you can't."

"An' yu'd fire me—honest to Gawd?"

"I—I've got to do something to—to protect myself," replied Terrill, choking up.

"It's got to be home to me—this hyar Lambeth Ranch, an' I'm shore powerful fond of yu."

"Shut up! That was a lie. I—I couldn't get along without you," flashed Terrill, with another kind of temper, and he ran away to the house, leaving Pecos relieved and glad, and uncomprehensibly moved. From that hour, nevertheless, Pecos realized he and Terrill were going to clash sooner or later. It only waited for the time and the place and the cause; and there was no use for Pecos to attempt to fend it off.

Terrill was subject to moods. He really was as-

tounding in that way, but most of them did not interfere with the work, which, after all, was Pecos'
heartfelt aim. Sometimes when Terrill thought he was
alone on the rocks or the banks of the river he would
sing at the top of his lungs. Pecos never got close
enough to him on these occasions to hear distinctly,
but he caught a sweet rising and falling contralto voice.
Then again Terrill would be wildly gay, and if opportunity offered where he was safe from attack, he
would torment Pecos unmercifully. At times he would
be profoundly melancholy and unapproachable, so
sad-lipped and somber-eyed that Pecos was glad to let
him alone. Again, and this was unusual and rare,
happening in the dusk or in shadow, when his face was
not visible, he would be provokingly curious about
Pecos' love-affairs.

"Dog-gone yu, boy, I told yu I hadn't had any,"
Pecos would reply, in good-humored impatience.

"Aw, you lie. A wonderful handsome vaquero like
you! Pecos Smith, you cain't make me believe you
haven't had ——"

"Wal, what? Yore so damn curious. Now just
what?"

"A wife, maybe. Sweethearts, shore lots of them—
and, like as not—more than one of those black-eyed,
bewitching little Mexican hussies."

"Wal, I'll be jiggered! Thet last's fine talk for a
clean-minded boy who cain't undress to go swimmin'
in front of men! . . . You got me wrong, Terrill Lambeth. I never had no Mexican hussy, nor any other
kind. Nor a wife. Gawd! thet's kinda funny. . . . An'

the nearest I ever come to a sweetheart was up heah at
the H H Ranch. . . . Mary Heald. I was a little sweet
on her, but I never told her. Course she might have
liked me—the boys swore she did—an' I knew I'd
shoot some fellar sooner or later an' have to go on down
the long trail. An' thet's just what happened."

"Forgive me, Pecos. I—I was just curious. . . . I
suppose then—I—we've only to look forward to the
day when you shoot Breen Sawtell or Don Felipe—
and ride away from Lambeth Ranch?"

Pecos was not so dense but he caught a faint bitterness in the lad's words, and it touched him. In the
shade of the trees—it was twilight under the canyon
wall and they were riding home. Pecos reached out a
hand to clasp Lambeth's shoulder.

"Terrill, didn't I say I'd never leave yu? Would it
have been honest of me to go in partnership with yu
when I might have to go on the drift? But it cain't
happen now. An' if I shoot Sawtell an' Felipe—which
I'm damn liable to do if they come foolin' in heah—
it'll be for yu."

Terrill made no response to that unless riding on
ahead could be construed as one.

Terrill had a sulky mood now and then, the only
kind that Pecos found it trying to put up with. Without any reason whatever, that he could grasp, Terrill
would get as sulky as a spoiled pup. It chanced one
day that such a state of temper encroached upon an
occasion when Pecos was as exasperated as he could
well be. Things had gone wrong all day, even to the
burning of his thumb with a branding-iron. This was

serious. It was his trigger thumb! To be sure, he could shoot fairly well with his left hand, but if he ran into some of the vaqueros he suspected of brand-burning T L stock, he would be in a pretty pickle.

An argument arose over the matter of driving again to Camp Lancaster. Pecos wanted to put it off, and he was reasonable about it, though he did not mention the particular objection, which was his sore thumb. Terrill tossed his tawny head—happening for once to be without the omnipresent battered sombrero—and said he would be damned if he would not take Sambo and go alone.

"Yu will not," replied Pecos, shortly.

"I will!"

"Ump-umm."

"Who'll stop me?"

"Wal, if yore such a dumbhaid, this heah little old Pecos Smith."

"Dumbhaid! . . . I shall go. I'd like to know who's boss around Lambeth Ranch."

"I reckon yore the owner of the ranch, Terrill, 'cause I have only a half share in the stock. But yu cain't boss me."

"I *am* your boss."

"Say, go away an' leave me be. Yore pesterin' me. Cain't yu see this is a particular job."

Terrill snatched the article Pecos was working on— no less than a wide leather belt he meant to carry money in—and threw it far down the bank.

"Wal, yu little devil!" ejaculated Pecos, nettled.

"Don't call me names and don't think you can work when I'm talking business," declared Terrill, hotly.

"Call yu names? Shore I will. Heah's a couple more. When yu air like yu air this minnit yu air a dod-blasted mean little kickin' jackass. Yu heah me? . . . Yore cranky, too, an' turrible conceited aboot bein' a boss. Why, yu couldn't boss a lot of mavericks. Yu make me tired, Terrill, an' I've a mind to spank you."

"*Spank me!*" shrilled Terrill. "How dare you?" And he gave Pecos a stinging slap in the face.

That settled it. Out flashed Pecos' long arms. He seized Terrill by the shoulders, heartily disposed to carry out the spanking threat. But sudden pangs in his sore thumb changed his mind. Instead he gave Terrill a flip that spun him around like a top. Then he swung his boot in a lusty kick to Terrill's rear. In any case a vaquero's kick was no trivial thing. This one lifted Terrill a little off the grass and dropped him sprawling. With astounding celerity Terrill sprang erect. Then Pecos met blazing eyes that took his breath. Many as had been the wonderful eyes of different-hued fury that had flashed into his, Terrill's were the most magical.

"*I'll kill you!*"

"Run along, yu little bullhaid," drawled Pecos.

Terrill did run off, screaming incoherently, and that was the last Pecos saw of him until dusk. Pecos was watching the last ruddy glow of sunset down on the river when Terrill came out to edge closer to him.

"Pecos." It was an entreating voice.

"Yeah."

"I—I apologize. . . . You treated me just—just as I deserved. It was temper. I used to lose my haid at Dad. I'm sorry."

Pecos and his two helpers rode the brakes of the river for twenty miles below Lambeth Ranch, and out on the slopes of the range for as many miles west. And Pecos' hopes were more than fulfilled. They had burned the T L brand on more than seven hundred mavericks. What a grievous blow this would be to Don Felipe and his new partner, not to include several other ranchers who lived in Eagle's Nest and ran their stock up and down the river! Soon the vaqueros of all those cattlemen would be riding out on full round-ups. Then Pecos expected some burned-out brands, if nothing worse.

In these three hot months of summer Pecos' vigilant eye had not been rewarded by a single sight of Indians, or any tracks in the brakes or up on the ranges. Men who knew that country were partial to spring and fall for their operations. Before long now anything might be expected.

Toward the end of August the drought was broken by occasional rainstorms, most welcome to Lambeth Ranch. Even the well-watered canyon had begun to grow dusty and gray. But the rains worked magic.

When Pecos rode down from the desolate ranges or up the lonely, silent river with its drab walls, its never-changing monotony, back into the one green canyon within his range it was like entering another world. Months of riding the Pecos brakes could not but have its effect upon any man. The contrast of Lambeth's Canyon counteracted this, and the vaquero would gain by night what he lost by day. Sambo was not affected by seasons, by heat or cold, by loneliness, by anything. "So long's I'se got my chewin'-terbaccer I'se all right," the negro was wont to say. Terrill was a difficult proposition to figure, and Pecos gave it up. Nevertheless, the lad never made one complaint about the hard work, the loneliness, and the confinement of the brakes.

Before undertaking a long siege of upriver riding, from which Pecos expected so much, he advised a week's rest for the horses. During this interval Pecos and his helpers dammed the stream up near the canyon head, and formed a fine little lake, from which they dug an irrigation ditch, with branches almost the whole length of the ranch. This was something Terrill claimed his father had always wanted to do.

The change from the everlasting seat in a saddle, riding the rough, ragged, dreary brakes, to work on foot with clear running water while eyes were rested and soothed by soft greens, and the lines of goldenrod, and the autumn coloring of vines and willows, turned out to be something so beneficial that Pecos saw the wisdom of frequently resorting to it.

The white clouds sailed up back of the rims to fill the blue vault above, and to thicken and change and darken, until a heavy black one would come trailing veils of rain across the ranch. At the same time the sun would be shining through somewhere, and lakes of azure showed amidst both the white and the black clouds, and rainbows arched down from the ranges

above to bend a gorgeous curve over the river, or drop
a fading end far down the canyon.

"Shore the lovely time heah is coming," said Terrill.
"Makes up for the rest."

"Pity we have to miss it," replied Pecos. "But I've
an idee, if it isn't too ambitious. Let's pack grub an'
beds an' work out two or three of them upriver brakes
at a time, then come home to rest up a bit."

That met with Terrill's approval.

"Sho yo's gonna find det upribber tough sleddin',"
predicted Sambo.

Pecos was destined to learn vastly more about the
river from which he had been named.

The country with which he had grown familiar
while trail driving for McKeever did not take in the
brakes of the river, but mostly the rolling ridges that
led up to the vast sweeping ranges.

From Heald's range, up and down the Pecos for
miles, the strange river had worn a deep channel
through dull red soil, and the places where cattle could
get down to drink were not many.

The part of the river Pecos was now to explore
proved to be the wildest and most dangerous reaches
along its whole length. Nothing marked the course of
the river. The cedar trees that grew sparsely were all
down in the narrow deep-walled winding canyon.
Cattle tracks led to the few breaks where it was possible to get down to water.

From time to time Sambo had told Pecos what he
had learned personally about the river below Horse-

head Crossing, and what had come to him through
other riders. Whole herds of cattle had been drowned
in the Pecos, and thousands had perished singly and
doubly, and in small bunches. Fords were so few and
far between that cowhands had often attempted a
crossing at a bad place and a bad time, only to be
carried down the swift current beyond a rocky wall to
death.

The savages, lying in ambush at Horsehead Crossing, which was the most important and the most
dreaded ford on the river, had often massacred an outfit of trail drivers and chased their cattle into the
breaks. Even a repulsed attack seldom failed of a stampede, which added to the number of unknown strays.

Pecos was of the opinion that most of these lost
cattle—for that matter all the cattle in this region
were lost and not only had to be found, but caught—
grazed gradually to the southward.

Three weeks of riding this hard country, allowing
for weekend rests at home, did not account for many
branded mavericks for Pecos' outfit, but the labor was
most valuable in acquainting Pecos with the haunts
of a surprising number of cattle, and in what could
not be done and what could. There was enough unbranded stock along Independence Creek alone to make
Pecos and Terrill rich ranchers, and that stream lay
between Lambeth Ranch and Camp Lancaster. Pecos'
visions of wealth and dreams of the future were not
inconsistent with possibilities. At night, round the
little camp fire, he would dwell on this and that aspect
of the business, finding in Terrill a rapt listener.

"Listen pard," said Pecos once, voicing a growing belief. "I shore don't want to set up yore hopes way sky-high an' then see them take a tumble. But, doggone it, I just cain't see anythin' 'cept big money for us."

"Pecos, you've got my hopes so high now I'm riding the clouds instead of my saddle," replied Terrill.

"Wal, I'll stick by my guns," went on Pecos, doggedly. "By spring we'll have twenty five hundred haid wearin' the T L. We've got the ranch, the water, the range. This country will *always* run cattle, an' a hundred times more'n what's grazin' heah now. It's so darn big an' so wild. Why, there's no cattle range in Texas thet can come up to our West of the Pecos range. Grass doesn't fail heah. Thet damned gray-green-yellow alkali-bitten river never went dry in its life. . . . We're *heah*, boy, we're *heah*!"

"But, Pecos, you've forgotten Don Felipe and Sawtell. It's so easy to forget anything here. I cain't keep track of days. It's *you*, Pecos, with all your talk of riches, that makes me remember poor Dad and his hopes. And then I come back to these slick devils who not only stole my stock but tried to steal *me*. . . . It cain't last, Pecos. Before October comes and goes these happy days will get a jolt."

Pecos was silent a long time. The lad spoke sense, but then he had no idea who his partner was. And naturally Pecos was brought face to face with dire possibilities. He pondered over them, one by one, and added others as far-fetched and unlikely as he could conceive. Not one presented any great obstacle to him!

Still, he could get shot in the back. If he would only sternly get down to the somber vigilance that had been natural to him in the past. But that was the opposite to being happy! He owed it to this orphaned lad, so lovable and fine, and so full of promise, to see that no tragedy ruined him.

"Terrill, yu handsome son-of-a-gun, listen," began Pecos, deliberately. "Yu don't know what I know. An' I've gotta brag some to convince yu. . . . Wal, I once rode for Don Felipe."

"Pecos! You did?" Terrill queried, in amaze, and he threw up his head so that the ruddy firelight played upon his tanned face.

"Shore did. An' when thet greaser sees me an' recognizes me, his black-peaked face will turn green, an' his little pig's eyes will pop out of his haid, an' them pigtails—shore yu seen how he braids his hair?— they'll stand up stiff. . . . Yu savvy, son?"

"Yes, I savvy," replied Terrill, soberly.

"Wal, to resoom. Don has got the same vaqueros he always had, 'cept two or three thet ain't ridin' for nobody no more. Ha! Ha! . . . An' do they know me? Wal, yu'll see some day, an' yu shore won't worry no more. . . . An' thet fetches us down to Breen Sawtell. . . . Terrill, thet man cain't cause me to lose the tiniest wink of sleep. Now do yu savvy thet, too?"

"No, I cain't. . . . Who *are* you, Pecos?"

"Wal, I'm yore partner, an' thet's enough. . . . Now listen to this new idee of mine. Next spring or fall, at the latest, *provided* we're free of worry aboot the Felipe-Sawtell outfit, we'll go south to the Rio Grande.

We'll pick up some honest-to-Gawd vaqueros thet I know how to find, an' we'll buy some fine hosses an' cows, an' particular some bulls, an' turn trail drivers ourselves long enough to get them heah."

"Oh, Pecos, there yu go again," declared Terrill, in despair. "Do you mean we'll drive and sell what cattle we have?"

"Not a darned hoof."

"But that would cost a lot of money."

"Shore it would, the way yu figure money. But I've got it, Terrill."

"Where?" gasped the lad, incredulously.

"Wal, I reckon yu ought to know," drawled Pecos. "'Cause somethin' might happen to me, an' in thet case I'd want yu to have the money. I hid all my small bills in a tin can back in the corner of thet loft where I sleep when we're home. The rest—the big bills—I pack around with me. Heah."

Pecos opened his shirt, and unlacing the wide leather belt he had made he handed it over to his partner.

"I reckon you remember this belt. It's to blame for my nearly kickin' the pants off yu thet day."

"I'm not—likely to forget that—Pecos Smith," returned the lad, in a low voice. "What'll I do with this?"

"Take a peep inside."

With eager trembling fingers Terrill complied; and then, utterly astounded, he fixed large dark dilated eyes upon Pecos.

"Fifty dollar bills! Hundred dollar bills! . . . I dare look no farther. . . . A fortune!"

"Not so bad, for a couple of young Texas vaqueros," replied Pecos, complacently, as he replaced the belt round his waist, and tucked in his shirt. "Yu 'pear more shocked than tickled."

"Pecos, if—if you turned out to—to be a—a thief—it'd *kill* me!"

"For Gawd's sake! I'm no bank-robber or rustler. I told yu," sharply returned Pecos, too keenly stung to weigh the strange significance of Terrill's words.

October waned. The sunny days were still hot, but no longer hot in comparison with those of midsummer. Lambeth Ranch presented a beautiful spectacle for that arid and rocky region.

The gray rock walls never changed. They were immutable in their drab insulation, though the sunrise and sunset took fleeting colorful liberties with them. But at their base a yellow-and-gold hue vied with the green, and circled the whole oval canyon, a warm fringe that had no regularity. In the notch of the walls, where the gulch opened, there were clinging vines with hints of cerise among the brown and bronze leaves. Across the green canyon floor shone lines and patches of goldenrod.

It was the season when birds and ducks had halted there on their southern migration; and there were splashes upon the blue lake and in the silver river, and flashes of myriads of wings, and music of many songsters.

Pecos was working the river canyon, with results

that delighted Terrill and brought the rolling white to Sambo's ox eyes.

"I done tole yo," he averred, time and again. "I'se de darky dat knowed all aboot dem cattle. Dey libes on dem ribber banks, up an' down so furs dey can git. An' dat's furder den we can go."

Nevertheless, keen as Sambo was about most things, he was wrong in regard to Pecos, for that vaquero could take a horse where any steer could go. And so at the low stage of water, and wading or even swimming their mounts around sharp corners of wall the three maverick-branders found places no white man had ever tried, and unbranded cattle by the score, and old mossy horns that took a good deal of hard chasing. Pecos had a knack of running them into the river, and if they did not venture to cross, which happened frequently, he roped them, dragged them ashore, and with Sambo's assistance, burned the T L on their wet flanks. Terrill built the fires and heated the iron.

With few exceptions all these cattle were driven downriver toward the ranch. Pecos had far-seeing plans. There were twenty miles of brakes below Lambeth Canyon, and a vastly wider range west of the river, which would one day run thousands of T L stock. Every time Pecos threw a lasso, and every several times Sambo did likewise, and once in half a dozen throws for Terrill, meant an added six dollars for the Smith-Lambeth combination. It was amazing how the thing grew. And likewise their appetite for work, and daring to encompass it grew in proportion to their reward.

"Wal, in the mawnin' we'll ride up this heah side, an' Sambo an' I'll cross the river while yu stay behind," said Pecos, at supper one evening.

"Like hob I will," drawled Terrill.

Pecos deliberated a moment. Often difficulties arose in the way of keeping Terrill from sharing real perils. To hint of danger a little too risky for his strength or horsemanship was to invite failure. And it struck Pecos rather strangely that now he should seek to deter the lad from ordeals that months past he had thrust upon him. There had been several narrow escapes for Terrill.

"S'pose yu tackle thet little brake just below where we'll cross?" suggested Pecos. "It hasn't been ridden yet an' there'll shore be a maverick or two. See what yu can do alone."

"Ump-umm," replied Terrill, imitating his vaquero's laconic expression.

"Gosh! I wish I could make yu mind," said Pecos, impatiently.

"Make *me* mind? Mr. Smith, you're desiring the impossible. You should obey me, and you never do."

"But, damn it, Terrill, I'm an old hand an' yu're a kid. I gotta confess yu're shore gettin' good."

"Who's a kid?"

"Yu are."

"I'm—well, you never mind *how* old I am. You wouldn't believe it, anyhow. But I'm going wherever you go. Savvy?"

Pecos saw the hopelessness of that tack. So he adopted another.

"Very wal. Course yu're my boss," he replied, sadly. "I'll just give up brandin' them mavericks across the river. 'Cause I care too much for yu, Terrill, to let yu try things thet might give me an' Sambo our ever-lastin'."

That was tremendously effective. Terrill looked queer and averted his face, as always when embarrassed. Pecos saw a constriction of the round throat.

"Then you do—care something for me, Pecos," he asked.

"Wal, I should smile I do—when yu're good."

"Don't spoil it by whens and ifs. . . . I'll do as you want me to."

They were stirring long before the red burst of sun glorified the eastern wall. Sambo had the horses up before Mauree called them to breakfast. Soon they rode down to the river, in the flush of dawn, and headed up the shore, where they had worn a trail.

Flocks of ducks got up with a splashing start and winged swift flight up the canyon; the salt-cedar trees were full of singing birds; buzzards soared overhead; and cattle made a great bustle to climb out of sight or disappear in one of the brakes.

At last they arrived at the place Pecos had marked as an easy one to ford the river.

"Wal, bub, heah's the partin' of the ways," announced Pecos, jovially. "Yu can shore keep busy all day. An' meet us heah aboot sundown."

"Bub!" ejaculated Terrill, scornfully.

"Huh? . . . Aw, excuse me, Terrill. I shore do forget."

"Wal, you shore do forget," drawled Terrill, tantalizingly. "For instance, you forget Don Felipe and Sawtell are due any day now. Suppose while you're way across there, chasing mavericks, they trailed me up heah—and nailed me."

"No, I didn't forget thet," denied Pecos, vigorously. "They couldn't come up this river any distance without me seein' them."

"They might. And if they did and caught me— neither you nor anyone else would ever see me again."

"See heah, boy, what the hell kind of talk's thet?" demanded Pecos, roused by the singular look and tone of the lad. Terrill knew something that he did not know.

"Have yu been honest with me—about those calf thieves?" went on Terrill.

"Shore. As far as I went. Are yu tryin' to scare me so's you can go along with us?"

"No. But I'm scared myself. I've become used to being with you, Pecos. It's so—so comfortable."

"All right. Stay comfortable an' come on," rejoined Pecos, tersely. But he was not satisfied with himself or with Terrill. "Grab yore rifles if it gets deep over there."

Without more ado Pecos headed Cinco into the river, taking a diagonal course downstream toward the opposite shore. Cinco was a big and powerful horse; moreover he had enjoyed a rest of several days. And he liked water. He crossed without swimming. Pecos

got only his feet wet. Sambo dismounted halfway over
and waded, to ease his own horse and lead Terrill's.
The pony was small. He broke away from Sambo and
lunged back.

"Rake him good!" yelled Pecos. "Yu're goin' too
low down! . . . It's deeper! . . . Dig him—come on!"

Sambo had to wade up to his neck to make it, and
Terrill's pony had to swim. He was a poor swimmer.
There was one moment when Pecos thought he would
have to spur Cinco in to go to Terrill's assistance. But
the pony floundered to a foothold and soon gained the
bank, with Terrill in high glee.

Pecos had observed in crossing that the water was a
little roily. And he thought this had been caused by the
disturbance his horse had made in the stream; however,
the water was flowing toward him, and a second glance
discovered to him that it was slightly discolored as far
as he could see. He did not like it, though perhaps cattle had been wading in above.

This side of the Pecos, at least as far up as he could
see, differed considerably from the west shore. Rough
wooded steps and benches rose to the rim wall, which
was insurmountable though only one-tenth the height
of the sheer cliff in other places.

They rode up along the edge of the water until
halted by the usual barrier. This point was surely a
couple of miles above where they had crossed. Pecos
did not need to thresh out the brushy terraces to flush
mavericks, as had been necessary in the thickets of the
brakes below. Here it was possible to see calves, yearlings, two-year steers, and old mossy-horns.

"Build yore fire, boy, an' red up the irons," shouted Pecos, almost excited at the prospect. "Million mavericks along these benches. Looks hard to ride an' rope, but they'll be easy to corner."

The work began fast and furiously. Terrill had to run from one spot to another with the red-hot branding-iron. Soon the air grew rank with the odor of burnt hair and hide. Pecos cornered a miscellaneous bunch on a bench where they could not get by him. They were stupid or tame; they had never been chased by a vaquero. Only the old wide-horned steers made any trouble. Pecos branded them all in time and number that was record for him.

"Seventy-eight pesos in less than thet many minutes," he yelled. "Aw, I don't know. . . . Yippy-yip! . . . Yore fire's not hot enough, Terrill. If yu wasn't so slow we'd shore get rich faster."

Sambo likewise did the best work Pecos had ever seen him do. Terrill was not only supposed to heat and run with the irons, but also keep track of numbers. This he soon failed on. Pecos and Sambo came to the point of dragging calves down off the upper benches, thus saving time. To keep one iron heating all the time and dash hither and yon with the others was about the toughest job Pecos had ever seen Terrill attempt. They not only lost track of numbers, but likewise of time.

"All de whole day long," sang Sambo. "All de whole day lo-on-ng."

"Pecos, I'm about ready to drop," cried Terrill, and he looked it. "Let's rest and eat."

"Nope. We shore gonna be hawgs today. 'Cause we don't want to cross over hyar again till next summer," replied Pecos. "Stay with us, Terrill, old pard."

Thus stimulated, Terrill saved his breath and went his limit. They worked downriver, and to Pecos, absorbed and thrilled at this unparalleled day, the hours were as minutes. Most of the time he was back of the trees and brush, out of sight of the river.

The first indication that time was flying appeared to be a darkening of the light. Indeed, the sun had gone behind the western wall, and the day three-fourths spent. Pecos wiped his grimy, sweaty face so that he could see. Terrill was staggering back down off the wide bench with his smoking irons. He had built a score of fires this lucky day.

The river appeared black-streaked gold instead of green. But it struck Pecos that the sinking of the sun over the rim could scarcely account for the changed color. Suddenly his heart leaped, as his quick eye registered the muddy hue of the water, and his ear caught a low, sullen, chafing murmur. A flood had come down. That explained the roily water in the early morning. Pecos cursed as he spurred Cinco along the brushy bench.

"Jump on an' ride!" he yelled, piercingly, to Terrill.

Terrill dropped everything to run for his mustang. Leaping astride, he hurried to meet Pecos coming down

"What's up?"

"The river, by Gawd! Lood at it! . . . Ride now an' don't break yore hoss's leg."

Sambo had seen and heard from above. He was dragging a calf by his rope. He got off to release it.

"Rustle, Sambo! If thet river's up a foot we're shore stuck."

Pecos could not tell how much the water had risen. But he was scared. Besides, he had to guide Cinco over the roughest kind of going. They had half a mile to travel to reach the place where they had come over. Cinco sensed danger and his blood was up. He was hard to hold. He crashed through the brush and sent the rocks rolling. In a few minutes of perilous riding Pecos got off the lowest bench to the sandy shore. Already the water had half covered it. Looking back, he saw that Terrill was behind, and that Sambo was in sight. Pecos rode at a gallop the rest of the way to the ford.

When he halted to look at the river his excitement was augmented by dismay. The channel had wholly changed. It had been fairly swift when low, but now it was swollen and fast, with swirls and eddies, and ridges of current. Logs and sticks and patches of debris were floating down. Close at hand the low sullen roar had a growing ominous sound. It reflected a strange black-and-gold sky, where broken clouds were taking on stormy colors of sunset. The whole scene, river, sky, walls, seemed strangely unreal and full of menace.

"Damn yore greaser soul!" yelled Pecos, shaking a fist at the treacherous river.

He deliberated a moment, while Terrill was splashing toward him. To be cut off from the ranch was a serious matter. With meat and water they would scarcely starve, but the prospect of being marooned there for months, probably, was something Pecos could not entertain for a moment. At that season when the river got high it stayed high. Pecos saw the theft of their cattle and the ruin of their hopes, if they were barred from the west side of this river.

Terrill came galloping down to halt the mustang beside Pecos.

"Don't wait—Pecos!" he panted, pale with excitement.

"Boy, can yu make it?"

"Shore I can—if we start quick. . . . She's rising fast—Pecos."

"—— —— luck! . . . A foot rise, maybe, wouldn't been so bad," ejaculated Pecos. "Keep above me."

Pecos eyed the river again, to get his bearing, then with a word made Cinco take to the water. Terrill spurred the mustang to a point a few yards above Pecos. Soon they were off the shallow bar. Terrill's horse had to swim before Pecos' lost his footing. They breasted that deep channel. But Terrill got behind. Pecos could not hold hold the iron-jawed Cinco, but as it happened, the horse soon found found bottom again. Another plunge took him to shallow water, on the edge of the big bar. Here Pecos held Cinco.

Terrill was in difficulties, and Pecos made about to go to his assistance when the mustang touched the bar. But the water was swift and there appeared a chance of his being swept below the bar. Pecos spurred Cinco, to snatch at Terrill's bridle just in time to drag the mustang out of danger.

"I'd have—made it, Pecos," shrilled Terrill.

"Maybe yu would. But thet's the worst place, unless the damn river's changed. . . . Work above me
now, so if he founders I can grab yu."

Pecos turned to see that Sambo had arrived at the
point to take to the river. "Haid upstream, Sambo!"
he yelled. "Allow for current. Haid upstream!"

To Pecos' further dismay and increasing alarm he
found that the water was fully two feet higher than
normal and so swift and thick that the horses could
not be kept to the line.

Halfway across the mustang slipped and rolled,
dumping Terrill out of the saddle. There was a terrific floundering and splashing before the lad reap-
peared. Then he floated face up and inactive on the
surface. In the struggle, the mustang had bumped or
kicked him.

It took tremendous effort of arms and legs to turn
Cinco in that current. But Pecos accomplished it in
time to stretch a long arm and catch Terrill before he
drifted out of reach. The ensuing wrench almost
jerked Pecos out of his saddle. Cinco, up to his
haunches in the dragging current, kept his feet. He appeared more thoroughly angered than frightened, and
once headed right again he made a magnificent struggle
to keep to the line Pecos wanted. But that was only
possible where he could wade.

Pecos had not attempted to drag Terrill across the
saddle, fearing to burden Cinco too greatly. With a
powerful grip on Terrill's coat under his chin Pecos
kept the pale face above water.

Then suddenly Cinco plunging into deeper water,

went under, and was swept downstream. The water came up to Pecos' waist. Cinco came up, swimming vigorously.

"Stay with it, old boy!" rasped Pecos, hard as iron, as he pulled the horse a little to the right. "Steady! Nothin' for yu, Cinco!"

But it was increasingly manifest that the ordeal was a great one, almost too much for the wonderful horse. They were off the bar in deep water sweeping like a mill-race. If Cinco could keep from being carried out of line before they passed a shallow point Pecos was heading for they would be saved.

There was no use to beat him. Seeing that he would probably fail, Pecos slipped out of the saddle and with right hand holding Terrill up he dropped back to seize the tail of the horse with his left. That move relieved Cinco of the weight which had handicapped him. It did not impede him to drag Pecos behind.

Pecos had extreme difficulty in keeping Terrill above water. Already the lad's head had been under too often and too long.

Suddenly something jarred Cinco. He snorted and lunged. The yellow current roared in seething foam around him. He had struck the rocky shore. He lunged again, sending the water in flying sheets. Then his black shoulders heaved up. At this juncture, Pecos let go to find he was about waist-deep. As he gathered Terrill up in his arms he looked back to see that Sambo had fared better. He had started farther upstream and had kept to the bar.

Pecos carried Terrill up on the bank and laid him

on the grass. Bareheaded, white, motionless, with eyes closed, the lad looked dead.

Pecos tore at the loose coat buttoned up to the neck. "Damn this heah coat!" flashed Pecos, passionately. "No wonder you cain't swim. . . . Terrill! . . . Oh, lad, yore not daid!"

Frantically Pecos ripped open the wet shirt to feel for Terrill's heart. It beat. Terrill was still alive. A cold, sick horror left Pecos. But what was this?

With shaking hands he spread wide the lad's shirt, suddenly to be transfixed. His staring gaze fell upon round marble-white swelling breasts.

"*My Gawd! . . . A woman!*"

At that instant Terrill's beautiful breast heaved. There followed a gasping intake of breath. Consciousness was returning. Then Pecos awoke from his stupefaction. Emotion such as he had never known flooded over him. With wildly swift hands he closed and buttoned the shirt over that betraying breast, and likewise the coat.

Then he waited, on his knees, calling on all his faculties to keep Terrill's secret inviolate. He could meet that, as he had met so many desperate situations. But what of this strange and tumultuous rapture of his heart?

Terrill stirred. The long eyelashes quivered on the pale wet cheeks. Pecos fortified himself to look into eyes that must somehow be different. They opened. But he was scarcely prepared for the dark humid mystery of the reviving mind and soul—for the purple depths of beauty and of passion.

"Pecos," Terrill whispered, faintly.

"Heah," drawled the vaquero.

"The river—the flood! . . . I went under. . . .
There was a gurgling roar. . . . All went black. . . .
Oh, where are we?"

"Wal, Terrill, yu 'pear to be lyin' heah on the
goldenrod, an' comin' out of yore faint," drawled
Pecos. "But I ain't so damn shore whether I'm in
heaven or not."

"Sambo!"

Pecos had forgotten the negro. But Sambo appeared, wading, his horse ashore some distance above.

"Good! Sambo made it fine, Terrill. . . . An' shore
there's yore pony climbin' the bank below."

Terrill sat up dizzily, with an instinctive hand going to her breast, where her fingers fastened between
the lapels.

"Pecos, I shore owe yu heaps," murmured Terrill,
dreamily. "First at Eagle's Nest, from I—I don't
know what . . . . Then at home—the black nights—
the terrible loneliness . . . and now from this awful
river. . . . I—I don't know how to ——"

"Wal, what's a pardner for?" interrupted Pecos,
once more his cool drawling self. "I'll fetch yore hoss
an' we'll meander home. . . . All in the day's ride,
lad, it's all in the day's ride."

Chapter XI

IT WAS mid-November. Early frost had severed
yellow willow leaves from the branches, and
seared the goldenrod and killed the scarlet of the vines
on the rocks. The melancholy days had come. Birds
and ducks had long bade farewell to Lambeth Canyon; and the coyotes were sneaking down off the
bleak range. Wary of the watchful Sambo, they kept
to the thickets and rocks until night, when they
pierced the solitude with their wild barks.

A norther was blowing, the first of the season, and
the wind moaned up on the rims. Drab clouds scudded
low toward the south and scattering rain pattered on
the cabin roof.

Terrill stood in the doorway, watching as always
when she was alone, for Pecos. He was in the canyon
somewhere. Sambo often rode or hunted out of reach
of call, but Pecos, since the flooded river had ended
branding operations for the season, worked around
the ranch. It was time for vaqueros to ride in from
Eagle's Nest or the several ranches below. And so
long as Terrill could remember they had made use
of the trail down the gulch. Her father had complied
with the hospitable custom of the Southwest, even
in case of vaqueros whom he suspected of stealing
from him. It was safer not to appear suspicious.

But Pecos Smith would not be hospitable to Don Felipe's outfit, or any other questionable one. And long had Terrill dreaded the day.

Somewhere around this time came her birthday. She knew that it fell upon a Wednesday and that she would be nineteen years old, incredible as it seemed. But she did not know which day Wednesday was. Or was it her twentieth birthday? She had difficulty persuading herself that she was only nineteen, and over and over again she calculated events of the fleeting past. How swift the years! Yet what ages she had lived since the day she rode away from the old Southern home! Whenever she saw moss on a tree she suffered an exquisite pang.

"Mauree, how old am I?" she asked as the negress came by from her cabin.

"Honey, yo is eighteen."

"No. I'm more than that. Nineteen at least."

"How come yo tink ob dat, after all dese years?"

"I don't know. But I feel terribly old."

"Shucks, Rill, yo ain't old," replied Mauree, and then, after a careful glance around, to see if the coast was clear, she whispered, "Honey, is yo gonna keep on forebber bein' a—a boy when yo's a gurl?"

Terrill knew she had prompted this broaching of a long-forbidden subject. She could not scold Mauree and be honest, though the mere mention of her secret terrified her. But she had failed herself. After her father was gone she had accepted the deceit as the only defense possible to her. It had become endurable to live perpetually in fear of discovery—until that fateful day when she burst through the broken door of Brasse's abode prison to look into the face of Pecos Smith. What had she not lived through since then?

"Oh, Mauree! Don't whisper it! I'd fall dead in my tracks if—if *he* ever found me out."

"But, chile, fer de good Lawd's sake, it ain't natchell. It ain't right. Why yo's a woman! How yo gonna hide dat bosom any longer? It's heavin' right dis minnit like a plate of jelly."

Terrill pressed her hands to her tumultuous breast. Without and within that cried her sex. And it seemed to cry more than a physical secret, more than the lie she had lived—the strange emotion that had insidiously, imperceptibly grown upon her, until all-powerful, it had flung at her the terrifying truth of love.

"Mauree, I must hide it—I must," she cried, and she meant this consuming torture, this thing that made her hot and cold by turns, that toyed with her peace, that ambushed her every mood, that awakened in her longings she had never dreamed of.

"But, yo fool chile, yo cain't hide it," ejaculated Mauree. "Yo nebber growed up in mind, but yo sho is a woman in body. I sew till I'se mos blind makin' yo clothes to hide yo real self. But I can't do it much mo. Why, if dis Pecos wuzn't blind himself—a simpleminded boy who nebber knowed woman, he'd 'a' guessed it long ago."

"Oh, do—do you think he will—find me out?" faltered Terrill, in despair.

"He sho will, sooner or later."

"What on earth can I—I do?"

"I dunno. Why yo so scared he'll find you out?"

"It would be—terrible."

"Chile, yo lub dis Pecos. Dat's what ail yo so. De doomsday ob woman has done fell on yo."

"Hush!" whispered Terrill, and she fled.

In the darkness of her room Terrill suffered an anquish of fact that had been but a dream. Mauree had called her child. If that were true, she grew out of childhood in this hour of realization. And when the wild shame and the nameless pang had eased, Terrill tried to face the crisis of her life. If she confessed to Pecos that her claim of masculinity had been a hoax, that for years she had worn the garb of a boy, first to please her father, and later to protect herself in that wild country—if she confronted him with the truth, would he not be so disgusted and alienated that he would leave her? It seemed to her that he would. And anything would be better than to be abandoned to the old fears, the lonely nights, the dreaded days—and now to this incomprehensible longing to see Pecos, to hear him, to know he was near, to shiver at a chance contact and to burn for more. No—she could not bear to lose him.

She must keep her miserable secret as long as she could, and when the unforseen betrayed her, if Pecos despised her unmaidenly conduct and left her—then there would be nothing to live for.

Terrill went back in retrospect to the last years of the war when her mother had trained her to meet the very part her father had forced her to play. Her mother had divined it. Hence the lessons and the talks and the prayers that had shaped Terrill's spiritual life, that had kept her a child. Terrill's sharpened intelligence told her that if she had not hidden her sex in the guise of a boy she never could have lived up to those aloof and noble teachings. To be a boy had earned the solitude she imagined she had hated. Her mother had the wise vision of the dying. Terrill would not have had it different.

But she was a woman now and this love had come upon her. What could she do to avert calamity? She had suffered through love of mother, love of father, and suffered still. This thing, however, was different. And she realized that now, with the scales dropped from her eyes, she would be uplifted to heaven one moment and plunged into hell the next. Still, if she were a woman she could find strength and cunning to hide that. Else what was it to grow into a woman? If she were clever Pecos might never find her out and never leave her.

Then came another startling thought, like a lightning flash in the night, and it was that she wanted him to find out she was a woman. Longed for it almost as terribly as she feared he might! Between these two agonies she must live and fight for what she knew not. A woman's intuition of hitherto unknown powers of subtlety or reserve, of incalculable possibilities, paralleled in her mind this sense of a tragic suspension between two states.

Outside on the porch a step sounded—a step that had never failed to thrill or shake her, and now set her stiff on her bed, with a heart that seemed to still its beats to listen.

"Mauree, where's thet darned Terrill?" drawled Pecos, at the door.

"I dunno," lied the negress, nonchalantly.

"Dog-goneit! Nobody knows nothin' aboot this hyar shack," complained Pecos. "Hyar I slave myself damn near daid while Sambo goes gunnin' around, an' thet boy sleeps or loafs on me. I'm gonna bust up the outfit."

Of late Pecos had talked in that strain, something unprecedented. Yet his solicitude, his unfailing watchfulness, and a something indefinable that was so sweet to Terrill—these belied his complaints. Terrill trembled there in the darkness on her little bed.

"Yo is?"

"Yas, I is," snorted Pecos.

"Pecos, yo done pretty good hyar wid us. Yo be a damnation idgit to throw us away lak rags now."

"Say, who said thet?"

"Not Mars Rill. No, suh. It was dat no-good yaller niggah of mine. He sed it."

"Ahuh. Wal, Mauree, it's true. An' I'm a liar. Why, I couldn't no more leave Terrill than go back to thet old life of driftin', drinkin', shootin'."

"Mars Pecos, I'se sho glad. For why yo talk dat way, den?"

"Wal, I gotta talk to somebody or I'll bust. Sambo runs off huntin' like a canebrake nigger. An' Terrill lays down on me, all day long."

"Nobody to lub yo, huh? Mars Pecos, what yo need is a woman."

"Ha! Ha! Thet's a good one. . . . Lord! who'd ever have me, Mauree?"

"Yo's a blame handsome vaquero, Pecos."

"Wal, if I am, it never did me any good. Mauree, I never really had a—a woman, in my life."

"Lawd amercy! Yo *is* a liar."

"Honest, Mauree."

"I believes no man, Pecos, white or black."

"Yu wouldn't believe this, either. I'd give my half of our T L cattle to have a decent pretty girl to love me. One yu know thet hadn't been pawed familiar by some man. I reckon I'd hug an' kiss her 'most to death."

"Pecos, I'se sho yo could git some black-eyed greaser wench fer less'n dat."

"Hullo, heah's Sambo," said Pecos, at the sound of heavy steps on the porch.

"Whar yo been, niggah?"

"I'se been huntin', woman."

"What fo' yo hunt when yo cain't hit nothin'?"

"Pecos, I'se hung up a fine fat deer."

"Good. I'm tired of beef. How's supper comin'?"

"'Mos' ready. Yo kin call Rill."

"Sambo, put on some wood so we can see to eat. . . . Hey, Terrill! . . . Are you shore he's in?"

"Yas, Mars Pecos."

Pecos called again, louder this time. But Terrill, secure in some delicious late-mounting sense of power, lay perfectly silent.

"*Terrill!*"

Ordinarily such a stentorian yell from Pecos would have scared Terrill out of her boots. All it did now was to send the blood rushing back to her heart.

"Ughh-huh," replied Terrill, drowsily.

"Yu come out heah."

Terrill got up, and slipping on a new blouse Mauree had given her that day, she stepped from the darkness of her room into the fire-lit living-room.

"What's all the hollering aboot, Pecos?" inquired Terrill, demurely, and with a yawn she stretched her arms high, and looked him straight in the eyes, with her new-found duplicity.

But a glance was all he gave her. "I've been worried aboot you. An' supper is ready."

No meal had ever been so enjoyable as this one to Terrill, so fraught with the delicious peril of her situation, so monstrously intriguing with a consciousness of her falsehood.

"Boy, you don't eat much. What ails yu?" said Pecos, before they had finished.

"Can't I fall a little off my feed without worrying you?" demanded Terrill, petulantly.

"I reckon yu cain't do anythin' off color without worryin' me."

They got up presently. Terrill pulled a rustic armchair closer to the fire, while Pecos filled his pipe. Sambo and Mauree sat down to eat their meal. Pecos took a long look out into the black night, then closed the door.

"Yu hyar thet wind, boy?" queried Pecos, as he drew the other chair up. "Blowin' the real *del norte* tonight. Heah thet rain!—Dog-gone if it ain't nice an' homey hyar! Fire feels so good. . . . . Terrill, if it wasn't for them damn rustlers I'm lookin' for I'd come darn near bein' happy heah with yu."

"Same heah," murmured Terrill, trusting her gaze on the fire. "But I'd 'most forgot Don Felipe's outfit. . . . Pecos, will those vaqueros of his dare to steal our stock *now*?"

"Shore. Even if they did know Pecos Smith was on the job they'd take watchin'. Yu see we've a string of old cattle and new branded mavericks for twenty miles an' more down the river. We've put our brand on aboot every maverick in the brakes. Thet's goin' to rile Felipe's outfit. They'll take to brand-burnin'."

"But we could recognize any burning out of our brand," protested Terrill.

"Shore we could—if we ever see it. There's the rub. Thet outfit won't burn a strange brand on our cattle an' turn them out, as has been the custom of brand-burners. They'll throw a herd together an' drive it pronto."

"Oughtn't we ride down the river and see? They don't have to come through our place to get down into the brakes."

"Shore we'll go, soon as this norther blows out. . . . Come to think of it, I'd better work some on yore rifle. I saved it from rustin', but thet darned sand is shore hard to get out."

"Say, I filled myself full of water and sand that day," retorted Terrill.

"Pretty close shave, son," responded Pecos, shaking his head.

Sambo fetched the rifle to Pecos, who worked the action. There was still a grating sound of sand inside.

"I reckon some boilin' water will do the trick."

"Pecos, can't you get me a smaller rifle? This one almost kicks the daylights out of me. Bad as that old Sharps of Dad's."

"Shore, when we take thet trip next spring with our herd of cattle."

"Oh, it's so terribly long. Let's go now."

"An' leave our stock for those outfits to clean up? Not much. We'll go next spring after we've done some cleanin' up ourselves."

When Pecos drawled one of his cool assumptions like that, Terrill had no reply ready. She could not repress a shudder. This vaquero spoke of a fight as carelessly as of a ride. That dampened Terrill's spontaneity for the time being, and rather than have Pecos see that she was downcast she went to bed. But sleep was not to be soon wooed. She had done nothing to make her tired physically, and her emotions seemed to have transformed her into another creature. Wherefore she lay snug in her warm blankets, wide eyes staring into the blackness, thinking, wondering about the future and Pecos. He filled her whole life now. There was no one else; there was nothing else.

Meanwhile her senses were alive to the *del norte*. The norther was a familiar thing to Terrill and she hated it, especially at night, when the conformation of the canyon and the structure of the cabin made sounding-boards for the gale. It moaned and shrieked and roared by turns. During these lulls Pecos could be heard talking to Sambo. After a while, however, this sound ceased and the cabin was silent. Then the monstrous loneliness of Lambeth Canyon assailed Terrill as never before, even in the far past, when she had first come there. She was not a man. It was solemn black night, full of weird voices of the storm, fraught with the menace of the wild range, and she had been forced into womanhood, with a woman's love and hunger, which she must cruelly hide, flooding her wakeful hours with the inexorable and inscrutable demands of life.

Next day the norther blew out of a clear sky, and the sheltered sunny spots in the canyon were the desirable ones.

Terrill got around to work again with Pecos, and no task frightened her. Moods were of no use. It had done her no good to brood, to sulk, or dream, unless to incur Pecos' solicitude, which was at once a torture and a delight to her. When he came searching for her, patient, kind, somehow different, she had to fight a wild desire to throw herself into his arms. She would do that some day; she knew she would. Then—the deluge!

She could do justice to any boy's labor for a day. And since she had discovered that what little peace of mind she achieved was when she was working with Pecos, she embraced it. She never did anything in moderation. And toward the close of this day she got scolded for overdoing.

"Say, I can pack a log with any boy," she retorted, secretly pleased at his observation, yet becoming conscious again of a slight difference in him. Perhaps she imagined it. Whereupon she reverted to a former character, just to see if she could rouse him as she used to. But Pecos did not lose his temper; he did not chase her, or slap her on the back, or make any objection to her omissions.

The norther passed and the warm days came again. Then it was delightful weather. Working about the ranch was pleasant. Terrill marveled at the improvements and wished her father had lived to see them. Pecos could turn his hand to anything.

"When are we going to ride down the river?" Terrill asked more than once. But Pecos was evasive about this. And she observed that though he had always been watchful, he seemed to grow more so these late November days.

Time slipped by. And every night Terrill said her prayers—as she had never ceased to do—and wept, and hugged her secret, and dreamed wild and whirling dreams. And every morning when she awakened she made new resolves not to be such a little fool this day and to avoid the crazy incomprehensible things she had done in the past. Only to find that she grew worse!

She could not leave Pecos alone. She was unhappy when he was out of her sight. She was unhappier when she was with him because the sweetness of it, the havoc that threatened, were harder to bear than loneliness. Lastly Terrill detected a new mood in Pecos, or one she had never noticed before. Either he was worried or melancholy, or both, but neither of these states of mind was evinced by him while Terrill was present. It was only when he thought he was alone that he betrayed them. Terrill got into the habit of peeping through a chink between the logs of her partition, when she was supposed to have gone to bed and when Pecos sat before the fire. Something was wrong with him. Was he growing sick of this tame life around Lambeth Ranch? Terrill grew cold all over, and longed for something to happen, for rustlers to raid their stock, for that horrid Breen Sawtell to come, and even Don Felipe. Everything, however, served only to add fuel to the fire of her love, until she felt that it was consuming her.

For a long while Terrill had kept faith in the belief that it was enough just to have Pecos there. But this grew to be a fallacy. One of her particularly impish moods betrayed this to her. A weakness of Pecos' had been hard to find but he had one. He simply could not bear to be tickled. Terrill had found it out by accident, and upon divers occasions had exercised the prerogative of a boy to surprise Pecos and dig strong little fingers into his ribs. The effect had been galvanizing; moreover, it proved to be something she could not resist.

Pecos was husking corn and did not know Terrill had stealthily stolen up behind him. He was sitting on a sack back of the corral. Sambo was packing the cornstalks up from the field and depositing them in front of Pecos. Both of them were tremendously proud of the little patch of corn they had raised. It was a fine warm day and Pecos sat in his shirt sleeves, husking the sheaths off the ears and tossing the latter into a golden pile.

Terrill's step was that of a mouse. She got right behind Pecos before he had the slightest inkling of her presence. Then, extending two brown hands with fingers spread like the claws of an eagle, she shot them out to rake his ribs with a fiendish glee.

Pecos let out a yelp. He fell off the sack in a spasmodic wrestling, with Terrill on top of him.

"You little devil!" he rasped, snatching at her.

Terrill would have been frightened if she had not been in the throes of other sensations. But her usual nimbleness failed her, although she got clear of Pecos. However, before she ran twenty feet she fell upon her face in the grass. Pecos pounced upon her. He knelt astride of her and dug his long steel-like fingers into her ribs. Terrill passed from one paroxysm to another. Even if she had not been exquisitely ticklish, such contact from Pecos' hands would have driven her wellnigh crazy. He was yelling at her all the time, but she could not distinguish what the words were. Then, letting up on her ribs, Pecos boxed her ears and got up.

Terrill lay there on her face until she had recovered. The wonder of it was that she was not furious, not outraged, not frightened, not anything but blissfully happy. Presently when she arose to flee she took good care that he did not see her face. She ran to the cabin and hid; then it was that she learned Pecos' mere presence no longer sufficed. Such a subterfuge as the tickling episode had been a shameless excuse to get her hands on him. In her heart, however, she knew she had not anticipated such a devastating response, and suddenly she found herself weeping violently.

Presently voices disturbed Terrill. She raised her head from a tear-wet pillow. Could Pecos have returned so early from that important task of corn-husking? She heard Sambo, then a strange voice, and finally Pecos. Terrill lost no time in getting to the living-room door.

Sambo was helping a rider off his horse. Evidently he was wounded or at least injured, for Terrill espied blood. She had seen the man somewhere, probably in Eagle's Nest. He must be one of the cattlemen who shared the range. Sight of Pecos then startled Terrill more than had the stranger. It had come, then—war over cattle that Pecos expected.

"Yu bad hurt?" queried Pecos.

"I reckon not," replied the man, rather weakly. "But I had to ride—bleedin' like a stuck pig. . . . Guess it's loss of blood."

"Help him to the bench, Sambo," directed Pecos. "Terrill, yu fetch some blankets, then yore dad's kit. . . . Mauree, we'll have to have water an' clean rags."

Terrill, having rushed to fulfill Pecos' order, did not stay out on the porch to look on, but stepped inside and listened. Despite what the man said, she was afraid he would die. She leaned against the door, quaking. That might happen to Pecos any day. What a coward she was!

"Wal," said Pecos, cheerfully, after a few moments, "yore pretty bloody for a gunshot no worse than thet. Shore there's nothin' else?"

"No."

"Yu bled a heap an' thet's what put yu off yore pins. I'm glad to say yu'll be all right in a few days. We'll take care of yu heah."

"Lucky I made it. Course I knowed where Lambeth's Ranch was, but it 'peared a damn long ways."

"Ahuh. How aboot some questions?"

"Okay. Gimme another drink."

"Water or whisky?" drawled Pecos.

"I'll take whisky, this time . . . thanks. My name's Watson. Hal Watson. Hail from the Gulf. Rockport. I've been runnin' stock out of Eagle's Nest fer a couple of years. Thet's how I come to get pinked."

"Hal Watson? Heahed the name somewheres?" replied Pecos.

"I reckon you're the fellar who got young Lambeth away from Brasee last spring?"

"Shore was. Smith's my name."

"You haven't dropped into Eagle's Nest since?"

"No. But never mind aboot me. Yu runnin' cattle below heah on the river?"

"Yes. I started in with a thousand head."

"What's yore mark?"

"It was a diamond, but it looks like a star now," replied Watson, meaningly.

"Diamond, eh? Wal, I shore saw a lot of yore stock last spring. Some close as five miles below heah. Reckon we might have branded a few of yore mavericks. Ha! Ha! But I didn't see any diamond brands burned into stars."

"All fresh done, Smith. I reckon thet outfit hasn't been operatin' long."

"What outfit?"

"I don't know. Some white cowhands an' greaser vaqueros. They come across the Pecos from the east."

"Wal. . . . Did yu see anythin' of Don Felipe's outfit?"

"They's workin' upriver, so I was told at Eagle's Nest. They're worryin' Stafford a lot. He sold out his Y stock an's runnin' only one brand, the old Double X X."

"Thet brand is mixed up with ours, too."

"Smith, there are some new brands that will make you think. But let me tell you how I happen to be here. . . . I left home a week or so ago with two of my boys, a Mexican an' a cowhand I recently hired. Said his name was Charley Stine. I'm satisfied now he was in with thet new outfit. We had two pack-hosses, an' we dropped off into the brakes above Stafford's. I hadn't ridden in there for months an' I was plumb surprised. More stock than I ever seen, but my brand was as scarce as hens' teeth. We found about fifty head fenced in a brake an' then my eyes were opened. My small diamond brand had been burned into a clumsy big star. You can bet I was red-headed. Stine advised goin' back, an' then's when I got leary about him. You know thet big brake down ten miles or more below here? It has two branches, shape of a Y. Well, we run plumb into runnin' hosses, bawlin' calves, flyin' ropes, an' burnin' hair. When I rode out of the brush into sight an' yelled that outfit was shore surprised."

"Man alive! Yu should have kept out of sight an' let yore gun do the yellin'," declared Pecos, severely.

"I quit packin' a gun for fear I'd kill some one. An' if I'd had one I'd shore done it then. Well, they didn't wait to see whether I had one or not, but began to shoot. Stine disappeared an' the Mexican was shot off his hoss. I had to ride for it, an' as they had me cut off from below I lit out for upriver. Two of them, both white cowhands, chased me a mile or more, shootin' to beat hell. They shore meant to kill me."

"Wal, yu don't say so," drawled Pecos, dryly. "It shore takes a lot to convince some men. I don't need to ask if yu're a Texan."

"No, that ain't hard to guess. I've been only about five years in Texas. . . . Well, I outrode those men an' got away by the skin of my teeth. Never knew I was shot till I grew wet an' felt all wet an' slippery. That's all. . . . Gimme another drink."

Pecos took to pacing the porch, his hands behind his back, his brow knitted in thought. Terrill was almost repelled. He was no longer her smiling, cool, and kindly Pecos. She stared as if fascinated. Vague recollection of the story he had related about himself now recurred. Either she had not believed it or had forgotten the bloody details. Then she did recall her first sight of him at Eagle's Nest, and somehow that picture faintly resembled this somber Pecos.

"Honey, yo is sho pale round de gills," remarked

Mauree, drawing Terrill away from the door. "Now yo lissen to yo' Mauree. They ain't nothin' bad gonna happen. I'se got second sight, chile, an' yo can gamble on it."

Sambo came in at that juncture, apparently as unconcerned as usual.

"Yo lazy perdiculous wench! Whar's dat supper? We is hungry men."

"Sambo, I done had it 'mos' hot when dis Watson fellar come."

The early twilight soon fell. Sambo revived the smoldering fire and then helped Mauree hurry the evening meal. Terrill kept away from the door, but still she saw Pecos pass to and fro. Presently Sambo called him.

"Boss, is dat fellar able to eat?"

"I reckon, Sambo," replied Pecos, seating himself. "Terrill, I'm shore sorry I cain't lie to you."

"Don't ever lie to me, Pecos," she entreated.

"Wal, we're due to lose some stock."

"I heard every word he said to you," went on Terrill, hurriedly. "Pecos, if we don't lose anything but stock —I won't care. We're no better than other ranchers."

"Terrill, thet's shore sensible talk from yu. Maybe yu'll grow up yet."

Pecos spoke no more, ate sparingly, and soon went outside again.

"How yu feelin', Watson?" he queried.

"Not so bad when I lay still."

"Wal, yu'll be settin' up in the mawnin'. An' as I'm

goin' to ride out early, I'd like to ask you some more questions."

"Where you goin', Smith?"

"I'm takin' the back trail, an' when the sun rises I'll be peepin' over my rifle down into thet Y Canyon."

"From the rim?"

"Shore. I can ride there in less than two hours."

"By Gawd! I'd like to go with you!"

"Nope. You need some rest. I'll be back before noon. Tell me where thet cow outfit is camped."

"Right in the middle below the forks."

"Ahuh. Thet's a long shot from the north rim, but I reckon I can burn some of them. I'll take two rifles an' scare 'em to jump in the river, if no more. Did yu see whether they had rifles or not?"

"Come to think of it, they wasn't usin' rifles, else I wouldn't be here."

"Ahuh. . . . Now what was yu aboot to tell me aboot Brasee?"

"He's dead. Killed by Jade, the barkeeper."

"I reckoned he'd not last long. Was it the same bartender I slammed the door on last spring?"

"No. Brasee or one of his greasers did for him. Place changed hands again. You wouldn't know Eagle's Nest."

"You don't say? What's happened? Somebody strike gold?"

"Stafford told me it was Texas gettin' a move on. Cattle have gone to ten dollars a head. Maybe it won't last, but Stafford thinks it will. Beginnin' of a new era, he says. You know when cattle were thick an' cheap there wasn't much movement, especially of rustlers. But this late summer an' fall all that changed. Trail herds drivin' north now, by Horsehead Crossin' in West Texas, an' the Chisholm Trail is a procession these days. Comanches on the war-path. Texans buyin' more stock than ever from Mexico, an' a hell of a lot of it is gettin' stolen right back again. Rustlers, gamblers, hoss thieves, gun-fighters, outlaws, loose women, all flockin' in with settlers, cattlemen, soldiers. It's one hell of a movement, Smith."

"Humph. I'm shore surprised. But yu cain't mean thet all this is affectin' it out hyar west of the Pecos?"

"Shore I do. Course nothin' like rumor has it for all the rest of cattle Texas. The Pecos has a hard name an' it's a far country. But if Texas is goin' to be a cattle empire—which Stafford swears is as shore as the sun shines—why, West Texas will soon be runnin' a hundred thousand head where now it's runnin' a thousand."

"'Ten dollars a haid!" Pecos whistled long and low. "More'n ever damn good reason to hang onto yore cattle. I told my young partner, Lambeth, dog-gone near thet very thing."

"Smith, if you can hang on to half your stock, or one-third—you're rich."

"I'm not countin' any calves before they're branded, but this heah news shore . . . But, say, what's this done to Eagle's Nest?"

"Woke it up, Smith. There's twenty-odd families now, not countin' greasers. Another store. Freighters every week. An' last but not least there's law come in."

"Law! What you mean—law?" queried Pecos, sharply.

"Thet's all. Law."

"Rangers?"

"No."

"Sheriff?"

"No. There's a little fat old duffer come to Eagle's Nest. Calls himself Judge Roy Bean. He built a home aboot a block from the corner Brasee had, you remember. An' this newcomer put up a sign—a good big one you can see—an' it says on it: 'Judge Roy Bean—Law West of the Pecos.'"

"Law West of the Pecos," echoed Pecos, incredulously. "For Gawd's sake! . . . Is this hyar Bean out of his haid?"

"Smith, it shore 'pears so. He's constituted himself sheriff, judge, court, law. Nobody knows if he has any papers from the government. He's been asked to show 'em an' he showed that fellar a big six-shooter. Thet ain't the best. He runs a saloon an' he's his own bartender. He stops holdin' court to sell a drink an' he stops bartendin' to hold court. He runs a card game, an' he'll bust into that to arrest a fellar for cheatin'. An', by thunder, I 'most forgot. He marries people."

"A parson, too?" whooped Pecos.

"No, he hardly claims to be a parson. A judicial right, an' moral for the community, he calls it."

"Judge Roy Bean! . . . I'll shore call on thet hombre. . . . An' he marries people?—Dog-gone!—I reckon I could get a wife now—if thet Mary Heald would have me!"

Chapter XII

TERRILL had to clap her hand over her mouth to keep from shrieking. It might have been hysterical laughter, but only she would have known how mirthless it would be. Flying to her room, nearly knocking her brains out in the dark, she barred her door, and awoke to more astounding proclivities of a woman.

"Find a wife!" she whispered fiercely to herself as she tore at the bed covers in the dark and kicked at nothing. "That Heald girl?—Merciful God! I thought he'd forgotten her. . . . The cold-hearted faithless wretch! He's what my mother told me to beware of. . . . But I'm his boss. He's working for me. What's partnership? This is my land, my cattle. He can't marry anyone but . . . Oh! Oh!"

Terrill slipped to her knees and buried her head in the pillows. Pecos had no idea she was a girl—that she could be his wife. But how could he love her if he never knew she was a girl? Who was there to tell him that she, Terrill Lambeth, loved him, adored him, worshiped him more than any woman ever had or ever could worship him? And the old torment rushed over her again, augmented a thousandfold by a new instrument of this terrible thing, love—jealousy.

She was in the midst of the worst hour she had ever

endured when a knock on her door sent her stiff and thrilling.

"Terrill, air yu in bed?" asked Pecos, in an anxious voice.

"I—I— Yes," choked Terrill.

"What's wrong with yore voice? Sounds sort of hoarse."

Terrill made a magnificent effort. "Must have had my haid under the blanket," she managed to enunciate clearly. "What do you want, Pecos?"

"Nothin' much. Only to talk a little. This man Watson upset me."

"Pecos, I'll get up and—and dress," returned Terrill, brazenly, anathematizing her silly falsehood.

"No. I'll come in," he replied, and to Terrill's horror and transfixing gush of blood, the bar of the door, which had evidently not slipped into place, dropped at Pecos' push and let him in.

"Shore dark as hell in this heah little cubbyhole of yores," he drawled. "First time I ever was in heah, come to think aboot it. Yu used to be such a queer lad."

Terrill never knew how she had accomplished the phenomenon, but when Pecos stumbled to her bed and sat down upon it she was lying on the far side with a blanket over her.

"Wal, son, I just wanted to tell yu thet I'm ridin' off before daylight an' won't see yu till I get back," said Pecos.

"But, Pecos—don't—you oughtn't go," cried Terrill.

"Listen, pard. We've struck some bad times. I reckoned we would. An' the thing for me to do is meet them. What's the use of us runnin' cattle if we cain't fight for them? If I needed yu or thought there was any risk leavin' yu behind I'd shore take yu along. But I'll be ridin' like hell in the dark. An' yu know Cinco. It's a thousand to one I'll get back pronto, but—an' see heah, Rill, I—I'm hatin' to give yu this hunch—if I lost out at such odds an' didn't come back, yu wait a reasonable time, then leave for Eagle's Nest with Watson an' the niggers. Savvy?"

Terrill's lips were mute. It was her arms she had to contend with—for they had a mad impulse to go up round his neck. To keep him home! She wondered if they would.

"Reckoned I'd jar yu," he went on. "Heah's my money belt. Hide it under yore bed. In case I don't show up, thet's yores. I'd advise yu to leave this Pecos country."

"Leave my—home!" gasped Terrill.

"Shore. Terrill, yu dunce, I'm only sayin' all this because somethin' *might* happen. . . . An' I've—I— I've been powerful fond of yu, lad. . . . Thet's all. Now adios, an' sleep tight."

His hand groped for her head, and finding it, fastened his fingers in her hair, as he had been wont to do, and gave it a tug. Then he was gone, leaving Terrill prey to such sensations that she made sure she would die with them. But they did not kill her then, and she concluded that she must be pretty tough.

The heavy money belt lay over her like a caressing arm. Terrill felt of it. How thick and soft! It was full

of bills. Where had Pecos gotten all that money? She
remembered Pecos' story of the two cowhands with
whom he had gone to maverick-branding, and who had
betrayed him by burning brands. There was all the difference in the world. A maverick belonged to anybody,
at least anyone who owned cattle on the range. But
these brand-burners and brand-blotters knew they were
guilty.

Terrill undressed and went to bed, with the leather
belt around her. The weight of it, or the consciousness
that it belonged to Pecos, disturbed her, so she finally
put it under her pillow. Then it gave rise to a fearful
dream, in which Pecos was about to be hanged for
rustling, and she rode up on thundering Cinco to snatch
him out of the very noose. They escaped very romanti-
cally and satisfactorily, but when Terrill awakened
the dream haunted her.

She was dropping off to sleep again when she heard
a thud of soft feet outside on the porch. Pecos had
jumped down from his loft. Her little window was a
mere gray patch in the black wall. She got up on her
knees to peep out. The stars were wan. It was a couple
of hours before dawn. Pecos' steps sounded faintly,
and after a considerable interval she heard a rapid beat
of hoofs on the trail. Pecos had ridden away on his
deadly errand. It gave her panic, yet in spite of that
there came to her a sense of disaster for those thieving
riders of the brakes. Neither her father, nor Sambo,
nor any of the other cattlemen between Horsehead
Crossing and the Rio Grande had ever presented any
obstacle to rustlers. But Pecos seemed of another stripe.

She crawled back into bed, and lay awake until dawn, after which she fell into a doze. Mauree awakened her. "Rill, air yo daid or jest gettin' like them lazy white trash in the towns?"

Terrill would have been out promptly after that call, had it not been for the need to hide Pecos' money belt. How heavy it was! And in the light it looked fat and bulky. She wished Pecos was going to marry her and take her to Rockport on a honeymoon. Just at that moment Terrill did not care where Pecos had gotten the money.

After breakfast Terrill went out on the porch to see how their wounded guest had fared during the night. He was sitting up, drinking a cup of coffee.

"Mawnin', Mister Watson. How are you?"

"Hullo, lad!" replied the cattleman. "I'm pretty good, considerin'. Little dizzy, but that's passin'."

"I'm glad you got off so easy."

"Wal, luck shore was with me. But I was on a fast hoss. Reckon he could run away from anythin' on four laigs."

"Ump-umm! I saw your horse. He's fine. But he could never run away from Cinco."

"Cinco. Is he your hoss?"

"Oh no. Wish he were. Cinco belongs to Pecos."

"Who's Pecos?" queried Watson, with more interest.

"Why, Pecos Smith, my partner."

"Smith! Oh, I see. He never mentioned his front handle. Wal, wal!"

"Had you ever heard of Pecos?"

"Reckon I have. I'm tryin' to recollect. But my haid's sort of buzzy this mawnin'. . . . So you're young Lambeth, eh? I knew your father. We had some dealin' together. He was a fine man—too upright an' trustin' for this country. Is it true that he was killed by Indians?"

"No, Mister Watson," replied Terrill, sadly. "It was a Comanche arrow that killed Dad, but it was never shot by a Comanche."

"Indeed! That's news. Some more of this Pecos deviltry. Wal, we've a lot to go through before we can have peaceful ranchin'. It's got to get worse before it can get better."

"We ought to band together."

"Lambeth, that's not a bad idee. But we're not ready for it here yet. Country too sparsely settled. Only a few cattlemen an' riders. Range too big. Distances too long. An' we're all too poor to hire enough help. It 'pears to me we got all we can do to keep from bein' shot, for a while yet."

Terrill sighed. Perhaps this rancher was right. "Until you came yesterday we hadn't seen a single rider for months, and not an Indian all summer. I'd almost forgotten we lived on the wild Pecos."

"Wal, it never rains but it pours, lad," laughed Watson. "I hope I'm not a bird of ill omen, but I'm shore afraid. . . . Hullo, what's the matter with your nigger?"

Sambo appeared, running up from the direction of the corral. The instant Terrill saw him she knew something was amiss. Her first thought was of Pecos. But he would be returning at noonday, or later. Sambo lumbered up to the porch.

"Mars Rill—dar's riders—comin'," he panted, and pointed up the canyon toward the gorge trail.

Terrill stepped to the edge of the porch. She saw horses, riders. She counted four—five riders and several pack-horses. They had turned the curve of the canyon and were coming down the trail half a mile distant. It was a sight Terrill's father had always greeted with dread, a dread which had been transmitted to her. This time, however, after the first start of dismay, Terrill reacted differently. It would not help Pecos for her to be panic-stricken. She belonged to Texas, too, and she was his partner. As she watched the riders leisurely approach, speculating upon their character and purpose, she determined they should not get the best of her. To the outside world she was still young Terrill Lambeth, son of Colonel Lambeth, and she could act the part.

"Dey's no vaqueros," said Sambo, finally.

"I reckon there's nothin' to do but receive them," suggested Watson.

"I dunno, suh, I dunno. Sho it hed to happen jest when dat Pecos Smith rid off."

"They're shore not backward aboot ridin' up here," replied Terrill, thoughtfully. "Maybe they are some of the new cattlemen you told Pecos aboot."

"Wal, either they're honest or plumb nervy."

When the trees and the barn hid the approaching horsemen from sight Terrill ran to her room. She threw off the light blouse, and donning her loose coat she buttoned it up. Then she stuck her gun in her hip pocket. The long barrel protruded from a hole and showed below the edge of her coat. But that was just as well, perhaps. Then before going back she paused to consider. Sambo and Pecos, and she, too, had always been expecting unwelcome visitors. Well, let them come. Whatever their errand, Terrill's first care was to conceal her sex, and after that meet the exigencies of the case as Pecos' partner.

"Where are they?" she asked when she got outside.

"Must be havin' a parley or leavin' their hosses," returned Watson.

"Heah dey come on foot. An' dey's walkin' arsenals," said Sambo, who stood out from the porch. He returned to sit down on the step. "Mars Rill, dis is no friendly call."

Presently the men came into Terrill's range of vision. "I shore know that tall one," she flashed. "Breen Sawtell."

"So do I," rejoined Watson, not without excitement. "Met him at Eagle's Nest last summer. Talks big cattle deals. . . . Can't say I liked him, Lambeth."

Terrill uttered a little laugh, which got rid of the last of her nervousness. "I can't say I'm in love with him, myself."

"Has he been here before?"

"Twice. Last time I took to the brush till he left. He's a new partner of Don Felipe's."

Watson whistled significantly, and no more was said. Terrill watched her visitors approach. Well she remembered the tall Sawtell, even to his shirt sleeves, his black vest and sombrero, his long mustache and deep-set black eyes. On his right stalked a short thick individual, ruddy of face and pompous of bearing. The other three men were cowhands, young, unshaven, hard-faced, not markedly different from any other cowhands of West Texas. They were all heavily armed, except Sawtell, who showed only a gun strapped to his hip. He halted some dozen or so steps from the porch and swept its occupants with his deep-set basilisk eyes.

"Howdy, folks."

Watson replied, but neither Terrill nor Sambo offered any greeting. Sawtell, after a moment, appeared most interested in Watson. He took a few more steps forward, while the stout man followed rather hesitatingly. Terrill had eyes for everything. She noted that only Sawtell looked over-eager.

"Don't I know you?" queried Sawtell, fixing Watson with his greedy eyes.

"Met you at Eagle's Nest last summer. My name's Watson," replied Watson, shortly.

"Sure. I remember. Talked cattle sale with you, but you wanted cash. . . . Say, sort of pale an' sickish, aren't you?"

"I ought to be. Got shot yesterday. Lookin' my stock over an' run plumb into some brand-blotters. They darn near did for me."

Sawtell's change of expression was not marked, but it was perceptible to Terrill.

"Shot! Brand-blotters! . . . Where aboot, Watson?"

"Downriver aboot ten miles. I outrode them an' got here, pretty much all in."

"So I see. All alone, eh?"

"No. I had two cowhands. A Mex an' fellow named Stine. I didn't see them after the first shots."

Sawtell seemed to proceed gropingly in thought. Terrill divined his next query.

"Downriver outfit?"

"I reckon not. There were several white cowhands mixed in with vaqueros. New outfit from across the Pecos."

"Like as not. They're driftin' in from all over." Then Sawtell turned abruptly to Terrill. "Howdy, Lambeth. I hear you lately went in partnership with one Hod Smith."

"Not Hod Smith. My partner's name is Pecos," rejoined Terrill.

"Where is he?"

"Out," replied Terrill, laconically.

"When'll he be back?"

"No telling. In aboot a week, maybe."

"Bill," said Sawtell to the stout man, "I reckon Smith is the hombre we want. Them cowhands at Heald's called him Pecos. But we never heard of it."

"Pears to me there's a Hod Smith an' a Pecos Smith," replied the other, ponderingly. "We don't want to get our brands mixed. The man we're after is the Smith who shot your brother an' went to burnin' brands with Williams an' Adams."

"Shore. An' we're on the right track," replied Sawtell, confidently.

"Excuse me, gentlemen, but if you ask me I say you're shore on the wrong track," spoke up Watson.

"How so?" retorted Sawtell.

"Wal, that's aboot all from me."

"It's enough. Are you a friend of Hod Smith's?"

"I don't know any Hod Smith."

"Fellers, we might have known we'd get up against a stall like this," said Sawtell, spreading his hands to his men. "So just drape yourselves around an' be comfortable. . . . Get up, nigger," he went on, addressing Sambo, and giving him a kick. "You can feed us after a bit."

"Thet's up to Mars Lambeth," replied Sambo, sullenly.

"Boy, order your niggers to cook up a feed for us."

"You go to hell," drawled Terrill, from where she leaned in the doorway.

"No Southern hospitality here, huh?"

"Not to you."

"Wal, we'll help ourselves."

"Bill, meet young Terrill Lambeth. This is Bill Haines, sheriff from up New Mexico way."

Terrill eyed the stout man. He would not have been unprepossessing if he had been minus the odious prefix. Terrill was playing a boy's part, but she was looking out with a woman's intuitive gaze, with the penetration of love. Haines had a smug, bold front; he had a bluff laugh; but his shifty gray eyes did not meet Terrill's glazing ones for more than a fleeting instant.

"Glad to meet you, young feller," he said, in a hearty voice.

"Are you a Ranger?" queried Terrill.

"Used to be, sonny," was the reply. "I'm now an officer for private interests."

"Have you come heah to arrest Pecos Smith?"

"Wal, yes, if this Pecos Smith is Hod Smith."

"Then you might as well leave before you get into trouble, because Pecos Smith is shore Pecos Smith."

"Breen, this young jackanapes has got plenty of chin," growled Haines.

"Wal, you can arrest him, too," declared Sawtell, with a guffaw. "He's in with Smith."

"Arrest *me*!—You just try it," flashed Terrill.

"Listen to the kid!"

"Excuse me, gentlemen," spoke up Watson, evidently prompted by Terrill's spirit. "Is this a legal proceedin'? I never heard of a sheriff west of the Pecos. It's none of my business. I'm as much a stranger to Lambeth an' Smith as I am to you. But I've a hunch you're barkin' up the wrong tree."

"Wal, for your edification, Mister Watson," sneered Breen Sawtell, "an' as you're a Pecos River cattleman, I'll tell you. . . . This cowhand Smith rode for the Healds. He was implicated in shady deals with two riders named Williams an' Adams. My brother rode down to the H H an' asked the Healds to fire Smith. An' he got shot for his pains. Shot when he wasn't lookin', so it runs up on the Pecos. Wal, then Smith lit out for the brakes. His pards drove small herds of stock to a certain New Mexico market. They were fetchin' out herds of a hundred haid or so, part mavericks just branded, and the rest yearlin's an' steers thet

had burned brands. Beckman, a cattleman I was foreman for a little while back, was the biggest loser. An'
after six months or more of this thievin' he took three
good riders an' trailed Williams an' Adams down in
the thickets of the Pecos. This was in the Alkali Lake
country across from Tayah Creek. . . . Wal, they
never came back an' nothin' was ever heard of them.
Then Haines an' I, with our men, took up the trail.
We found the decomposed bodies of six men. One had
a lariat round his neck. That one we figgered was Williams. Adams we identified by his front teeth. He had
been shot. Beckman we recognized from his clothes. He
had an arrow stickin' through his ribs. But, hell! no
Comanche killed him. There was a dried-up hoss carcass with some arrows stickin' in it. . . . Now here's
how we figger it. This man Smith was campin' alone.
He never went anywhere with his pards. An' expectin'
them back from a drive, he come in time to see Williams hangin' to a tree, an' no doubt Adams aboot
ready for his. There was a fight, an' Smith was the only
one left. He shot a lot of Comanche arrows around to
make it look like the work of Indians. Then he searched
all the dead men for money, took it, an' rode away. We
kept on down the river trail to Eagle's Nest. There we
learned a rider answerin' the description of Smith rode
into town early last spring, broke open Brasee's jail,
where this young Lambeth was locked up for somethin', an' left with him an' the nigger for this ranch.
In this case it's shore easy to put two an' two together."

"Sawtell, take this from me," ejaculated Watson, feelingly. "This Pecos Smith is not your man."

"An' why not?"

"There's some mistake."

"Hell! didn't we find out thet he'd paid a big bill for young Lambeth? Two hundred dollars. Lambeth had been locked up for debt. The greaser said Smith had a roll of bills as big as his laig."

"That may very well be. But this *Pecos* Smith is some one else. He's not the kind of a Texan who'd burn brands an' murder for it."

"Say, how'n hell do you know this Pecos Smith ain't our Hod Smith?" demanded Sawtell, angrily.

"Wal, I can't prove it. But I'd gamble on it. An' what's more, I wouldn't be one of the outfit to accuse him of all this—not for a million dollars."

"Aw, you wouldn't? Watson, your talk ain't so convincin'. How do we know you ain't in cahoots with Smith?"

"Sawtell, you're a damned fool, among other things," declared Watson, in amazed heat. "I'm a respectable rancher, as everybody on this river knows."

"Ahuh. So you say. But *we* don't know ——"

"Breen, you're goin' a little too fast," interrupted Haines, sourly. "I told you we might be on a wild-goose chase. An' if we are we want to know it before makin' any moves."

Sawtell fell into a rage at this and stamped up and down, cursing. He was a passionate and headstrong man, evidently determined upon a certain line of conduct, and he meant to stick to it.

Terrill had suffered a horrifying conviction. Pecos really was the man they were after. He really was a rustler. All that money, surely thousands of dollars, part of which Terrill had in her possession—had been the combined profits of the three brand-burners. Pecos' story had omitted a few little details, but it dovetailed with that told by Sawtell. Terrill could easily supply the discrepancies. She had a rending, sickening agony in her heart. Was it possible that the man she loved was a cow thief? Terrill's impulse was to run and hide to conceal her hurt, but she dared not act upon it, because any moment Pecos might ride in sight, and she had to see him meet these men. She shook at the very thought, and was hard put to it to stand there.

"Haines, are you afraid to go through with this job?" demanded Sawtell, after his tirade.

"No. But I'm not arrestin' any unknown vaqueros. You can lay coin on that," replied the sheriff, testily.

Sawtell plainly was handicapped by the presence of others. He fumed, and chewed his long mustache, and glared at his ally as if he suspected hitherto unconsidered possibilities.

"After all, the money is the main thing we're after," he burst out, as if unmasking. "Agree to thet?"

"Yes. There's some sense in makin' the money our issue. Why didn't you come to that long ago?"

"No matter. . . . Wal, I've a hunch this money is hid right in this cabin," went on Sawtell, with passion. "An' if we find it you can bet your life I'll have the truth of Hod Smith's identity."

"Yes? You're a positive man, Sawtell, but that ain't enough for me. How will you have it?"

"I was the market for Williams an' Adams. I paid them for all their stock. I know every greenback of thet money. Haw! Haw!—Now what do you say?"

Haines appeared not only thunderstruck, but slowly growing enraged.

"I'll say a hell of a lot if thet's a fact."

"Wal, it is, an' you can just swaller it, hook, line, an' sinker. I bought thet stolen stock cheap, you bet, knowin' I could realize on it. An' of course I meant to trail Williams an' Adams an' get all my money back. I kept advisin' them to stay out of towns, to rustle all the stock possible, to save all their money, an' they cottoned to thet. My plans would have worked out fine. But while I was away, one of Beckman's cowhands rid plumb on to Williams an' Adams with another bunch of cattle. They shot him. Thet put Beckman on their trail, with the result I told you."

"Sawtell, that deal doesn't hold water," protested Haines, red in the face.

"Wasn't I dealin' with rustlers?"

"Shore. An' buyin' in stolen stock once for evidence was all right. But keepin' it up! What'll the cattlemen whose stock you bought say to this?"

"Wal, to hell with them! If it came to a showdown I'd let them pick out their burned brands. . . . You got any more kicks to make?"

"Little good it'd do me if I had."

"We come down here to find that money an' hang

thet Hod Smith, an', by Gawd, we're goin' to do it!"
declared Sawtell, black in the face.

"Sawtell, I'd say there was little chance of either,
with you holdin' the reins," returned Haines, with sarcastic finality.

Suddenly Sawtell whipped out his gun and presented
it at Sambo. "Nigger, do you want to be shot?"

"No, suh. I'se not hankerin' fer dat," replied Sambo,
rolling his eyes.

"Turn round an' stick your black snout against thet
post," ordered Sawtell. . . . "Hey, Sam, fetch a rope.
Rustle. . . . There's one on thet saddle. Take it. . . .
Now a couple of you hawg-tie this nigger to thet post.
Make a good job of it."

In a few moments Sambo was securely bound, after
which Sawtell confronted Watson, as he sat pale and
composed on the porch bed. He flinched as the gun was
carelessly waved in his direction.

"Tie this feller hands an' feet."

"See here, Sawtell, that's goin' too far. I'm a crippled man. Besides, I'm absolutely neutral in this
fight."

"Neutral be damned! . . . Tie him up!"

His further protestations were of no avail. The three
cowhands roped him fast to the bed he sat upon.

"Now then," went on the leader. "Sam, you an' Jack
go down by the river. There's a trail under thet far
wall. Hide in the brush an' hold up any man who
might ride alone. . . . You, Acker, hop your hoss an'
ride up the canyon to thet thicket below where the trail
comes out of the gorge. Hide your hoss an' yourself, an'

you be damn shore to stop any rider comin' down. You
all savvy?"

"Ahuh. But I reckon we all better have our hosses,"
replied Sam.

"Wal, yes, if it suits you. Now rustle," finished Sawtell, and sheathed his gun. "An' now, Bill, it's for you
an' me to go through this cabin with a currycomb."

Chapter XIII

TERRILL heard this byplay between the two men and watched them with clouded eyes, while almost sinking in the throes of stupefying misery at the renewed doubt of Pecos. But when Sawtell announced his intention of ransacking the cabin she conquered the blinding weakness. Whatever Pecos had been in the past, he was honest and fine now; he had saved her and he was her partner; but even if some of these things were true, she loved him so wonderfully that she would fight for him and share his fortune.

"Come on, Bill," sang out Sawtell, his heavy boots creaking the porch boards.

"Not me. Search the shack yourself," replied Haines, ill-temperedly. He did not like the situation. Terrill's hopes leaped at the chance of dissension between them.

"Wal, by thunder! if you ain't cross-grained all of a sudden," snorted Sawtell, in disgust.

"I hired out to arrest a criminal, an' not to risk pokin' around in his shack. Like as not, if there wasn't anybody here with sense enough to keep a lookout, you'd turn around presently to have a gun poked in your belly."

"But, you thick-headed ———! The boys are guardin'

the only two trails into this canyon. We cain't be surprised."

"That's what you say. My idee of your judgment has changed."

"Ha! It's your nerve thet's changed. A few words from this peak-faced cowman an' you show your white liver."

"Sawtell, your remarks ain't calculated to help this deal," rejoined Haines.

"I shore see thet. Wal, in a pinch I can do the job myself."

"Haw! Haw!"

That sardonic ridicule widened the breach. Terrill made sure now that these two men would clash.

"Haines, this man has fooled you all the way and means to double-cross you in the end," interposed Terrill.

The sheriff's frame vibrated as if it had been surcharged with a powerful current.

"Kid, you don't say much, but when you chirp it's somethin' worth thinkin' about," returned Haines, with a harsh laugh.

"That'll do from you, Lambeth, or I'll slap the tar out of you," growled Sawtell. "Haines, I'll give you one more chance. Are you goin' help hunt for thet money?"

"Bah! You're loco, Sawtell. If this Hod Smith ever had any money it's gone by now. Why, it's 'most six months since that last cattle drive was made."

"Wal, it's a forlorn hope, I'll admit, but if I do find thet money you shore won't get a dollar of it."

"The hell I won't. Find it an' I'll show you."

Sawtell gave him a long gaze. "You may be surprised pronto," he said, in another tone. Then he
wheeled to stamp toward the door.

"Get out of my way, Lambeth," he ordered.

For reply Terrill extended the gun, which she had
drawn and cocked. Sawtell recoiled away from it.

"By Gawd! . . . Look here, Bill. . . . This kid
has throwed a gun on me."

The sheriff showed a disposition to get out from behind Sawtell.

"You can't come in heah," rang out Terrill. The
man's close, raw presence, his blood-red eyes, the hard
amaze he showed, added a last force to her will. She
meant to kill him if he tried to enter. And on the instant Terrill was thinking that the hammer of her gun
would fall on an empty chamber.

"Ahuh. So, Lambeth, you're givin' yourself away.
Cub partner of a rustler an' murderer, huh?"

"Breen Sawtell, you bet I'm Pecos' partner," flashed
Terrill, and pulled the trigger. The hammer fell with
a sharp metallic click. Sawtell flinched. Terrill cocked
the gun again. "Look out for the next one. I'll kill you.
. . . You can't ——"

Sawtell's hand flashed out to throw up the gun.
Terrill screamed and pulled the trigger. The gun went
off in the air, but it was a narrow escape for him. Holding her arm up, he wrenched the gun loose, and tossing
it back he knocked Terrill into the cabin. As she went
down her head struck hard.

When Terrill came to she found that she had been

bound to a chair. Sawtell had taken down a jug of liquor that had stood on the shelf for years, and after smelling it he took a long gulp.

"Aggh! . . . Bill Haines don't know what he's missin'."

Whereupon Sawtell began a search of the room. This did not take many moments, for there were such few places to hide anything. Meanwhile Terrill had fully recovered her wits. She had been hastily tied with some soft rope hobbles that had hung just inside the door. She could twist one small and capable hand so as to reach the knot, which she believed she could loosen. There were two rifles in the living-room, of which hers was loaded. If she could get hold of that! Then she grasped the fact that her feet were bound to the legs of the chair. Even if she did free her hands she could not get up. Then she espied Sambo's hunting-knife on the table, within reach. After that she watched the ransacking ruffian while she redoubled her efforts to free her hands. She wondered what had become of Mauree. Probably the negress had run off in fright to her cabin and baby.

Sawtell got through searching the living-room. Then he gave the pole partition a vigorous shake. Terrill's door flew open and Sawtell entered her little room. No one was ever permitted to go in there. Any thorough search must discover that there was something strange about Terrill Lambeth. But on the moment Terrill had no qualms about this. It was the money Pecos had intrusted to her. Why had she not hid the belt in the barn or a crevice in the cliff. For Sawtell would most surely find it.

"Haw! Haw! Haw!" roared in husky accents from Terrill's room. Then Sawtell appeared with the money belt clutched in his hands. There was a radiance about him, but it appeared far from beautiful. His eyes emitted a wolfish hunger. "By Gawd! . . . I've got it," he crowed as he laid the belt on the table. His big shaking hand, with its tobacco-stained fingers, tore out sheafs of greenbacks that had been neatly and compactly folded. "Oho! I guess I didn't have a hunch. . . . All the big bills—fifties—hundreds! . . . Mister Hod Smith, you shore are a savin' hombre."

The doorway darkened to the wide frame of Haines, who suddenly halted, pop-eyed, at sight of Sawtell and what he was doing. As if by magic, then, astonishment appeared swept away.

"Breen, so help me Gawd, you found it!" he exclaimed.

"I shore did," replied the other, in grim exultance. "There's twenty thousand, anyway. An' that was worth comin' for." Whereupon he moved the belt and piles of bills back to his left on the table, interposing his body between it and Haines. Then he poured out a cupful of red liquor from the jug. "Here's to your bad luck, Haines, an' poor judgment!"

He tossed off the drink with a flourish. "Aggh!— That's stuff for you. Have a drink, Bill. It's as old as the hills."

Neither of the men seemed aware of Terrill. Haines took a stiff drink, though his gray eyes, now with a blaze in them, never left the belt and money for an instant.

"Good likker, all right," he coughed, and edged along the table. "Breen, I was wrong. You shore had a hunch. But I was only sore, an' worried aboot this Hod Smith mebbe bein' Pecos Smith. . . . Do you recognize the money?"

"Yes, if it's anythin' to you," responded Sawtell, dryly, and he began stowing the flat packets of bills back into the belt.

"Shore it's a lot to me. I'm as tickled as can be. If you know your own money we're justified in takin' it. An' I say let's let well enough alone an' rustle out of here before this Smith person gets back."

"An' why for, Bill?"

"He might be Pecos Smith?"

"Hell! S'pose he is? What do we care? Wouldn't he look as fine danglin' from a rope as anyone else?"

"You don't seem to savvy somethin'," retorted Haines. "If he is Pecos Smith he won't be easy to string up."

"Haw! Haw!"

"Man, you've lost your head completely."

"Nope. Thet applies to you, Bill. I'm figgerin' shore close. There's only two trails into this canyon, an' I've got two men hid on the river trail an' one man hid on the gulch trail. Smith will be held up either way."

"Then we ought to help guard. There's many a slip, you know. . . . Give up your crazy notion to hang Smith an' let's go."

"He shot my brother."

"What'n'hell if he did?" shouted Haines, stridently. "There's some who say that wasn't such a loss. You make me sick with your braggin' loyalty, when all the time you was double-crossin' him yourself."

"You're a —— liar!" returned Sawtell, ominously.

"Now, Breen, don't bluster that way an' go back on what you know."

"What I know is my business," returned Sawtell, doggedly. "What you think you know concerns me when you get to gabbin' in front of strangers. You forget that nigger tied up out there. An' this cattleman who calls himself Watson. You talk too much. You haven't one damned proof that I double-crossed my brother."

"No. It's just my hunch. But you can bet your pile this Smith vaquero knows. An' that's why you're so keen to hang him."

"Air you goin' to shet up?" demanded Sawtell, threateningly.

"Wal, there's no use in arguin' any more since we've got the money."

"*We?*" shouted Sawtell, derisively.

"You heard me correct, Breen. I consented to take up my old Kansas job as sheriff to serve your ends. I rode down in this Gawd-forsaken Pecos country with you. I'm riskin' my skin right this minute, an' you bet I'm in on everythin'."

"Haines, you're in on nothin'. I told you thet a while back. You shot your chin off once too often."

"You mean you're not goin' to divide that money?" yelled Haines, hoarsely, his ruddy face changing color.

"Get out! Your fat greedy face hurts my sensitive feelin's," retorted Sawtell, and he shoved Haines out of the cabin. For a moment his tall form obstructed the light. Terrill espied Sawtell's hand creeping down toward his gun. Her heart nearly burst. The fight was coming. These ghouls would destroy one another. Terrill's right hand came free. If she could only get up! She tore at the knots. The men had forgotten her. Her rifle leaned against the wall. Sawtell had left the money belt on the table.

"Breen Sawtell, you're as crooked as a rail fence," replied Haines. "But crooked or not, I want my share of that cattle money. You agreed to divide it."

Sawtell stepped out on the porch, so that all Terrill could see was his left side. His left hand was stiff, with the long fingers quivering.

"Shore. But you lost your nerve an' you wouldn't help me. So I'm justified in not makin' a divide."

"———! I'll show you up all over New Mexico," hissed Haines.

"No you won't, Bill."

"Of all the thick-skulled men I ever seen! Do you think you can soft-soap me out of this deal?"

"All I'm thinkin' now, Bill, is that you won't be goin' back."

"He-l—!" A shot cut short Haines' yelp of fury. The thundering report appeared to clamp Terrill's eyes tight shut. Then her ears vibrated to the crash—crash —crash of guns. Both men must have emptied their weapons. As Terrill opened her eyes she heard a groan that appeared to come from the left side of the door.

Sambo or Watson had been hit. Then a boot grated, the porch boards creaked—and there followed another bursting report.

Terrill's strung faculties broke to sight of Sawtell stepping before the door. He was sheathing a smoking gun. Terrill had wit enough to grasp that Sawtell had not had time to reload the gun. His face was black and terrible. He felt of his left arm where blood showed near the shoulder.

"Barked me, huh," he soliloquized, and pulled a bandana from his pocket. Then as he stepped to the threshold he espied Terrill. "Ha! 'most forgot you, Lambeth."

"Is—he—dead?" gasped Terrill.

"Who? Bill? . . . I reckon so, for all intents an' purposes. . . . Tie this arm up for me." And taking the hunting-knife off the table, he cut the hobble that bound Terrill's hands, not noticing that one of them was already free. "What you shakin' aboot, youngster? A little while ago you was steady enough. I thought my day had come."

Terrill at last succeeded in knotting the bandana securely. Sawtell stuck the knife upright in the table and made no move to retie Terrill's hands. "Now what?—Aha! Another little drink for my nerves."

When he threw back his head and tipped the jug to his lips, Terrill snatched the knife, and quick as a flash freed her feet. He saw her out of the corner of his eyes. Down the jug thumped. Terrill flashed her hand for the money belt, and securing it she whirled to flee.

But as she leaped through the door Sawtell's hand

fastened on the back of her coat. He gave such a tremendous jerk that not only did he drag Terrill back across the threshold, but he ripped both coat and shirt almost off her body.

"You —— little devil! Must I kill you, too?" And with his free hand he twisted the belt out of her now nerveless hands and tossed it back on the table.

Terrill sank to her knees, almost fainting. To be suddenly snatched almost nude paralyzed her. Sawtell pulled at the split garments, which divided and slipped off Terrill's white shoulders.

"Fer Gawd's sake!" he rolled out, in breathless amaze, his bold eyes feasting on the curved white breast Terrill could not hide. "A *girl!*"

He let go the half of Terrill's garments, and dropping heavily into the chair he placed a hand on each of her shoulders. He shook her. Terrill's head wabbled back and forth. She was almost swooning.

"Come out of it!—You ain't hurt. . . . Let me look at you. . . . Terrill Lambeth, heh? . . . Wal, I'll be . . . ! I reckoned you was damned pretty for a boy."

"Let me—go!" wailed Terrill. The end had come. She would rather have died. This man's horny hands! His hot eyes! Her faintness left her. There was more horror than shame. She tried to get up. He held her down with hands like lead.

"All the time you've been a girl?" he ejaculated. "When I was here—twice before—you was a girl?"

"Yes—yes. I've always been. . . . It was Dad's fault. He—he hated girls. He would dress me as a boy

—when I was little. . . . And so—out heah—I kept to boy's clothes. . . . For pity's sake—let me—cover myself!"

"That —— half-breed Felipe—he knows you're a girl," declared Sawtell. "I savvy now. *That's* why he wanted me to stay away from here. . . . Wal, if this ain't my lucky day!"

Terrill, with returning strength, plucked at her rent garments, so obviously agonized by her nudity that Sawtell let go and flung some of them in her face.

"Why, you damned little hussy!" he rasped in sudden passion. "Awful ashamed, ain't you, half undressed before a strange man? Puttin' it on thick, huh? . . . You damned lyin' cat. Livin' here with this rustler, Smith. Pretendin' to be a boy!—Why I ought to strip you an' drive you up an' down this canyon."

Something about this remarkable revelation, no doubt the sight of the girl, had inflamed Sawtell into a frenzy. He jerked the torn coat out of her hands and flung it aside. He pulled at the shirt, but she clung desperately to this.

"Kill me—and be—done!" she whispered.

"Kill nothin'. You're too pretty to kill. But I'll beat hell out of you if you try any more tricks with me."

Terrill would have sagged to the floor but for his pressing knees.

"You've been livin' here with this man Smith?"

She thought she understood him.

"Answer me," he went on, and cuffed her sharply over the head. "You're livin' with this man Smith?"

"Yes—I—I'm living—heah."

"You're not married to him? . . . An' you're in love with him? . . . Haw! Haw!—You bet you air. . . . An' you know he's a rustler—a cattle thief? He told you where all this money come from?"

"Yes. But he wasn't brand-burning. . . . He was only—branding mavericks."

"Aw, hell! You're not an idiot. You didn't swaller that old guff?"

"I did—I did. I believed him."

"Wal, I furnished thet money to him an' his pards. I paid it into his hands."

"But you—you said Pecos wasn't—with those men?"

"I lied to fool Haines. It served my turn. . . . Yes, you been livin' with a low-down rustler. Shore you're no lady to be proud. Sooner or later you'd seen him hanged. An' it's just as well that I come along when I did. You're young yet. You'll get over it. . . . Now when this Smith feller comes back we'll swing him up. An' I'm goin' to stay here all night—with you. An' to-morrow I'll be takin' you away with me."

Terrill was past speech and almost power of vision.

"Wal, if you ain't pretty ——"

He broke off suddenly. He seemed to listen, and his fondling hands dropped from her person.

"What the hell?" he muttered.

Terrill's ears—that had been strained to breaking all these interminable hours—caught a low swift rhythmic patter of hoofs.

"A hoss comin'. . . . Must be Sam."

When he got up Terrill slid forward, her head toward the door. Sawtell strode over her.

"Sam's shore tearin'. . . . What's he runnin' his hoss like thet for?"

Terrill tried to rise, rose to one elbow, slid back again. She recognized that horse. Cinco! And shuddering death seemed to run along her reviving nerves out of her body.

Sawtell leaped out of the door, off the porch, to face up the canyon. His legs stood wide and bowed. His hair bristled.

Terrill whispered: "*It's—Pecos!*" And she got up on one hand. Suddenly her stunned faculties reasserted themselves. But she was still so weak that she could scarcely slip into the two halves of the split shirt, and hold the front together.

That swift clatter had become a thrumming roar.

"My Gawd, it ain't Sam!" yelled Sawtell.

Terrill's sight caught the black Cinco against the gold of the sunset sky. He scattered dirt and gravel against the cabin. Then Pecos leaped out of the very air, his spurs jangling, his boots thudding, as he hit the ground to confront the stricken Sawtell.

Pecos was hatless. A white band spotted with blood bound his head. He was also coatless, vestless, and there were other stains of blood visible. His face was stone gray, except the leaping terrible eyes.

"Who'n hell are yu?" queried Pecos, piercingly.

"Sawtell. Breen Sawtell," replied the other hoarsely. He licked his lips.

"What are yu doin' heah?"

"We come down to arrest one Hod Smith."

"Ahuh. Who's we?"

"Haines there, an' my men. Maybe you met Sam —up at the gulch trail."

"Mebbe I did. Who shot these men?"

"There was a hell of a fight. Young Lambeth was in it."

"*Terrill!*"

"Oh, Pecos—I'm—all right," replied Terrill to that devastating call.

"Sambo, you daid?"

"No, boss. I ain't daid atall. But I'se damn near daid."

"Watson! . . . Who killed him?" flashed Pecos.

"Must have stopped a stray bullet," replied Sawtell, his voice huskier.

"Haines, yu called him. . . . Shot to pieces. Who did thet?"

"Wal, me an' Bill had a little duel."

"If yu came down heah to arrest me, why'd yu fight?"

"We come to arrest Hod Smith."

"There's no Hod heah. I am Pecos Smith."

"*Pecos*—Smith!"

"I said so. Are you hard of heahin'?"

"Did you shoot my brother—at Healds' Ranch?"

"I beat him to a gun. He forced me to draw."

"Was you a partner to Williams an' Adams?"

"Yes. I'm the man."

"Then—Pecos Smith, you're the man I'm after."

"So I reckon. What're yu goin' to do aboot it?"

"Pecos, he swore he'd hang you," rolled out Sambo, passionately.

"Wal, Sambo, I'm wastin' a lot of time in gab, but I'm shore curious."

"Boss, dis white trash sho treated our Rill turrible low down."

"*Terrill!*—Yu said yu were all right?"

"I am, Pecos . . . only scared—and weak. He tore me—to pieces . . . and he found out I—I'm . . . Oh, Pecos, I can't tell you."

Sawtell quailed. His eyes had been locked with Pecos'. At last he sensed what Watson had hinted at and Haines had warned him of.

"Can't tell me what?" called Pecos.

Terrill was mute. If she had not been frozen there, leaning on her hand, she would have flopped down. But Pecos did not see her. His dancing gold-flecked eyes never oscillated a fraction from Sawtell.

"Smith, I'm on to your dodge," spoke up Sawtell. It was the brazen voice of desperation. "This Terrill Lambeth is a girl. You been livin' with her—pretendin' she was a boy. Don Felipe had a hunch. . . . If any more comes of this meetin'—you'll be spotted all over the Pecos country. . . . But you ought to marry the girl. She must have been a decent little thing once."

"Are yu—talkin' yet?" queried Pecos, in a strange, almost inaudible voice. And perhaps that weakness spurred the desperate Sawtell on. Perhaps his mind grasped at straws. If he infuriated this Pecos Smith beyond control he might gain an instant's advantage.

"But whatever she was—she's shore a hussy now," rasped on Sawtell, his body flexing.

"Ahuh."

"She knows you're a rustler—a brand-burnin' cow thief. She admitted that."

"Terrill—believed—thet?"

"Shore. She's on to you. That money now."

"Ahuh!" There might have been, to the strained sight of a madman, an indefinable break in Pecos.

"That money! *By—Gawd!*" Then Sawtell bawled and lunged.

There was a red flash, a burst, a boom. A cloud of smoke. Sawtell's gun went flipping high. He staggered back to fall upon the porch, a great spurt of blood squirting from his heart.

Chapter XIV

PECOS leaped out of his set posture. He glared around, particularly toward the mouth of the canyon. And on the instant he espied two men running along the thicket under the west wall. Their clumsy gait betrayed cowhands unused to such locomotion. They tallied with the number of saddle horses Pecos had counted.

"Ahuh. Thet's aboot all," he muttered, and slowly sheathed his gun, to turn to Sambo.

"Boss, if yo ain't speculatin' on nuthin' particular, jest cut me loose," spoke up that worthy, turning his head as far as possible.

Pecos drew a knife, and cutting the hard knot of the lasso he unwound it from Sambo's long frame. There appeared to be considerable blood from a gunshot high up on Sambo's shoulder.

"Hit any other place?" queried Pecos, sharply. "This heah is only an open cut."

"Boss, if I hadn't played 'possum I'd shore got more hits dan dat," replied the negro as he stepped free. " 'Cause dat black mustached gennelman was sho out to kill eberybody."

"How many in the bunch, Sambo?"

"Five was all I seen."

"There's the last two—across under the cracked

wall." Pecos pointed until Sambo had located them.
"We don't want them hangin' around. Take my rifle,
Sambo. Go down an' drive thet outfit of hosses up the
trail. Let those men see you doin' it. Then take a few
shots at them just for luck.—Rustle now an' get back
pronto."

Cinco had edged back from the cabin and now had
his head up as he nervously pawed the ground.

"Whoa dar, Cinco—whoa, old hoss," called Sambo,
as he approached. The horse stood, allowing Sambo
to unsheath the rifle. Whereupon Sambo lumbered
away out of sight.

Pecos surveyed the ghastly scene, then he strode
over Sawtell's body into the cabin.

Terrill sat on the floor, holding to a chair. With
her other hand she was holding rent garments together
over her breast.

"Pe-cos!" she whispered.

"Yu all right?" he demanded, sharply, as he knelt
to take her by the shoulders and force her head up to
the light. There was absolutely no color in her face.
He gazed piercingly into her eyes. Stark horror was
fading. A rapture of deliverance shone upon Pecos.
After that one swift scrutiny his tight breast expanded
in passionate relief. For the rest, he could not trust
himself to gaze longer into those exquisite betraying
depths.

Terrill let go of the chair and clung to him wildly.
Her head dropped against him.

"Pecos! Pecos!" she whispered.

"Shore it's Pecos. What yu think? I reckon yu

mean I didn't get back any too soon. . . . There's a bruise on yore temple."

"He—hit me."

"Ahuh. Hurt yu anywhere else?"

"My arm's wrenched."

"Yu fought him?"

"I threw my gun—on him," replied Terrill, growing stronger. "Meant to kill him. . . . But he knocked it—up . . . grabbed me. . . . I didn't quite faint. I felt him tying me—to the chair. . . . Later I worked my hands loose—and when he was drinking—I cut my legs free—snatched your belt and ran. . . . But he caught me. . . . It was then he tore my—my coat and—shirt off . . . found me—out. . . . Oh, Pecos!"

Mauree interrupted this scene. Her eyes were rolling.

"Mars Pecos, dem debils sho turned our home into a slotterhouse. . . . Rill honey, say yo ain't hurted."

"I'm all right, Mauree."

"Yu take charge of Terrill," said Pecos, rising.

"Oh, Pecos—don't go!" implored Terrill, hanging to his knees.

He could hardly look into the sweet havoc-shadowed face.

"Child, I won't go far," he said, hurriedly. "Thet mess out heah—an' Sambo's chasin' what's left of thet outfit."

He disengaged his knees from clinging arms and got outside, feeling shaken and dizzy. It took strong will to counteract the softer mood, to face stern issues still, to fortify himself against the sickening reaction sure to follow.

Pecos scanned the opposite side of the canyon. Cattle and horses were running in fright. Then he heard Sambo shooting. It would be just as well, he thought, to have a look. Cinco came whinnying to him, whereupon Pecos remembered to scan him for a possible wound. There was a welt on his flank, sensitive to the touch.

"Wal, it's darn good fer yu, old hoss, thet yu can run fast."

When Pecos got beyond the trees where he could look up the canyon he espied Sambo trudging back down the trail. Apparently the negro had driven the horses clear out of sight. Pecos waited for him, straining his eyes to catch a glimpse of the last of Sawtell's riders.

Sambo arrived presently, puffing hard.

"Boss—I—sho—winged—one of dem."

"Thet'll help, Sambo. But I reckon those cowhands wouldn't hang around heah now. I shore peppered thet one who was layin' fer me up the trail."

"Pecos, I wuz worried aboot dat. How yo see him? Sam, dat Sawtell skunk call him."

"I ran into fresh hoss tracks before I got within miles of our trail down the gulch. Those fellers had been to Eagle's Nest. When they turned off down our gulch I got leery. An' when I rose into the canyon Cinco either seen or smelled a hoss. So I cut off the trail by thet thorn-bush thicket. It's good I did, fer there was one of them hidin' in it, an' he shot at me. Wal, I shot back, you bet, an' plenty fer good measure. Then I loaded up an' sent Cinco down the trail hell-bent fer heah."

"All de time I prayed yo'd come. An' den when I'd gone back on de good Lawd den yo come, yo sho come, Pecos."

"Wal, I'll heah yore story after a bit," replied Pecos, thoughtfully. "I reckon we've gotta begin a graveyard on Lambeth Ranch. Some graves with haidstones, Sambo. Damn good idee— Up there on thet level bench. Shallow holes, Sambo, 'cause we shore ain't goin' to sweat more'n we have to to cover them stiffs."

While conversing thus they had once more approached the cabin.

"Search 'em, Sambo. Take papers, guns, watches, money, anythin' worth keepin' an' put them all in a sack. Relatives an' friends of theirs might ride in heah some day. An' if they don't come a rarin' fer trouble we'll turn the stuff over. . . . Too bad aboot this cattleman Watson."

"Boss, I'se a hunch dat was sho no accident," spoke up Sambo.

"What?"

"Dis killin' of Watson. 'Cause after all dat bunch shootin' when I got my shoulder barked I seen Watson was alive. Den come anudder shot an' he sagged in dat rope."

"Wal! Wal! . . . Sawtell figgered this Watson had heahed an' seen too much. Shot him an' laid it to accident."

"'Zackly. Dat Sawtell was a hell of a man, Pecos."

"I reckon—among his kind. . . . But save yore story, Sambo, till our work's done."

"You some shot up yo'self, boss?" queried the negro.

"I stuck my haid up over thet Y Canyon rim, an' one of them vaqueros grooved me. This other cut heah is from a snag ridin' the brush. They won't interfere with my appetite none. . . . Sambo, yu'll want a pack-hoss, also an old canvas yu can cut up. I'll take pick an' shovel, an' go dig the graves."

"Yas, suh. Heah's yo' rifle, boss. Don' leave dat behind. Yo can nebber tell. . . . 'Kin sabby,' as the greasers say."

"Ahuh. . . . An', Sambo, after yu move these men, have Mauree scrub away all thet blood."

Pecos did not think he would need the rifle, nevertheless he took it, and burdened with this and the heavy tools he approached the bench he had chosen for the graveyard. It chanced to be situated where ambush from the rim above was out of the question.

Pecos applied himself vigorously and in an hour or more had three shallow graves dug. The labor had caused him to sweat and pant. Moreover, it had begun to operate upon the dark grimness of mind and the sick icy sensation in the pit of his stomach, reactions which always succeeded deadly passion. He kept on working even after the job was sufficiently done. Indeed, he would have welcomed much toil. There must be other ordeals after this mood had passed.

Presently he was interrupted by the arrival of Sambo, leading a horse over the back of which bent the body of a man roped up in canvas.

"Which is this heah one?" asked Pecos.

"Dis is Sawtell," replied Sambo, unceremoniously tumbling the corpse off the horse. "Pecos, yo sho hit him whar he libbed. . . . An' what yo tink! He wored a money belt chuck full."

"Did he?—Thet reminds me of mine. Where is it, Sambo?"

"Terrill got dat. . . . Boss, yo sho should hab seen ——"

"Rustle back after another daid man," interrupted Pecos. Still he had not arrived at the state of mind where he could listen.

"Wal, Sawtell," said Pecos, after Sambo had ridden away, "yu'll rot heah because you had no good in yore heart nor sense in yore haid."

Pecos had made a clean, swift job of killing the man, and he duplicated it in the burial. Then he searched about until he found an oblong stone, one end of which he imbedded at the head of the grave. Later he would cut a name in the stone.

Sambo made two more trips with gruesome burdens, and after the last one remained to help Pecos until the duty was accomplished.

It was mid-afternoon when Pecos wended a weary way back to the cabin. The shock had passed, as often it had before; the sickness lingered only faintly. Pecos had weathered another stern vicissitude of the wild Texas borderland. These things had to be. He counted himself a pioneer. He knew what had to be stood and done before a man could have peace along the length and breadth of that Pecos wilderness.

He must face another ordeal, a more difficult one for him, and he shirked it. He could not think how to meet the coming issue between him and Terrill. He could let only the exigencies of the hour decide for him. Only one certainty stood out clearly in his troubled mind, and it sustained him where otherwise he might have had no anchor at all. A wonderful affection for Terrill Lambeth as a boy had been transformed into a tremendous love for Terrill Lambeth as a girl. Pecos would far rather have had the inevitable revelation postponed indefinitely. He had grown happy with his secret. Terrill's sex, no longer hidden, might make a difference—he had no idea what. Certainly as a boy she had looked to him, trusted him, relied upon him, cared for him in a way, but as a girl ——

The first stranger who had wrung from Terrill the truth of her sex had likewise instilled in her a belief in Pecos' guilt. That was a blow. It stung, it flayed. It was bitter. It raked over the old sore. Perhaps his reasoning was vain, illogical, invalid, and he was indeed a rustler. That issue must be met, with himself and with Terrill; and he might as well face both at once.

To approach that cabin was now harder for Pecos than if it had contained ten men of Sawtell's ilk. Pecos made a stupendous effort, and he did not really know exactly what the effort was for. But he had to go on; he had to go back to that cabin, to work there, to eat and sleep there, to face Terrill a hundred times a day. And the prospect filled him with breathless tumult.

Sambo and Mauree had cleared and cleaned away every vestige of the fight. The old cabin looked as sleepy and lonely as always. Sambo had removed the rude bough couch that had been on the porch.

While Pecos lingered outside Sambo called from the door:

"Boss, what is I gwine do wif all dese waluables?"

Whereupon Pecos forced himself to enter. One end of the table was littered with guns, belts full of shells, watches, knives, wallets, and last a wide black money belt.

"Sawtell an' dat no-good sheriff 'peared to be well heeled," said Sambo. "But Watson had no money or nuthin'."

"Sambo, do yu think thet fat feller was a sheriff?" queried Pecos as he weighed the money belt.

"Wal, I tuk it he might have been once. I heahed them say somethin' aboot Kansas. But he sho wuz no mo' sheriff dan me. Dey gabe demselves away, boss. Dat was a trick."

"Ahuh. Wal, put all this stuff out of sight so we can forget the deal."

"Boss, I sho don't want to be 'sponsible fer dis money."

"All right. I'll hide it. Let's see." Pecos gazed about the room.

"Dere's a loose stone in de chimley low down," said Sambo, and kneeling he worked a large stone free.

"Just the place. Dig out behind it, Sambo," replied

Pecos. Between them they soon disposed of the belt, and the other articles Pecos stowed upon a triangular shelf in a corner. That done, Pecos breathed still more freely. Mauree had begun to prepare for the evening meal: there were iron pots and tin pots on the fire.

"Mauree, is that water hot?" called a voice, somehow Terrill's voice, yet not the same.

"Yas, honey, it's sho hot. An' de salve yo ast fo is on de table. Yo better hurry, chile, an' fix Mars Pecos up 'cause supper 'mos' ready."

There happened to be a chair close to Pecos, which he backed into weakly. He heard a step.

"Pecos, will you let me dress your wounds?" asked the soft changed voice.

"Wounds!—Aw, why shore, if they're worth botherin' with."

"But you look so awful in that bloody bandage and shirt," protested Terrill.

"So I must. Reckon I forgot."

Terrill appeared coming around the table, upon which she deposited some articles. Pecos did not look up, yet he saw her. It was Terrill and still not Terrill. The same small boots with the worn trousers carelessly tucked in the tops! But instead of the omnipresent loose coat or shirt she wore something white. He caught that without really looking.

"Pecos, have you another shirt?" she asked, standing thrillingly close beside him, with a hand on his arm.

"Yes, it's up in the loft. I'll put it on after."

"This one is gone. Today has shore been rough on our shirts." She uttered a wonderful little low laugh, deep and rich, that tingled Pecos clear to his toes. What could have made all this difference in a boy he had known so well?

Terrill cut his ragged bloody sleeve off just below his shoulder.

"This can't be a bullet hole," she said.

"Cut myself on a snag."

With deft capable hands Terrill washed the wound, anointed it with salve, and bound it securely.

"This one on your haid!—I'm almost afraid to look at it."

"Wal, never mind, Terrill, if it'll sicken yu. Sambo'll do all right."

"*I* shall dress it." She wet a towel in hot water and soaked the stiff bandage off and bathed the wound, which Pecos was sure consisted only of a shallow groove. "O my God!" she whispered, very low, as if to her inmost soul. "One inch lower—and life would have been over for me!"

"But, Terrill, it's my haid," said Pecos, rather blankly. That speech of hers would require long cogitation.

Terrill appeared slow over this task. Her touch was not so sure, so steady. Pecos felt her fingers tremble upon his brow. She hovered over him, from one side to the other. There was a slight soft contact to which his over-sensitive nerves reacted outrageously. He never raised his half-closed eyes. He saw the white garments as a blur, too close for clear vision. But her round arms were bare to the elbows, golden brown at the wrists, then white as milk. Once, as she leaned over him, to work with the difficult bandaging on the far side of his head, she had only to drop her arms a trifle and they would be round his neck. Pecos longed for this so dreamily, so poignantly, that when he awoke to it he thought he was crazy.

"There! If you don't roll in your sleep it will stay," she was saying.

"Sleep!—I'll never sleep no more around heah. . . . Thanks, Terrill. I reckon yore a fair doctor."

Pecos stalked out upon the grass without any definite aim. If he had kept on he would have stalked over the bank into the river. But he stopped. The sun was setting in wondrous hues; the river gloomed, a winding purple band with silver edges; the great wall stood up, receiving the golden blast of sunset; and the canyon lay under a canopy of spreading rays and dropping veils.

Where had it gone—the menace, the peril, the raw wild life that hid behind the beauty, the solitude of the Pecos? A vision came to him, not unlike the dreams of the pioneer, of a time when the hard lives of vaqueros and cattlemen, the brutality of the range, the mingled blood of rustler and avenger, the raid of the Comanche, all would vanish in a sense of security in neighbors up and down the roads, in the tranquillity of homes, in the prosperity of endless herds of cattle. That was the promise of the glory of the sunset. Otherwise all hope and strife toward such an end would be futile.

But the vast Pecos range must ever be lonely, gray, brooding, hot as a furnace in the summers, cold in winters, when the bitter northers blew, a barren land of scaly ridges for leagues and leagues, a grazing wilderness for numberless cattle, from which the coyote and the buzzard would never disappear. It was what this country was that chained Pecos to it. But for men like Watson and women like Terrill, whose destinies had set them there, Pecos could have foregone the dream of the pioneer to write a bloodier name across that frontier. Better men than he had done no less. Texas had been a battleground, and was blood-soaked from river to river. No Texans but had been born to fight—no Texans ever survived who did not fight! But the best of manhood survived in the longing for homes. This era of guns and nooses, of the burned brand and the hard-eyed outlaw, would pass some day.

In that moment of exultation Pecos divined he had always been on the right trail. If he had lost the letter of it at times and had veered from it in spirit, yet he had always come back to plant his feet right. His past tracks had had to be bitterly reckoned with; there might be more and worse before the years covered them with dust, but he would never again make a false step.

A voice called him to supper and it was that same changed voice. As he turned to go back to the cabin he espied a gleam of white moving away from the door. Terrill had been watching him.

Pecos went in resolved to be natural. If he had been wise and great enough to forestall events, there would never have been any reason to blot out this tragic day.

Sambo had put mesquite knots on the fire, as the bright ruddy light and sweet fragrance testified. Terrill sat at the other end of the table, as she had always done. But nothing else could ever have been so different.

Her hair was parted in the middle. It rippled and shone like the ripples of the river when the sunset fell upon them. Her face was as white as if it had never worn any golden tan. Her eyes were large, dark, luminous, windows of myriads of emotions. And under them shadows as deep and mysterious enhanced their havoc. But her features alone could not have accounted for the disturbing transformation from boy to girl. That white waist! It was old-fashioned—as compared with those Mary Heald had worn—and it fitted Terrill poorly. It had been a girl's waist and now it graced a budding woman. It was open a little at the top, no doubt because Terrill could not close it, and slightly exposed the graceful swell of her neck. For the rest there was the contour of breast that thrilled Pecos while it stabbed him with the memory of his unintentional sacrilege.

His prolonged stare, or something in his look, brought the vivid blood to Terrill's face. She appeared nervous, timid, shy, yet her eyes hung upon him hauntingly. What had she to fear in him? He knew now, and she must never know that he had long been aware of her secret. Then he remembered what Sawtell had said, and there came a break in his feeling.

"I can't eat," she said, after she had tried. "I—I can't be natural, either. . . . Pecos, are you shocked —angry?"

"Don't think aboot things," he answered, rather gruffly. He was thinking about things himself. What could he do if she looked at him like that, with such strangely hungry eyes?

"But, Pecos—if I—if we don't talk—it'll be harder," she rejoined, with singular pathos.

Sambo, who sat before the fire, came to their rescue. "Boss, I'se powerful curious 'boot whar yo got dat bump on yo' haid."

"Wal, I'll tell yu," replied Pecos, never before so willing to talk.

"Please, Pecos, tell us," added Terrill, eagerly.

"Wait till I drink this coffee," he replied, and presently got up to light a Mexican cigarette, one of the few he had smoked since the trip to Camp Lancaster. "I got down to the Y Canyon aboot sunrise. An' I found thet outfit camped where Watson said they was. Wal, my idee was to scare them out, if I couldn't do more. An' I figgered the way to work it. If you remember it's a queer-shaped canyon. I shot seven times into thet bunch havin' breakfast. Long range, but I hit one greaser, anyhow. He squealed like a jack rabbit. Yu should have seen them pilin' over one another. Then I run back, hopped my hoss, an' rode like hell as far as I could along the rim. Thet was when I got snagged. Wal, I jumped off with the other rifle an' made for the rim. Heah, if anythin', I was even closer than where I first seen them. An' I began to shoot again, as fast as I could load the old rifle. My idee shore worked. Thet outfit reckoned they'd been set on by men surroundin' the canyon.

Their hosses were ready for the day, an' they mounted an' made off through the thicket for the river. An' they kept shootin' steady. It was when I was climbin' along the rim thet one of them hit me. Wal, they shore rustled down the river, an' I reckon they won't come back very soon."

"Sambo, is yo' appetite done gone whar Rill's an' Pecos' is?" asked Mauree. " 'Cause if it is dis supper am wasted."

"Doan trubble, woman, doan trubble," replied Sambo. "Dar won't be no grub left. I'se so happy I could eat a hoss."

A fugitive happiness seemed to hover over Terrill. One moment she radiated eager young life, and the next she grew blank, as if suspended between hope and fear. Pecos became guiltily aware of her unconscious appeal to him. While he told his story she sat wide-eyed and open-lipped, absorbing every word, betraying her fears and her thrills.

Presently Pecos, driven by wonder and cruel longing, went out on the porch to sit in the dusk. How serene the canyon! The river moaned low out of the shadow. A coyote wailed from the heights. If avarice and lust and death had stalked there this day, there were no ghosts of them abroad now. He wondered if Terrill would follow him out. What did her actions, her brave and wistful glances, betray? She realized she had failed in faith. Her conscience tortured her. Or was it something else? He might make a pretense of hardening his heart, of holding aloof, but it was sham. How many interminable hours since morning!

His head throbbed from the bullet wound. At intervals a slight sigh, almost a gasp, escaped his lips, involuntary regurgitation of that hideous inward clamp on his vitals. Could he listen to the solitude, could he think of the tranquil dusk settling down, could he dwell upon this beautiful girl delivered into his keeping when he had ridden red death that very day? But that was hours, endless hours, past. Life seemed surging on, piling up, swelling to engulf him.

A light footfall creaked on the porch board. Terrill came out and sat beside him, close to where Sawtell had fallen that day.

"Pecos." She spoke low.

"Yeah."

"I—I'm nervous—that old fear of the dark. . . . Let me sit by you?"

"Yeah." He drawled it, but that was a lie, too. She sat down close beside him and gazed out into the gathering dusk. If she had any terrors of the place, of what she had escaped, these were not manifest. Her profile against the black cliff appeared chiseled out of marble, cold, pure, singularly noble, and as sad as her life had been. Pecos could not convince himself of the facts. His wandering rides, his ruthless hand, his unfailing service to the weak and unfortunate—these had landed him there in that lonely canyon, at the side of a girl as lovely as an angel—and as good.

"Terrill, go to bed," he broke out, abruptly.

He startled her. "Must I?" she asked, and the willfulness of the boy Terrill seemed gone forever. There was a suggestion of his word as law, never to be disobeyed.

"Suit yourself. But yu look so white—so spent. If yu'd sleep ——"

"Pecos, I cain't sleep this night unless you—unless I'm near you."

He could not reply. It was as hard for him to think clearly as to speak clearly. His nerves were on edge. His heart seemed thawing to an immense pity, and that meant a liberation of his love—which, surrendered to, while she sat so close, so tense and alive, meant only chaos.

"May I stay?" she asked.

"Yeah."

A bright line tipped the opposite canyon rim. The moon was rising behind them. Terrill edged a little closer to him. Once a timid hand slipped under his arm, to be quickly withdrawn. He caught her glancing up at his face, which he kept rigidly to the fore.

"Pecos, I'm all tight inside—on fire. . . . But feel my hands."

She put them in his and they were like ice. One lingered in his, and as no nerve or muscle of his responded, it slowly fell.

"Fever, I reckon," he said. "Terrill, it's been a tough day for a—a g— youngster."

"Horrible! . . . And just to think! If I'd had one more shell in my gun I'd have killed him! . . . I wish to God I had."

"Wal, Terrill, thet's queer. Why do you?"

"Then he couldn't have told."

"Ahuh." Pecos believed she meant that Sawtell could not have betrayed her sex. That seemed natural. Terrill over-exaggerated some kind of shame in this dual character she had lived.

She sat silent awhile and the warmth of her contact with him seemed strange in view of her ice-cold hands.

Across the canyon the moonlit line had grown to a broad white band creeping down, imperceptibly diminishing the darkness below. An owl hooted in the gloom and the insects kept up their low mournful hum. Sambo and Mauree came out, evidently having finished their work. Mauree bade Terrill good-night while Sambo tarried a moment.

"Folks, I sho gotta tell yo," he rolled out. "Yo know mah wife has second sight. An' she say good is comin' out of dis turrible day."

"Bless her, Sambo," cried Terrill.

"Shore there is, Sambo," drawled Pecos. " 'Cause there was a lot of bad went under the ground."

"Dey sho did, Pecos. Dey sho did. . . . An' now good-night Mars Pecos. . . . An' Gawd bless an' keep yo, Missy Rill."

Sambo moved away toward his cabin and the moonlight tipped his black head.

"Oh . . . he has not called me Missy Rill since I was a child," murmured Terrill, in mingled joy and pain. Perhaps that chord of the past vibrated in her frozen and inhibited emotions, for suddenly she clutched his arm, she slipped to her knees and crept close and lifted her face. Pecos' heart leaped up in his breast.

"Pecos, my only friend—you are angry—cold—you freeze me when I want—I need so much to ——"

"Yeah, I reckon," blurted out Pecos. How long could he resist snatching her to him? What would she do? Was he only blind, mad, a blundering vaquero who had never learned to know women?

"But I can't endure that," she wailed, and clung to him. "Is it be-because that beast tore my clothes off —saw that I wasn't a—a boy?"

"Yeah," replied Pecos, dully, as if by rote.

"But I couldn't help that, Pecos, any more than I can help being a girl. I was fighting for you—to save your money. I got it, too, and ran. But he caught me by my coat and shirt—and they tore off."

"You mebbe wasn't to blame. But why yu was there an' he seen yu half-naked. A girl! . . . Yu cain't deny he meant to make a hussy of yu then," declared Pecos, knowing full well how wild and unreasonable his statements were.

"No, dear Pecos," she replied, gravely. "I saw too late it would have been far better to let him take the money. But I didn't. . . . And you came in time to —to save me."

In all Pecos' life there had never been anything a millionth part so sweet as this moment. What was she pleading for? It must come out. Could he deny her whatever she seemed entreating for, so as to prolong this growing suspicion of her love? Prolong it only to keep back the inevitable truth of her affection

for a brother, a protector? After the whirling heights
of his hopes, could he bear that? But he must goad
her on.

"What if I hadn't come in time?"

"Then, when you did come you would have found
me—daid."

"Wal, we're wastin' breath on thet. I did come an'
yu ain't daid. . . . But I'd rather have seen yu daid
than to live to believe me a low-down rustler."

"*Oh, Pecos!*" She wailed.

That was the mark. He had struck home. The thing
which flayed him likewise flayed her. Almost rudely
he shoved her back. Yet that was of no avail. She
swayed again to catch at his hands.

"Terrill Lambeth, you believed me a thief?" he
queried, sternly, and he laid rude hold of her.

"Yes—yes. I cain't lie aboot anything so terrible.
I *did*. . . . But he was so shore. He seemed to know
all. He recognized that money—the very bills you
had. . . . He'd paid you, he swore. And God forgive
me! I thought it the truth."

"Aw!" breathed Pecos, huskily.

"There! It's out. It was killing me. . . . But, Pecos
—Pecos, dear Pecos, don't look so black and fearful.
Listen. The minute I saw you again—the very instant
—I knew Sawtell was the criminal and not you. I felt
it. I saw it in your eyes. . . . Let that plead for me."

"But you believed!" he flashed, harshly.

"I did, but I don't. Cain't you be human?"

"I'm human enough to be powerful hurt."

"But what is a hurt?"

"You went back on me."

"Pecos!"

"You betrayed yore pard."

"Not truly."

"You double-crosser."

"No—no. I deny that. If—if it *had* been true, I would still have stuck to you."

Pecos gazed at her spellbound. The moon had long since topped the rim and had just then come out from behind the corner of the cabin, to shine in its silver radiance upon her face. Something sustained her in spite of the monstrous barrier Pecos had cruelly raised. There was no bottom to the tragic abyss of her eyes, as there was no limit to her loyalty. She belonged to him. She was a leaf in the storm. But her strength consisted in the bough from which she would not be separated. She clung.

"Yu failed me, Terrill Lambeth," he went on, hoarsely, and his true pain was easing out forever in these accusations. "In my hour of need yu failed me."

"In faith, but never in heart."

"I'm a Texan. An' I hate a cow thief as bad as a hoss thief. I've helped to hang both. An' yu believed I was one."

"But I confessed it to you. I could have lied," she cried, driven desperate.

"Yu never cared."

"O God—hear him! . . . Pecos Smith, I've loved you from the moment I laid eyes on you."

"As a big brother, mebbe."

"As a girl hungry for she knew not what. As a girl

who must hide her longing and her sex. As a girl driven into womanhood. Oh, I could never have learned to love you so well but for my secret."

"Terrill, yu've been a bogus boy. Yu've lived so long untrue thet you cain't be true."

"Pecos, I love—you—now," she cried, brokenly, her spirit following her spent strength.

"Yu beautiful fraud!"

She made one last effort to clasp him in failing arms. "If you—do not—love me—there's nothing left—but the river."

"Liar!"

"Pecos, this flint man cain't be you. My Pecos ——"

"Yu double-crossed me."

"No—no!"

"Yu failed me."

"Have mercy, then!"

"Yu believed me a thief."

"Forgive me. My heart—is breaking. I have only you—in all this world."

Pecos could hold out no longer. He drew her to his breast and lifted her lax arms round his neck.

"Wal, I reckon thet'll be aboot all," he said, in a voice so vastly changed that it seemed a stranger had spoken. She lay still in his arms, but he knew she had not fainted. He could see those great dark eyes. He felt the slow-stealing warmth of her breast on his, and the quickening pound of her heart.

"Pecos," she whispered.

"Yeah."

"You forgive?"

"I reckon I was only punishin' yu for lack of faith. You poor kid."

"Oh, wait! Pecos. This *will* kill me. Don't tell me too quickly—you didn't mean all—those—horrible names."

"Wal, I meant them for the moment. I shore was mad. But I saved another for the last."

"Oh, Pecos—what?" she implored.

"Terrill darlin'."

"Then—you—love—me?"

He spent his answer on her cool sweet lips. It was then that his reward came unasked, unexpected as had been the treasure of her love. For all that had been innate in Terrill Lambeth, the femininity that had been suppressed, the emotion that had been denied so long, and the fostering of the lonely years of that wild country, where she had been kept as secluded as a cloistered nun, and the hunger which such a life must only magnify, now burst all bounds in an abandonment as pure as her thoughts had ever been, and which blindly sought his lips in kisses and his arms in embraces that broke off only to be renewed.

At last her lovely face fell back in the hollow of his arm and it was no longer white or tragically convulsed.

"Pecos, how can you love me so—so much as that, if only these few hours you've known me to be a girl?"

"Wal, it shore seems a whole lot of love on such short notice," he drawled. "But the fact is, honey, thet I've loved you more an' more all the time ever since I—I found you out."

Startled, she leaped up in his arms.

"Pecos Smith! . . . You deceitful wretch! . . . O Heaven—since when?"

"Darlin' Rill—since the day you nearly drowned."

"That day—that day!" She hid her hot face on his breast and hugged him tight. "But since you love me ——"

Chapter XV

AS FAR as Pecos was concerned Rockport or any
town would have been good for a visit, but the
Gulf cattle town in its heyday was no place for Terrill.

Pecos had not seen its like. It appeared to be surrounded on three sides by bawling cattle and on the
other by the noisy Gulf. There was a main street upon
which to ride or drive or walk at any hour of the day
and far into the night, but to do so was a most strenuous and uncomfortable undertaking.

The Gulf Hotel, where Pecos engaged rooms at an
exorbitant figure hummed like a beehive. Its patrons
appeared to be the same as the surging crowds in the
street—settlers, cattlemen, cowhands, buffalo-hunters,
soldiers, nondescript travelers, desperadoes, and the
motley horde of parasites who lived off them. It was
hot and dusty on this December day. What would it
have been in mid-August?

The spirit of the throng, the movement and meaning of it, permeated Pecos' blood. He had been only
a riding vaquero, a gun-throwing adventurer. He had
now become a part of this very thing. There were settlers' wives and daughters in that crowd, all of whom
had embarked upon the great adventure Terrill was
already living.

"Dog-gone it, Terrill," he drawled to her, "this heah is grand. Turrible for us to watch 'cause we shore know what those young men an' women are goin' up against. But we feel somethin' big an' wonderful with them. They'll *do* it, Terrill. Yu cain't fool me when I can see people's eyes. Thet's why I'm alive, 'cause I can see what men think."

"Pecos, it makes my heart come up in my throat. I'd like to go with them. Oh, I hope these young men can fight."

"I shore see a lot of Texans among them."

"But who are the white-faced men in black, an' the ghastly women all decked in flowery dresses?"

"Dog-gone if I know them, honey," replied Pecos, evasively. "But I reckon they ain't so good. Now, Terrill, don't yu leave me for a single minute. An' if I have to leave yu it'll be heah where yu can lock yoreself in yore room."

"Pecos Smith, you won't leave me even there for a single minute," she retorted. "Do you imagine I'd let a dashing, handsome vaquero, loaded down with money, go out in that crowd alone? Not much!"

"Say, thet ain't so turrible flatterin'," replied Pecos, dubiously. "You look like a kid, but yu got the mind of a woman."

"Pecos, I'm dependent upon you," she said, sweetly. "And aren't you dependent upon me?"

"My Gawd, yes! If I didn't have yu I'd be drinkin', gamblin', mebbe shootin', an' I don't reckon what else. But all thet's past an' I'm so happy I'm loco."

"I'm so happy I'm frightened."

"I shore wish thet Judge Roy Bean had been home. Then *I* wouldn't be so frightened, myself. Haw! Haw!"

"What do you mean, Pecos?" she asked, blushing scarlet. "We came here to buy cattle."

"Aw, I didn't mean nothin'. . . . Wal, come on. There are stores heah an' mebbe we can find some of those women's clothes you're cravin'."

But a breathless scramble through the crowd from one store to another failed to reveal any ready-made female attire that Terrill wanted. There was an abundance of material, some of it good, but it had to be made into dresses. So they had to resort to boys' apparel. After a mirthful foray they returned to the hotel with new fancy-topped Mexican boots, silver spurs, a buff sombrero in which Terrill looked so fetching that Pecos whooped, corduroys, shirts of various hues, a jacket, and other articles. While Terrill raved over these purchases like a boy, Pecos told her to change while he went downstairs to the office.

Pecos was perturbed because he had discovered that he was being followed by two men. This was no unusual thing in any crowded frontier post. But these men looked like Texas rangers to Pecos. And he could not take any chances with such men. Why were they following him? Pecos decided his right move was to find out.

Wherefor he approached the hotel desk and asked if there were any Texas Rangers in town.

"Captain McKinney is here with some of his Rangers," replied the clerk. "They're working on that Big Brewster cattle-steal."

"Where can I find him?"

"He's stopping here. Saw him here a moment ago."

The lobby was crowded with men. Presently Captain McKinney was pointed out to Pecos. He appeared to be about medium height, of the usual Texan complexion, had a fine stern face and piercing eyes. Pecos approached and stood respectfully waiting a break in the Captain's conversation with two men, evidently ranchers.

"Well, sir?" queried McKinney.

"Are you Captain McKinney?" replied Pecos.

It was characteristic of Texas and particularly of the Rangers that such a query invited a guarded reply.

Finally Captain McKinney replied.

"Yes."

"Wal, Captain, I reckon a couple of yore Rangers have been trailin' me all aboot town."

"Who are you?"

"Pecos Smith."

Well Pecos knew then that he had been wise to approach this Ranger Captain. Also he had further appreciation of the significance of his name.

"Come to my room," said McKinney, abruptly.

Pecos had the keenest of susceptibilities in his meetings with men. No matter what the issue, this meeting had been favorable, or most certainly a Captain of the Texas Rangers would not walk down a corridor in front of a suspected man.

Pecos was ushered into a well-lighted corner room.

"I'm glad you looked me up," said McKinney, inviting Pecos to a chair.

"What's the idee, Captain—Rangers trailin' me?" drawled Pecos, sitting back.

Then the two Texans locked glances. Pecos liked this man, saw in him the clean-fighting Ranger. He saw, too, that he was the object of such scrutiny as seldom fell upon him.

"Mind letting me see your gun?"

"Captain, thet's somethin' I don't do. But in yore case ———"

Pecos handed the gun over, butt foremost. McKinney received it with the thoughtful air of a man who knew what guns meant to Texans. He examined the butt.

"Seven notches—all old," he observed.

"Wal, Captain, reckon I could have added three more lately, but I had reason to quit."

The Ranger Captain returned the gun, also butt foremost.

"Smith, I've heard good and bad aboot you."

"I reckon. I've lived sort of a reckless vaquero life."

"Smith, could you by any chance be related to Bradington Smith? He was on the Ranger force before the war."

"Yes. Brad was my uncle."

"You don't say. That's interesting. You come of an old Texas family. . . . Smith, I have a letter here somewhere aboot you," said McKinney, searching among a pile of papers. "Here it is. From a cattleman

who ranges over the New Mexico line. Sawtell—
Breen Sawtell. Do you know him?"

"Wal, I reckon I *did*," replied Pecos, coolly. In
spite of his earnestness and his unforgettable relation
and duty to Terrill, he reacted subtly and coldly to
this approach.

"Like to read the letter?"

"No. I can tell yu just what's in it, Captain."

"Well, do so. Give me your angle. I don't mind
telling you that it's through this letter you were
shadowed by my men."

"I reckoned thet. How'd they know me?"

"Slinger knows you. Jeff Slinger. I'm glad to add
that he swears he doesn't believe one word of this
letter."

"Jeff Slinger!—Is he a Ranger?"

"He certainly is. Ten years' service."

"Wal, I'll be dog-goned. He never said so. I helped
him in a scrape with some greaser hoss thieves some
years ago. Just happened to run into him. We camped
some days on the Rio Grande."

"It may stand you in good stead. What's your angle
on this Sawtell letter?"

"He was tryin' to hide his tracks, Captain," replied Pecos, and briefly related Sawtell's relations to
Williams and Adams, and how he operated.

"That fits in perfectly with some information I got
not long ago from a trail driver. We'd better look
this Sawtell up."

"Wal, Captain, if yu do yu'll have to *dig* him up,"
replied Pecos, with a grim laugh.

"How so?" queried the Ranger, though he understood perfectly well.

"Sawtell's daid."

"You shot him!"

"Captain, I'd like to deny the doubtful honor, but I cain't."

"Perhaps you better tell me aboot that—if you will."

Pecos necessarily had to make this a longer narrative and he slighted nothing, though he did not go into detail about the Lambeth Ranch nor did he care to give any impression of a large amount of money.

"There were witnesses to this visit of Sawtell's?"

"Yes. Before I arrived an' after."

"The negroes and this young Lambeth?"

"Yes, sir."

"That is well for you, in case there ever is a come-back. But that does not seem likely to happen. . . . Smith, is the boy my Rangers saw with you this young Lambeth?"

"It's young Lambeth, all right. I'd shore like to fetch him in, Captain."

"Do so, by all means."

In his relief and exuberance Pecos ran up to Terrill's room to bang upon the door.

"Who's there?"

"Pecos. Rustle."

Evidently Terrill had been sitting on the floor. She opened the door with a boot in one hand. All the rest of the new things she had on. And if she did not look

bewitching, Pecos knew he had some magnifying ail-
ment of his eyes.

"How do I look?" she beamed, eagerly.

"Wal, girl, I'd hate to say," he replied. " 'Cause it
might go to yore haid. . . . Heah, let me pull on
thet boot."

"It's new—and a little tight. . . . Ouch! . . .
Pecos, are you shore I'm ——"

"Heah. Don't climb all over me. You'll muss yoreself. Leave the jacket off. . . . There. Now you're
a girl in spite of them pants. . . . Come to look at
them, though, any man with eyes could see ——"

"I won't wear them," flashed Terrill.

"Honey, yu got to, or we cain't go on."

"Then don't hint and don't look," she pouted.
"Here—where are you taking me?"

"Terrill, I've had some more good luck. There's
a Ranger Captain heah. I went in to see him. Reckoned
it a good idee to tell aboot Sawtell. Wal, he was fine.
An' he asked to see young Lambeth."

"Young Lambeth!"

"Some of his Rangers saw you with me. Took you
for a boy. An' I didn't give it away. Oh, this will be
fun. Now, Terrill, you be just as sweet an' nice as you
know how. Put on a lot of—of swank. Savvy? It
won't do me no harm."

Terrill seemed quick to divine that there had been
something amiss and her spirit rose to meet it.

At Pecos' knock he was bidden to come in. The
Ranger sat at his table.

"Captain McKinney, heah's my pard, young Lambeth," announced Pecos, and he certainly reveled in McKinney's stare.

"How do you do, Captain McKinney?" said Terrill, with just the right tone of deference.

Hastily the Ranger stood up, as if his eyes were poor while sitting. He certainly used them. "Young Lambeth!—Ah! . . . Er. How do you do? . . . Say Smith, this is no boy!"

"Captain, I didn't say young Lambeth was a boy," drawled Pecos. "She's a girl, all right. Terrill Lambeth."

"Oh!—My mistake. Well, I—I am delighted to make your acquaintance, Miss Lambeth," he replied, making Terrill a gallant bow. His eyes shone with pleasure succeeding amaze. "Do you ride rodeo today?"

"I'm pleased to meet you, Captain McKinney," replied Terrill, shyly. "You see, I've been a boy for a long time, and we couldn't find any women's clothes to fit, so I kept right on."

McKinney was plainly mystified as well as captivated.

"Terrill Lambeth? . . . Well, I remember that name Lambeth. Are you any kin to Colonel Templeton Lambeth?"

"His daughter," replied Terrill.

"Well, of all things!" exclaimed the Captain, profoundly stirred. "His daughter! . . . Templeton Lambeth and I were friends. We went through the war together. I never heard of him afterward. Where is he?"

"He is daid, Captain," returned Terrill, gazing away through the window. "He was murdered. . . . After the war, my mother being daid, and Dad ruined, we drove to West Texas, and settled on the Pecos River below Horsehead Crossing. I was nearly fifteen then. . . . It was a lonely place, our ranch. But wonderful for cattle-raising, until the rustlers came. . . . Nearly two years ago they murdered Dad. Made it look like the work of Comanches. Of course I have no proof, but I believe Breen Sawtell and his partner, Don Felipe, were behind it. They tried to steal *me*, as they did my cattle, and they would have done so but for Pecos here."

"I am shocked, saddened," declared McKinney. "Yet so glad to get news of Temple. . . . What a story! Oh, that is Texas of these hard years. . . . And you lived on alone there in that wild Pecos country? It's almost incredible for a girl of your class."

"Alone except for my negroes, Sambo and Mauree, until Pecos came last spring. And you must remember, no one knew I was a girl."

Pecos drawlingly interposed: "Captain, young Lambeth is goin' to be Mrs. James Pecos Smith."

"I wondered. I had a hunch. . . . Of all the romances! . . . Terrill, I congratulate you. I wish you happiness. But—but is this Pecos fellow ——"

The Captain halted in grave embarrassment.

"Captain McKinney, if he had not been Pecos Smith he never could have saved me," replied Terrill, lifting her head with pride. Love and faith did not need to be spoken.

"Terrill, I am glad he *is* Pecos Smith," returned McKinney, with strong feeling. "I believe my old friend would be glad, too."

Then he turned to Pecos to extend a hand.

"You will marry the best blood of Texas. . . . You will get one of the most lovely girls I ever saw. . . . I swear she is as good and fine as she is beautiful. . . . Do you realize your wonderful fortune? . . . You gun-throwing vaquero—come of an old Texas family, too! . . . What luck! What duty! Pecos, I hope to God you rise to your opportunity."

"Captain, I'm shore prayin' for thet myself," responded Pecos, slowly and with emotion.

Later Pecos went out to purchase guns, rifles, shells, knives, all of the newest designs, and sadly needed wearing apparel for himself, two new saddles and various other articles.

And Pecos met settlers, trail drivers, cattlemen, ranchers from whom he learned many things. The settlers, perhaps, profited as much from the meeting as Pecos. He encountered Jeff Slinger again and they became friends. Captain McKinney devoted himself to their service, and was especially kind to Terrill. When he went away, having ended his duties there, he left Slinger and another Ranger, an experienced Indian-fighter named Johnson, to go back with Pecos on the long drive with the cattle.

Slinger knew of a cattleman named Hudson who ran stock out on the Frio River, and could be bought out. He was a bachelor, getting well along in years, and wanted a little peace and freedom from rustlers. Slinger had happened to encounter this cattleman in Rockport during Pecos' stay. The result was a meeting. Hudson appeared to be a hawk-eyed old plainsman from Brazos country and at once inspired confidence.

"Wal, I got aboot two thousand haid left—the finest breed of long-horns I ever had," Hudson said.

"Would yu sell?" asked Pecos.

"Reckon I would long ago if I'd known what to do with the boys. I've got two nephews who've been brought up on hosses, an' ridin' cattle is their especial dish."

"Ahuh. How many cowhands besides these boys?"

"Two. They ben with me long an' I shore hate to see them go up the trail with the drivers. Dodge an' Abilene are bad medicine."

"Would these four hands fit in with the kind of outfit I want?"

"An' what's thet?"

"A young, sober, hard-ridin,' straight-shootin' outfit to run cattle with me West of the Pecos."

"West of the Pecos! . . . Wal, Smith, I don't believe you could beat these four boys in all Texas."

"If I take them will yu sell?"

"Reckon I will. I can get ten dollars a haid at Dodge."

"Shore, but thet's there."

"Wal, to get down to bed-rock. . . . Eight dollars, Smith."

A deal was made. Slinger promised to find two more cowhands that he could absolutely guarantee. These were to go home with Hudson, and the herd was to be rounded up, and made ready for Pecos' arrival, when he would pay his debt and go on.

"Course thet means Horsehaid Crossin'," he pondered.

"Smith, it's your best bet. The west trail is not so good. Grazed off in places. Water little an' far between. My range is way at the haid of the Frio. You have a good road an' fine conditions this season all the way to the old Spanish trail thet takes off west for the Pecos. With eight good men beside yourself, all well armed, you needn't worry none aboot Indians. An' you won't lose a steer."

"Done. I'm much obliged, Hudson."

It took vastly more time to consider what else to buy and take back to Lambeth Ranch. Pecos wanted a home for Terrill and all the comforts possible to pack into the wilderness. For two days he had Terrill's pretty head buzzing. Yet in spite of her glee and enthusiasm, when it came down to selections she rendered a vast and sensible help.

Pecos bought three wagons, one new and the others second-hand, and twelve horses, all of which were acquired at a low figure. But when these three larger vehicles were loaded to the seats they represented several thousand dollars in value, not including Terrill's precious treasures. What with Pecos' armament, and food supplies for a year, furniture, tools, bedding, lumber, leather goods, boots, clothing, utensils, lamps, oil, and so many other needful articles that Pecos could not remember them all, the wagons were heavily laden.

"Gosh! My hair shore raises when I think of crossin' the river with these loads," ejaculated Pecos, in mingled concern and hope.

"Wal, yore hair might be raised afore we git thar," remarked Johnson, dryly.

At last they left Rockport early one morning with Slinger and Johnson each driving a wagon, and Pecos the third, with Cinco haltered behind. Terrill, back in her old blue jeans and jacket, and a battered old sombrero she had picked up somewhere, astride her buckskin mustang, rode beside Pecos for all the world, to his glad eyes, a boy again.

Chapter XVI

HUDSON's range took in the headwaters of the Rio Frio, and it was a rugged beautiful country that captivated Pecos' eye.

The very day Pecos arrived with his three wagons buffalo were sighted in the wonderful sheltered valley where Pecos' two thousand long-horns had been grazing. Buffalo seldom traveled west so far as the Rio Pecos, but according to Hudson isolated herds, probably separated by the hunters from the main body, often wandered up the Frio. Even before Pecos had arrived a buffalo hunt had been planned for him.

Hudson's ranch-house betrayed the bachelor and one who was used to the elemental life. It was located up in a pass, between two round-top hills, where the wind blew eternally. Terrill vowed it would have driven her crazy.

"Why wind!" ejaculated the old Texan, in surprise. "It wouldn't be home without wind."

"Lord! what'd a norther do heah?" replied Pecos. "Hudson, we live down in a canyon where it seldom blows. No dust. Never very cold, even when the northers blow."

"Wal, no one man can hope to know the whole of Texas," returned the rancher.

On first sight Pecos formed a most satisfying estimate of the outfit he had hired through Jeff Slinger and Hudson. The brothers, John and Abe Slaughter, were typical Texans, born on the range, stalwart six-footers, almost like twins. Texas Jack was a bullet-headed, jolly-featured, bow-legged cowhand who appeared to be one it might be well to have as a friend, and never as an enemy. Lovelace Hall was an extremely tall Texan, red-headed, and dark-eyed, an unusual type in Pecos' experience, and said to be "hell on hosses, cows an' other ornery things." These two had been trail drivers and had been secured by Slinger. Hudson's other two cowmen were strikingly different, as one was a Mexican vaquero and the other a negro. Lano, the former, was a slim lizard-like rider, darker than an Indian, stamped all over with incomparable horsemanship. The negro answered to the name Louisiana. In fact, Hudson had no other for him. He was medium-sized, but magnificently muscled, and had a pleasing, handsome face. These completed the sextette, and Pecos, seldom at a loss to gauge men, was greatly pleased.

"Fellers," he said, intimately, "before we come to terms I have this to say. Accordin' to Hudson, none of yu know Texas West of the Pecos. I wouldn't be square with yu if I didn't say it's a hell of a tough nut to crack. Hard all the time, harder in winter, an' turrible in summer. Lonesome as no other part of Texas. Even L'lano Estacado ain't so lonesome. Gray, rocky, scaly ridges runnin' forever down to the Pecos an' away on the other side. A buzzard now an' then, or a coyote, an' rarer a deer. Wild hosses on the lower reaches, but few along the fifty miles of my ranges. Comanches always, Kiowas an' Apaches occasionally. Soldiers few and far between. Rustlers bad an' comin' thicker. We'll have to fight. No law except an old geezer named Judge Bean at Eagle's Nest, an' he's a highway robber."

Pecos rested a moment to catch his breath and to let all that sink in.

"But West of the Pecos it's the grandest cow-country on the face of the earth. I am aimin' big. I know the game. I have the grass, the water, the start in cattle. What I need is a fightin', hell-rattlin', hard-shelled outfit. I'd be grateful alone for yu drivin' this new herd out there for me. But I want yu all to *stick*. There is a future out there for the right kind of men. If I make out big—as I shore could do with yu fellers all keen an' hot on the prod—I will give yu an interest, or help you to make a start yoreselves. An' for the present I'll pay yu more than yu're earnin' heah. Thet's all. Think it over while we're gettin' acquainted."

Later Hudson told Pecos that he had overheard Lovelace Hall say to his comrades: "Fellers, we've nothin' to lose an' everythin' to gain. Thet talk of Pecos Smith's was as straight as Slinger says he can shoot."

Next day they hunted buffalo as shy as wild mules, which were the wildest animals Pecos had ever hunted. Six bulls were killed, two by the Ranger Johnson, who knew the game. The cowhands accounted for three, and the other fell to Pecos and Terrill.

Pecos disclaimed the credit and Terrill did likewise.

"Wal, if I didn't see Terrill stagger thet bull my eyes are pore," remarked Hudson, with a twinkle in those members. "An' it shore fell before it got near enough to Smith for a last shot."

"Terrill, yu get that robe," drawled Pecos.

"What aboot all the robes an' the meat? I cain't use any more. Besides, I'm leavin' for Santone."

"Dog-gone! I never thought of packin' hides an' meat," declared Pecos. "We just haven't got the room. Hudson, will yu sell me a wagon an' team?"

"No. But I'll throw them in the bargain."

Half of the next day was taken up in skinning and cutting up the buffalo. And on the following day, at sunrise, Pecos' caravan of wagons, riders, and cattle set out on the long slow drive.

It was a leisurely procedure for the wagons, at least. Pecos drove one of the teams and Terrill sat on the wagon with him. They talked and planned, and made love, and dreamed of the future, and marveled at the long string of cattle grazing ahead, not so wild a bunch as was usual with that breed. The slow pace made Terrill drowsy, and finally, when Pecos rested the horses at the foot of a hill, she went to sleep. When she awoke the first thing she did was to make sure that her precious trunk was still on the wagon, carefully hidden and protected.

"Pecos Smith, if we run into Comanches and they get my trunk—you lose me," she averred.

"If they go thet far you bet yore sweet life we'll all be daid."

"We're going to be raided. I feel it in my bones."

"Terrill darlin', Comanches ride usually in bunches of thirty or forty. What chance would such a bunch have with this outfit, heeled like we are?"

Long before sunset the day's drive ended. The camp site was ideal; Pecos could look afar to the west and see the dim ghosts of the mountains, somewhere beyond the lower brakes of the river. The cowhands, eating supper in relays of three, were happy, which augured well for the state of the herd. With this the case, with grass and water abundant, and wood for fire and Terrill singing, Pecos gazed at the evening star and thought it was rising for him.

The next day, as far as action and result were concerned, seemed like the first. And so, one after another the slow days accumulated with only minor mishaps that occasioned no delay. The weather stayed fine, cold at night, stinging at dawn, warm at midday.

"Pecos, do you ever stop to think how—how strange and natural a long drive gets to be?" queried Terrill, dreamily.

"Don't I? Ha! It's life, Terrill, an' with yu it's heaven."

"Pecos Smith, I don't believe I could bake biscuits without you getting sentimental," she retorted.

"Wal, yu'll have to show me aboot the biscuits."

But he understood her. There grew to be something beautiful in such a long ride into wild country. The anticipation and labor of preparation, the endless gossip of accident, weather, scant grass and water, savages, the worries about what might happen and never did happen, the gradual fading away of the influence of towns and people—these things ceased magically to loom and were eventually forgotten. Storms and floods, stampedes and Indians, certainly could and did disrupt the peaceful tenor of such days as these. Terrill ceased to mention them; she even forgot her trunkful of delights that revived the memories of her old home. And Pecos dreamed while he watched the horizon.

He would have preferred to dream in his saddle, because the wagon seat was hard and uncomfortable and he was a poor teamster. Nevertheless, no journeying of his down into the wilderness had ever been comparable to this. The sun rose red, shone pale at noon, gold at eventide, and that was another day. That longhorn herd might have been especially trained for him. What little trouble they gave! How few had strayed! He had to award all praise to his riders.

Day by day the landscape imperceptibly changed. A mile was an atom on that vast western upheaval of Texas, yet to keen eyes each mile told of the approach toward the more barren regions that sheered north to the Staked Plains, and west to the brakes of the Pecos. Yet still there was good water to be had, and fair grazing. Pecos' herd gained weight. Now and then a bleached skull of a steer, ghastly reminder of less fortunate drives, gleamed under the pale sun.

A day came, however, that stood out like a landmark. The caravan cut off from old Fort McKavett toward the military road that stretched west toward the Horsehead Crossing of the Pecos. This sheering off was, of itself, a stirring change. But when Terrill came radiant of eye to cry out: "Oh, Pecos, I know this road! I remember the hills. I came by here . . . . I will show you the old camps . . . . It seems so long ago . . . . Oh, Pecos!"

Downgrade all day they drove, with the cattle moving faster, owing to a thinning of the grass. And that night they made dry camp, the first of the long drive. Next day they crossed water, and on the third made Dove Creek. A thicketed bottomland, with a clear stream, held the stock.

Terrill showed Pecos where she had slept in the wagon. She remembered a tree where she had sat at twilight, melancholy and sad, longing for home yet never wanting to go back, pondering doubtfully over the future, fearful of the ever-growing wildness of this dark-gray stone ledged land.

"Oh, I cried so hard," said Terrill, her eyes picturing that past hour. "It was a day when all had gone wrong. Dear old Dad—so seldom discouraged! But this day he was down, and I went down too. I could not see any hope in the future—anything but dreadful pain and loneliness. . . . Oh, Pecos, how terribly wrong I was! What a child! . . . Oh, if I had ever dreamed then that I was to meet you, love you, be loved by you—I would not have cried myself sick that day."

"Terrill, what do yu suppose I would have done in the past, if I'd ever dreamed I was to meet yu, love

yu, be loved by yu?" returned Pecos, in a passion of
regret. "I never dreamed of a yu, darlin', yet somethin'
kept me from goin' plumb to hell."

Another day set Pecos' caravan on the old military
road.

The sun hazed over. There was a chill in the air
and a wind rustled the brush. No living creature of
the wild crossed Pecos' vision. The coyotes had ceased
following the herd. Something, perhaps an instinct,
encroached the leisurely travel. Pecos felt a slight restlessness. Despite the weeks and leagues behind, the
way still was long. The horses lagged less; the cattle
plodded on sometimes without looking for grazing.
That night at Kinway Creek, after the best and longest
day's journey of the trip, the cowmen did not sing on
guard or joke around the camp fire.

Johnson had picked up Indian mustang tracks not
many days old.

Pecos decided to put Louisiana on the wagon and
take to the saddle next day. He talked with Jeff and
Johnson.

"Wal, it ain't anythin' to see Indian signs," said
Slinger. "Not up heah, anyway. The land is shore
heavin' an' grayin' for the Staked Plains."

Johnson was not sanguine. He did not appear to be
a talkative man. Pecos decided the chances were ever
that they would have a brush with the Indians. The
Slaughter boys and Lovelace Hall were out on night
guard. Texas Jack lay asleep in his blanket, his head
on his saddle. Lano and Louisiana stood beside the
fire, toasting one side, then the other.

Pecos walked away from camp toward where the herd rested and slept. In the main the steers were quiet. Calves born on the way bawled drearily. Travel was hard on them. The guards sat their horses, or rode to and fro, to edge in a stray. All seemed well. It was only the silent night, the cold wind, the encroaching monotony, the long, long way.

Terrill was still awake. She called to Pecos as he was passing. The little tent was just barely large enough for her bed and duffle.

"Lady, one bad thing aboot you, anyhow, is yu cain't sleep with yore boots on," said Pecos, reflectively, as he sat on the bed. Terrill had felt for his hand and found it.

"Pecos, you are worried," she whispered.

"Not a tall, dear. But I'm just thoughtful."

"Well, the men are. I heard Johnson talking to Slinger. But how much easier we are than Dad's out-fit when it camped here years ago. Pecos, I think the country grows on you."

"Ahuh. Wish we could drill right on instead of waitin' for the cattle."

"But we cain't. All our hopes are in that herd. Pecos, I feel like Mauree when she has 'second sight,' as Sambo calls it. We are going to get across."

"Shore we are, honey. Dog-gone, but yore a game kid. I don't mind admittin' thet it's yu I buckle on. But for yu, this drive would be apple pie. Last day or so it's come home to me. Yu're the real stuff, Terrill. But yu're a *woman*, an' no man ought to risk yu on this cussed Hosshaid Trail."

"Dad risked me. All the settlers risk their wives and daughters. We can't be left behind. Besides, Pecos dear, don't you exaggerate this woman idea? I can ride and I can shoot. I'm not the least bit afraid. I will not be in the way. And I'll bet I can keep my haid under better than you."

Pecos rose with a fervent: "Thet's just it, Terrill. Yore nerve, yore spirit, yore faith. Yu beat me all hollow. 'Cause yu have other an' finer feelin's. More courage. Thet's what kills me. . . . I'm prayin' Gawd to see yu through safe. . . . Good-night!"

Dead Man's Water Hole was the next camp, reached late in the evening of a dark and dismal day. If a norther threatened, it did not materialize. That night Pecos stood hours on guard at camp, giving way to Slinger after midnight. Wolves mourned from the ridges above the restless herd. There were four cowhands on duty. Terrill was awake when Pecos noiselessly crept past the little tent. She called a good-night to him. Then he sought his own bed under a tree.

One more day to Wild China Water Holes, then a long drive to Horsehead Crossing. That second day would be the rub. Again the signs of Indian mustangs had perturbed Pecos. And in the morning Johnson informed him that a score or more of Kiowas or Comanches had camped right on that spot two, or at the most, three, days ago.

"Take charge, Johnson," replied Pecos, curtly.

Lano was fetching in the saddle horses; it was Texas Jack's day with the cooking chores; Slinger was greasing the wagon wheels; Johnson strode off to a high point with his field-glass; the cattle grazed down the road.

A wintry sun shone fitfully through the dreary clouds and lighted the winding road down toward the Pecos. Out of the gray blur showed dark-spotted hills and blank spaces and white streaks, all forbidding, all the menace of the Pecos.

At breakfast Johnson unfolded his first surprise. "Men, we'll stay heah today, rest an' graze the stock. Everybody sleep some. We'll make the long drive into Hosshaid tonight."

It was a wise move, no doubt, but it enhanced suspense and wore upon all. Pecos had to find what work offered to counteract his restlessness. He was no trail driver, and he marveled at those doughty Texans who had endured the waits, the stampedes, the toils and fights of the Chisholm Trail.

Terrill, however, slept at least half the day. When she was about camp she seemed quiet, a little strained, but always that ready, beautiful smile flashed for Pecos.

At sunset the caravan was on the move, with the cattle far in the lead. Terrill rode her mustang and kept close to Pecos. Lano returned on a scout far back along the road. The sun came out dully red before setting and the barren world grew ruddy. Then it faded under a steely twilight and black night.

No stars showed. The black hills stood up against a dark sky. The wagon wheels rolled downgrade and sometimes the brakes creaked startlingly. The herd walked and trotted three miles an hour, never being allowed to graze. The dumb brutes were silent, as if they knew of the stampedes and massacres that had occurred on this lonely road.

Terrill sat her mustang for ten dark hours, without complaint, and when the gray dawn began to lighten she had a reassuring smile for the anxious Pecos.

Word came back to halt the wagons.

"Hosshaid Crossin', Terrill," exclaimed Pecos, huskily. "Now, if we can only cross I'll ask no more."

It was almost daylight when Johnson rode back alone. Pecos needed only one glance at the Ranger, even in the gloom.

"We cain't hold the herd," he said. "They smell water. They'll go down an' drink, scatter shore, an' mebbe stampede."

"What's the deal?" asked Pecos.

"Drive the wagons off the road, down behind thet bank of brush. Take Terrill, Louisiana, Jack, an' Lovelace, an' climb thet bluff there. Take water, grub, plenty of shells. An' hide in the rocks till we come back."

A few minutes later when the gray gloom began to show objects dimly at a distance, Pecos had his several followers upon the low bluff to which he had been directed.

The flat summit with its rim of broken rock and fringe of brush was just about large enough to afford protection to a party of six. Pecos was swift to appreciate it as a natural defense. A few good shots with an abundance of ammunition could hold it against a considerable force without undue risk. It stood somewhat above the road and about two hundred yards or more distant. Behind was a deep ravine. To the west the land dropped off to the gray thicket-patched valley of the Pecos. On the left sheered down the brushy ravine in which the wagons had been fairly well concealed. At least they would have to be searched for, and considering that they were close under the bluff, it would go rather hard for the discoverers.

"Terrill, yu lay low behind this rock," ordered Pecos. "An' if yu get careless I'll bang yu on the haid."

"Don't worry, Pecos," she retorted.

"Wal, I'm worried already. Cain't yu see this means a scrap? . . . Jack, yu watch the river side."

"Si Señor," replied Texas Jack, crawling toward his stand.

"Lovelace, yu an' Louisiana face the road. An' now let's all get set for whatever Johnson has a hunch aboot."

Day had broken, meanwhile, a morning with good visibility, but no indication of sunshine. It was still too early for sunrise, though by this time there should have been a ruddy glow on the horizon. But the east was black.

Pecos felt a reluctance to look at the river. If he had ever felt love for this God-forsaken secret river that feeling was in abeyance now. Nevertheless, he raised himself to peep over the rock, quite aware of Terrill's tugging remonstrance. There! The well-remembered river-sweep in the shape of a horse's head. It gleamed dark in the cold morning light. It meandered out of gray obscurity into the wide open break of the valley and meandered on into the gray confines. That river had a treacherous soul. It seemed to know that this ford was the only sure one for hundreds of miles, that in itself and the few fountains it drained out of the stony earth, there hid the only allaying of thirst for beast and man in all that aloof and inscrutable country.

It was this soul, this sublime arrogance in its power, that lay like a mantle over the endless banks of sand, its gray ridges, its patches of green. For that dominated.

Up from the river thin pale lines, broken here and there, paralleled the road. Bleached bones. Skulls of cattle. For three hundred years, ever since the Spaniards had staked off the stark and deadly *L'lano Estacaco*, cattle had perished there. They had dropped within sight of the river they had killed themselves to reach. It was a place where death stalked. No Indian teepee, no herder's tent, no cowman's stone shack, no habitation had ever marked Horsehead Crossing. Men had to cross the Pecos there, but they shunned it as a pestilence. As it had been, so would it always be, used but hated, a dire necessity. On the sunniest of days this place could not but repel. And on this drear dawn the dominance of loneliness and solitude, with its attributes of ghastly gray, prevailed to weigh down the heart of man, to warn him that nature respected only survival; to appall his sight with desolation, to flaunt the invisible shadow of the Pecos over all.

"Look, boss," whispered Texas Jack.

There was that in the vaquero's voice which caused Pecos to start and duck down to roll over to the watcher's side, a matter of six feet.

"Kiowas," whispered Jack.

Through a crack in the rock they could see into a ravine that paralleled the road. It curved round the mound from behind and had a high fringe of brush on the left bank. In fact the narrow gully could not be seen from the road. Jack's finger indicated this place, which was no doubt one of the coverts the Indians used to ambush travelers.

"Bunch sneakin' up the gully," whispered Jack. "Leadin' their hosses. They're behind the brush now."

Pecos beckoned Lovelace and Louisiana to crawl over on this side of the narrow space. And he had to make a fierce gesture to keep Terrill from following suit.

"Where'nhell did Johnson an' his outfit go?" queried Pecos, impatiently.

"Boss, you can bet they're watchin' them Injuns," replied Texas Jack. "Johnson was a buffalo-hunter an' Injun-fighter before he became a Ranger. He's had fights with Comanches right heah, an' he's up to their tricks."

"Last night's drive put us right, boss," interposed Lovelace. "Shore as shootin' these redskins never expected us till tonight. An' they've just heerd an' seen our cattle. So they're sneakin' up to see what it's all aboot."

"Boss, I see color again," whispered Texas Jack, pointing. "Hey, keep your noodle low."

Pecos had been searching the lower end of the gully, which part was within rifle range of their position. But it was toward the farther end that Texas Jack pointed.

Suddenly Pecos' burning eyes caught a movement of something through the bushy bend of the gully.

"I see 'em, boss," whispered Lovelace, as cool as if he had just espied some deer they were hunting.

"How aboot you, Louisiana?"

"I'se sho waitin' fer orders, boss," replied the negro vaquero.

It increased Pecos' excitement and impatience to realize that all his men had gotten a line on these skulking savages before he had. Yet their positions behind the rocks were not markedly different. Pecos had kept his gaze glued to that brushy bend, behind which the movement and color had disappeared. Then so easily did a bunch of lean redskinned forms creep into view that Pecos had to stifle a yelp.

"Kiowas, all right," said Texas Jack, in a low voice. "Wasn't shore, but now I am. I know them birds. Suits me they ain't Comanches."

"Hold on, boys. Thet's a long shot for these rifles," warned Pecos. "We might spoil Johnson's idee, whatever thet is."

"There ain't so many in thet bunch," whispered Lovelace.

"Aboot a dozen, but shore there's more around thet bend," rejoined Jack. "Looks to me like it's taps fer these reddys."

"Taps. What's thet, Jack?" asked Pecos.

"Boss, I served three years in the army."

"Ahuh. An' thet's where yu had yore Injun-fightin'?"

"Most of it. But I rode with— Say, look, boss. *Look!*"

"Yes, I see. Somethin' scared 'em. They was leary enough before."

"More comin' along. Must be twenty. . . . Wal, if Johnson has draped his outfit where I reckon he has the boot will shore be on the other foot."

Pecos watched the dark line of Kiowas with mingled emotions.

"I see them, Pecos," whispered Terrill, tremulously.

"Be careful, yu little devil," ordered Pecos. He did not see how she could be any more careful, as she was lying flat and peeping low down between brush-screened rocks. She should have been thoroughly frightened, but she was not. She had her new rifle and did not look averse to breaking it in.

Then Pecos sheered his gaze back to the Kiowas. From some source they had become acquainted with imminent peril. Their first movements had indicated that they were bent on ambushing the drivers of the cattle herd now spilling over the banks of the river. But now there had come a great difference. First Pecos had noted the arrival of a lean tall Kiowa, evidently a leader, for as he glided round the bend the others wheeled to him. What violent, eloquent, significant gestures! They might have been surrounded, to judge from this chief's expressive arms and hand. From the ambushers they might have become ambushed. Still it was evident that they still believed that they were unseen. They were particularly apprehensive of the winding sweep of the ravine below. But to Pecos' position they paid scant attention. For one thing, it was too far distant to be a menace, and secondly it was from the river that they sensed danger.

"Funny deal, ain't it?" queried Texas Jack, amused. "The reds are goin' to get a dose of their own medicine, an' I'd say it was aboot time."

"If Johnson drives them down thet gully or up on the road this way it's ———"

"Boss," interrupted Louisiana, "I sho seen somethin' black bob up ober de bank. Sho's I libe it wuz one of dem Slaughter boys' noggins."

"Where?" queried Pecos. What was the matter with his eyes, anyway, that he could discover nothing? One distraction was caused by the slender Terrill lying prone behind him. His attention was divided.

"Way down de gully, boss," replied Louisiana.

"Look out yu don't take one of our outfit for a redskin," warned Pecos. "There! . . . My gosh! it's Abe Slaughter. He's wavin' his hat at us."

"So he is. Thet's to post us to his whereaboots. Wal, Abe, we're wise, but yu gotta guess it 'cause we cain't get up heah an' dance for yu."

"Two fellers thar, boss. Both the Slaughter boys," said Lovelace.

"Thet leaves Johnson, Slinger, an' Lano somewhere else," mused Pecos. Then he glanced back at Terrill. She gave him a bright look from her darkly purple eyes. "Terrill, somebody shore will open the ball soon, but we want to keep out of the dance at first."

"Thet's a good idee, boss," agreed Texas Jack. " 'Cause if them Kiowas come pilin' either down the gully or the road under us it'll be most damn bad for them."

"They won't go down the gully," averred Lovelace. "They'll be quick to get lines on where the shootin' is comin' from. An' they'll break away in the other direction."

"Darn if Johnson didn't figger this nice," ejaculated Pecos, gratefully.

"Boss, them Kiowas has given up ambushin' us," rejoined Jack, gleefully. "If it just ain't too slick for anythin'!"

Pecos entertained something of the same enthusiastic acclaim of Johnson's coup. It was easy to see through the situation now.

The Kiowas had gotten wind of Pecos' caravan or some other, and had proceeded on to Horsehead Crossing, where the facilities for ambush were particularly favorable. All day long they would have had lookouts on the watch for cattle in the distance. But Johnson's night drive had been an innovation. These savages had been in camp somewhere back from the river and had been surprised by a vanguard of cattle at daybreak. Whereupon they had made haste for their ambush, only to meet with uncertain and puzzling circumstances which now had augmented to either hearing or sight of white men who were hunting instead of hunted men.

Obviously the three avenues of escape were up and down the gully, both of which the Kiowas showed a decided reluctance to approach, and the high brushy bank to the road, which they likewise feared because it might bring them into sight of enemies located behind the high bare bank toward the river.

Pecos' sharp eyes caught stealthy movement of one Kiowa scout working under the lea of the bank down the gully. No doubt the same reconnoitering was being done in the other direction.

"Ah—h!" came from Texas Jack.

Pecos saw a puff of bluish-white smoke spout from behind the bank at the head of the gully. Next instant, crack! went a rifle.

"She's opened, boys," said Pecos, grimly.

"Pick your partner," added Lovelace.

"No. Hold your fire. *Wow!* Listen to thet!"

Five or six heavy rifle-shots spread along the bank, and instantly pandemonium broke loose down in the gully. The horrid screams and snorts of wounded and frightened mustangs, the threshing, hideous war-cries and gunshots. Pecos saw Indians stagger and fall into the brush before a dust cloud obscured that bend of the gully behind which the Kiowas had concentrated.

"They'll break an' run, fellers," said Texas Jack, disgustedly. "an' we won't git a chance."

"Sho will. They're gonna come by heah," replied Louisiana.

"Let's pile down an' bust 'em comin' up," suggested Lovelace.

"Say, yu roosters, listen to the boss," declared Pecos.

Indian-fighting had been out of his line. What a fire-eating outfit he had collected! It added mightily to the thrill of the moment.

"Pecos, come here," piped up Terrill, just as coolly as either of the three who had spoken. "I see horses breaking the brush down there."

He lost no time crawling to Terrill's side. After that first heavy volley the shooting from the gully had become desultory. Smoke and dust hid the bend. Johnson's men were pouring as rapid fire as possible into that cloud.

"Look out, Abe, old boy, or you'll git it," said Texas Jack, from his side.

"Damn fool! What's he want to show himself thet way for?" ejaculated Lovelace.

"I doan see no more arrers," added Louisiana.

Pecos had marked the flight of arrows, like swallows streaking up from the gully, but in the excitement he had not made note of when this defense ceased. From beside Terrill he could not see down into all the gully. She had a perfectly steady finger pointing toward the heavy thicket of brush that lined the road. It was not altogether Terrill's finger that directed Pecos' attention to the important spot, but a shaking of brush, and then lean, dark, wild heads of mustangs.

"Heah, boys, quick," called Pecos, sharply. "They're shore goin' to make a dash." The three men crawled swiftly to his side. "Now look. See thet yellow rock with the cow skull stickin' on top?—Look beyond it a hundred steps, mebbe, on this side of the road where ——"

"Whoopee! I got 'em," shouted Jack, under his breath.

"Me too!—Gosh, if they was only closer!"

"Dey's close enuff fer dis nigger," remarked Louisiana, dryly. "I sho doan lub dem red debbils."

"Terrill, yu shore did a good piece of scout work," said Pecos, with great pride. "Heah I been thinkin' aboot yore blueblooded grandmother an' the delicate feelin's yu inherited! An' all the time yu're one of them greatest of women—a Texas pioneer's wife-to-be!"

"Haw! Haw! She's shore Texas, all right, boss," declared Jack.

"I reckon from this heah day she'll be Texas Terrill," drawled Lovelace.

"She doan gib me no creeps," added the negro vaquero. And thus the status of Terrill seemed established by practical hard men during a time of stress, at the wildest place along the wild Pecos.

The shooting ceased. No doubt Johnson's men were expecting the Kiowa band to burst out somewhere from under that pall of dust.

All of a sudden the dark, lean mustangs leaped out of the brush into the road.

"They're comin'," called Pecos, stridently. "Wait! —It's a long shot. Wait till they're even with us!"

Shots pealed from across the gully.

"Fellers, there's ridin'!" ejaculated Texas Jack, admiration wrung from him.

"Move boys! To the left! Don't shoot over Terrill!" ordered Pecos.

"—seven—nine—eleven," Terrill was counting.
"Heavens Pecos, look at them come!—Poor naked,
skinny things!"

The Kiowas strung up the road with mustangs
stretching low. No painted, feathered, colorful riders
these! . . . They fitted the wildness of the place. The
spirit of that ghastly country pervaded them. They
strung out in single file, dark, gleaming faces glancing back, rifles and bows aloft, their lean figures erect
with that incomparable horsemanship of the plains
Indians.

"My Gawd! cain't they ride!" exclaimed Pecos.
"Wal, boys, it'll be short an' sweet. . . . Get ready!
. . . *Let drive!*"

With the heavy boom of guns the erect forms on
the mustangs appeared to go over like tenpins. The
Kiowas at the flash and bang from that quarter slid
down on the off side of their mustangs and rode by
magnificently, with only an arm and a foot visible
over the backs of their racing steeds. In a few seconds
they had passed the zone of danger. Bullets kicked up
dust beyond. Then the string of Kiowas, as if by
magic, flashed behind a projecting bank and were gone.

"Wal, the boss had it figgered," said Lovelace, who
was the first to get up. "Short an' sweet."

"I never was no good at wing shootin'," declared
Texas Jack. Pecos rose from his kneeling posture, to
wipe the perspiration from his face.

"Didn't even skin one!" he ejaculated.

"Boss, it'd been a tolerable good shot to hit one of

them reddys standin' still from heah. An' these was goin' like greased lightnin'.''

"I never got a bead on nuthin'."

Pecos looked at Terrill, who had not moved. She lay with her rifle to her shoulder, pointing over the bank. "Get up, Terrill. It's all over. No scalps for us!—How many times did yu shoot?"

Terrill sat up. She was quite pale, but her eyes were dancing darkly.

"Pecos, couldn't they ride?—Oh, it was wonderful! —I guess I was too—too fascinated to shoot."

"Wal!—Say, young woman, just suppose they'd rode right up heah an' one of them was aboot to lift my hair! . . . What then?"

"You shore have beautiful hair, Pecos, and I wouldn't want you bald-haided. . . . Oh, my legs are weak!"

"Fellers, Johnson is yellin' fer us. An' there go the Slaughter boys down into the gully," said Texas Jack.

Pecos stood up to survey the scene.

"Yes, an' he means for us to rustle. Pile down to the wagons, men. . . . Terrill, give me yore hand. We'll make a run down for our horses."

In quick time Pecos and Terrill were in the saddle again. The horses were hard to hold. And the extra saddle horses, once unhaltered, broke and ran down the road. But the other men were appearing down there.

Presently the two factions of Pecos' party were re-united. Johnson, sweaty and dust-begrimed, talked while he tightened his saddle cinch.

"It worked jest as I'd planned. Must have been aboot twenty of them. We ain't hangin' around to see. Now drive the wagons right across. Tie them three saddle hosses behind the wagons. Leave the wagons over there an' come back to help us cross the stock. . . . Let's all work fast while our luck holds. I don't never feel good on this side of the river."

The wagons rolled downhill at a brisk trot. Pecos saw that the cattle had spread up and down the river, but none appeared to have strayed more than a quarter of a mile. They had drunk their fill and were now grazing. Watching the wagons splash into the water, Johnson said the river might be a little high, but would not give them any trouble. This was a wide, shallow, gravelly ford. The wheels scarcely sank over their hubs. In short order the wagons were across and up on the bank off the road.

"Come on, Texas Terrill; we gotta ride now," shouted Pecos, gayly, though anxiety vied with his hope. They joined the riders rounding up the herd. It proved to be far less trouble than Pecos had anticipated. They crowded the cattle gradually to the ford, then with ten riders in a half circle the wedge-shaped start was at last effected. Once the leaders had been forced into the water the greatest difficulty was passed. The river ran a little high and swift, with water slightly roiled.

"Look, Terrill, thet's the color of the water the day we got trapped. Remember?" called Pecos, as they splashed along in the rear of the herd.

"I reckon I've cause to remember, Pecos Smith," declared Terrill, dark meaning eyes on his.

Pecos had the satisfaction of crossing his herd in less than half an hour from the start.

"Say, Smith, do you know we picked up a couple hundred haid of stock over there?" queried Johnson, with a broad smile.

"No!"

"Wal, we shore did. There was a bunch on the downriver side. All wearin' an XS brand. I reckon some trail driver had a stampede here an' mebbe got wiped out. I seen burned wagons an' not so old."

Soon the long caravan was strung out on the west side of the river. From the highest point Pecos gazed back. The scene appeared the same as from the other side. Horsehead Crossing gleamed pale and steely under the wintry sun. There was no evidence of life. The white skulls of steers stood out distinctly, striking the deadly note of the place. It brooded there in its loneliness. Nature was inhospitable. It had allowed Pecos' caravan to pass; perhaps the next would be added to the tragedy of the past.

Chapter XVII

ALL the way from Independence Creek to the head of the Gulch Trail that led down to the ranch Pecos distributed his stock. When the last batch of weary cattle were turned loose Pecos and his cowhands rode back towards the river to join the wagons.

Eight days' drive from Horsehead Crossing! Pecos had to recall the camps to make sure of the number. How the days had flown! The long, long drive was over. Before sunset the wagons would be on the rim above Lambeth Ranch.

"It shore makes one think—all this good luck," soliloquized Pecos, solemnly. "Ever since I met thet boy Terrill—who was a girl. . . . Gawd bless her an' make me keep her safe an' happy. . . . No more of some things for me, an' one of them is Hosshaid Crossin'!"

From a high point on a ridge Pecos came out where he could see down the river. The scene gave him both shock and thrill. He seemed to have been long absent, and all at once to be plunged into the old, wild atmosphere of the brakes. The wide, bone-dry jaws of the canyon yawned beneath him, and stretched away with the green river showing. There was a white rapid close enough for Pecos to hear its low roar. The river bottom held wide green bands of mesquite, salt cedar and arrow-weed, and from these the gray brush-spotted slopes rose gradually to the ragged cliffs. Above spread the land for leagues and leagues, with grass and stone prevailing far as the eye could see.

As always, Pecos tried to find a way to climb out of the brake. It was a habit which operated instinctively. On either slope there was no place to which he would have put Cinco. Trapped there, he would have to go up or down the river. He gazed again at the boundless rolling range, with its gray monotony, its endless physical manifestations of solitude. West of the Pecos for him! It filled every need of his adventurous soul. And down there, ahead of the wagons, rode the little woman who had taught him self-reverence, self-control. Life loomed so sweet, so great that it stung him to humility.

The sun was still above the range when the wagons reached the rim above Lambeth Ranch. But it was sunset down in the canyon.

Terrill had dismounted to run wildly to the rim, where suddenly she stood entranced. Pecos followed. He hoped to look down upon the old tranquil place unchanged. How his gaze swept the opposite rim, the golden cliff, the purple caves and thickets, and finally the green meadows dotted with cattle and horses, the brook that was a ruddy streak of sunset fire, and lastly the old green-roofed cabin with its column of blue smoke winding upward.

"Looks like all was well, Terrill," said Pecos, feelingly.

Terrill squeezed his arm, but she was mute. One by one the other members of Pecos' caravan lined up on the rim. And just at that moment a flare of gold deepened on the bold face of wall across the river, to reflect its wondrous warmth back into the canyon. Low down the purple veils appeared to intensify and show caverns and gilded foliage through their magic transparency. From the cracked and cragged rim of the opposite canyon wall down over the seamed face and the green-choked crevices shone the mystic light, down the grassy, boulder-strewn slope to the second wall, and then sheer down this cracked and creviced form to the shining foliage, and the gold-fired flags and rushes that fringed the blazing brook.

This ephemeral moment held the watchers entranced. Then the glory and the beauty began to fade. And with that the practical Texans turned to necessary tasks.

"Smith, you never could have convinced me there was such a pretty brake along this gray old Pecos," observed Johnson.

"More'n pretty. It's a gold mine," vowed Slinger.

"Skins the brakes of the Rio Grande all holler, boss," added Texas Jack. "We'll shore stay with you heah till the old mossyhorns come home."

"Thanks, boys," replied Pecos, finding speech difficult. "Unhitch an' spread around. We'll camp on top heah tonight."

"How'n hell are we ever goin' to git the wagons down?" asked Lovelace.

"We'll take the old one apart an' let it down piece by piece," replied Pecos. "The others we'll leave up heah. Reckon we'll build a shed for them. . . . Cut a long pole, somebody, a good strong one thet we can fasten the pulley an' rope to. I fetched them along so we can lower our outfit easy."

"*Mauree-ee! Sambo-oo!*" Terrill was screaming in wild sweet peal down into the canyon.

Pecos ran to the rim. The echoes pealed back, magnified in all their sweet wildness, to mourn away in the distance.

"*Sambo!*" yelled Pecos, with all his might. *Samm-mbooo!* cracked back the echo, wonderful and stirring, to bang across to the great wall, and roll on, on, on down the river.

"*Mauree-ee!*" cried Terrill, in ecstasy.

"There they are!" exclaimed Pecos, in great satisfaction.

"Oh! Oh! Oh!" screamed Terrill, beside herself.

"Boss, dat yo come back?" rolled up Sambo's deep bass.

"Yes, Sambo, we're heah."

"Ah, Missy Rill, is yo all right?" called Mauree.

"All safe and well, Mauree."

"Is yo done married to dat Pecos man?"

"No-o! Not yet, Mauree!"

"How's everythin', Sambo?" shouted Pecos, gladly.

"Boss, I'se done hab trubble. New calves an' colts an' pickaninnies ——"

Pecos let out a roar, but it did not drown Terrill's shrill cry of surprise and delight.

"What yo sayin', Sambo?"

Mauree had disappeared around the corner of her little cabin, and when she hove in sight again with a black mite of humanity in each arm Sambo awoke the slumbering echoes once more:

"Dar yo is, boss. Two mo' black cowhands!"

"*Whoopee!*" bawled Pecos, giving vent to all that was dammed up in him.

Louisiana, like the other cowhands, had come to the rim again, drawn by curiosity. When the echoes of Pecos' stentorian climax had died away the vaquero yelled down:

"Hey dar, niggah."

"Hey yo'self," replied Sambo, belligerently.

"Seems lak I know yo. Is yo' name Sambo Jackson?"

"Yas, it am."

"I sho yo how glad I is when I come down dar."

In the dusk Pecos and Terrill sat on the rim above the canyon. Lano was singing a Spanish love song, the men were joking around the camp fire, a cow was lowing in the dark meadow.

Terrill had her head on Pecos' shoulder and at last she was weeping.

"Wal, darlin', what yu cryin' for now?" he asked, softly, stroking her hair. "We're home."

"Oh—Pecos—I'm—so—so happy. . . . If only—
Dad knows!"

The last gleam of the afterglow faded off the river.
Shadowy rifts of blackness marked the brakes of the
Pecos, in their successive and disappearing notches.
Night fell upon the lonely land. A low murmur of
running water soared upward. The air grew chill.
Wind rustled the brush. And a crescent moon peeped
over the dark bold canyon rim. The Pecos flowed on,
melancholy and austere, true to its task, unmindful
of the little lives and loves of men.

Chapter XVIII

PECOS moved the supplies down into the canyon
the next day, a strenuous job that left no time
for the sentiment that might have overcome him upon
returning to the ranch. Another day dawned with him
in the saddle, guiding this merry and bold outfit into
the brakes of the river. And that evening, finding Terrill rested, he yielded to his yearning and faced the
tremendous issue at hand. But he did not tell her then.

After Terrill had gone to bed, Pecos strolled up
and down, listening to the wild night sounds, watching
the moon slide down to the opposite wall, peering
into the river gap, slowly surrendering to the emotion
that had dammed up within him. He marveled why
God had been so good to him. Forgotten prayers
learned at his mother's knee came back to him. His
happiness and his responsibility, realized so stupend-
ously now in these lonely moon-blanched hours, magnified all the forces of his mind. On his lips still
lingered the sweet fire of Terrill's kisses, and he gazed
up at the watching stars with a breathless sense of
his ecstasy, while all the time he had the eye and the
ear of a hunted wolf. He had been trained in the
open. He did not trust the dreaming solitude. If some
raw wild spirit had spurred him to a tenacious grip
on his life, when he had nothing but the bold, reckless

pride of the vaquero, what now must transport him, make him invulnerable, to protect the beautiful and innocent life dependent upon him? He felt a mighty passion that swept him up and up, like a great storm wind, and rent asunder the veil of the mystery of love. He seemed to be illumined by the meaning of love, home, children, life, and death. He who had dealt death so ruthlessly!

In the gray dawn Pecos had met and solved his problem. He was a Texan. He was one of the moving atoms of the great empire he envisaged. He realized the chances; he knew the cost of success on that frontier. All could be met and vanquished, but only through an eternal vigilance, a lion heart and iron hand.

"Queer idees for a vaquero," he soliloquized, possessed with a sense of power.

The day broke beautifully to the melody of a mockingbird in the mesquite. The river slid on like a ribbon of red and gold. Pecos called the negroes and his riders to their tasks, while he went for the horses. Cinco came at a whistle, but the little buckskin mustang, as always, obeyed only a rope. It was when Pecos was on the back of one of these bewhiskered little beasts that his respect was roused. The mustang never tired, he lived on little grass and water, and he could climb or go down where even Cinco balked.

Pecos turned the horses in at the corral and strode on to the cabin. He smelled wood smoke and savory meat. Was Terrill really a girl? Had she been spirited away in the night? What queer pranks his imagination played him? He went in eagerly. After all, his eyes never deceived him.

"Terrill up?" he queried of Mauree.

"I done call her. Breakfast on de table."

There came a thumping of little hard boot-heels on the floor. Pecos wheeled from the fire. All was well with his world! Here was the glorious embodiment of all the night had brought in dreams, hopes, plans, beliefs.

"Mawnin' Pecos." The rich sweet voice had been the magic almost of a day.

"Sleepy-haid!" was all he said.

"Oh, I slept a thousand hours away."

"Thet's good. It takes yu a long way from yesterday. . . . Let's eat. We've shore got lots to do." And he placed a chair for her.

"Do?—I cain't do anything but run after you—all the livelong day."

"Thet'll be enough."

Where was the havoc wrought by the long trip? His keen eyes had to search for a little pallor, a little thinness in her cheeks. But youth had returned triumphant. Happiness shone in opal glow of skin and luminous eyes. She was hungry, she was gay, she was inquisitive. But Pecos gave her no satisfaction until the meal was finished, when with a serious air he led her out of the cabin, across the open grassy plot to his favorite seat under a tree. Here, surrendering momentarily to her charm, he drew her close.

"Pe-cos, some one might—see," she said, with what little breath he left her.

"See us? Heah?" He laughed and released her.

"Not that I object," she laughed. "But, you know, Comanches ride out on that rim sometimes. . . . If you want to—to hug me, let's go in."

"Terrill, we must rope an' tie up our problem," he said, earnestly.

"Problem? Why, we settled that all, didn't we?"

"It seems long ago an' I'm glad," agreed Pecos. "I stayed up all night. An' I thought, Terrill, I thought as never before in my life. . . . Come, sit heah by me, an' we'll talk aboot everythin'."

"Pecos dear—you're very—serious," she replied, almost faltering.

"Wal, don't yu reckon I've enough to be serious over? . . . When will yu marry me?"

She gave a sudden guilty start and red blushes waved from neck to cheek and brow. But he struck fire from her.

"Soon as we can ride to Eagle's Nest. Three hours if we push the horses, Pecos Smith," she flashed.

"Darlin', thet sounds like yu were callin' my bluff. But I'm in daid earnest. Yu will be my wife?"

"Si, Señor! . . . Oh, Pecos. . . . Yes—yes—yes."

"Wal, we won't run the hosses haids off, but we'll go today."

"*Today!*" she whispered, awed.

"Shore. Thet's the first step on our problem. Accordin' to thet—to what we heahed, this Judge Roy Bean can marry us. . . . By the way, Terrill, just how old air yu?"

"Guess."

"Wal, I said fifteen when I met yu an' I reckon I stick to thet yet."

"Way wrong, Pecos. I'm nineteen."

"No!"

"I am. Ask Mauree. I'm certainly my own boss, if that worries you."

"I'm yore boss, child. . . . So you're a grown-up girl, after all. Dog-gone! Thet accounts. I'm shore glad. Wal, thet's the second step on our problem. We're shore gettin' along fine. But the next's a sticker."

"Pooh!"

"Thet damned money. We've got a lot left. I've had a notion to burn it up. But thet's nonsense. Now Terrill Lambeth, use yore woman's haid an' decide for me. . . . I held it honest then an' I hold it honest now to brand mavericks. What brandin' I did with Williams an' Adams was straight. I never knew till it was all over thet they'd been burnin' brands. Then all the money fell to me. What could I do with thet any better than buildin' up a ranch for us? It all came from Sawtell. He was crookeder than Williams an' Adams. Made rustlers out of them. Led them on, meanin' to track them down, hang them, an' get his money back."

"Pecos, we shall keep what's left of that money and forget where it came from," replied Terrill, deliberately, almost without pause. "I know Dad would have done so."

"Honey, yu shore are a comfort," replied Pecos, huskily. "My conscience is clear on the moral side. There ain't any other. . . . So thet third step on our problem wasn't such a sticker, after all."

"Go on. We'll build a whole stairway, right to the sky."

"Terrill, we'll spend some of thet money."

"Spend it!" gasped Terrill.

"Shore. Squander a lot of it, if yu like," he drawled, watching her closely.

"*Where?*"

"Wal, say San Antonio."

She squealed in a frenzy of glee, mauled him with strong brown little fists, kissed him in a transport, all the while babbling wildly. Pecos could not keep track of the breathless enumeration of things to buy and do, but he gained a startling idea of what she had been used to back on the old plantation home. That gave him more insight into the family she had sprung from. He realized it had been one of blood and wealth.

"Say, sweetheart, if thet means so turrible much to you, we'd better hang on to most of this money, so we can go to town occasionally while we're gettin' rich."

"Oh, Pecos. I was just carried away. I would come to my senses and not buy everything. But I must have a woman's clothes."

"Shore. I savvy. Yu shall have all the damn linens, silks, laces, ribbons, all the flimsy stuff an' fine dresses yu want, a pack-saddle full of toothbrushes, hair combs, powders, an' all the jimcracks yu raved aboot."

"Oh, Pecos! . . . And to think I'll start off on my honeymoon in boy's pants!"

"Shore. An' yu'll come back in them, too."

"San Antonio!"

"Listen, honey, the seriousness is this, I reckon. We're goin' to stay heah always?"

"Why, Pecos!" she ejaculated, suddenly down to the earth of practical things.

"Yu love this place?"

"I love my Pecos River and my Pecos Vaquero.— Listen. I'll be serious, too. I suffered here. But I came to love the loneliness—all that makes this Pecos country. I have lived outdoors. I could never be happy in a city. I don't want to live among people. I couldn't think or be myself. . . . If it's for me to say, then this shall be our home—always."

"Terrill, yu've all to say aboot thet," returned Pecos, with strong feeling. "An' yu've settled it as I hoped yu would. . . . Now, little girl, let's face it as I see it. . . . As a cattle-raisin' proposition this range of ours cain't be beat in all Texas. The grass is scant, but the range is wide. We have pure water heah, an' a fine spring in Y Canyon. Halfway between an' back up on the rollin' ridges there's Blue Lake, a cold spring-fed waterhole where thousands of cattle drink. If cattle have pure water they don't need a lot of grass. When the river runs so salty the stock cain't drink, we have our other water, always steady an' pure. Thet means we can run fifty thousand haid of cattle in heah. It means what I so often joked you aboot when yu was a boy. Our fortune's made!"

"I believe you, Pecos. But, oh! the obstacles!"

"There's only one obstacle, honey, an' thet's the rustler," went on Pecos, thoughtfully. "He's heah an' he'll come more an' more. For years yet rustlin' will increase as the number of cattle an' prices increase.

I could hold my own, mebbe, but as yu've consented to be my wife—bless yore brave heart!—I'm not goin' to take the risks I've taken in the past. . . . We'll go get married. . . . Gosh! it's sweet to see yu blush like thet! . . . We'll have our honeymoon an' our little squanderin' fit. I shore have an outfit of cowhands who are the real Texas breed. I'll drill them into the hardest-ridin', hardest-shootin' bunch thet ever forked hosses. We'll ride these Pecos brakes together an', by Gawd! we'll make it tough for rustlers."

"Oh, Pecos! All Dad's life that was his dream. Wouldn't it be strange if he realized it through me? . . . And *I* shall be your right-hand vaquero."

"Terrill, yu're goin' to be a wife," he replied, forcibly.

"Shore. But I want to ride, too," she said, spiritedly. "If I cain't, well, I won't be your wife. So there!"

"Yu can ride yore pretty little bull-haid off! . . . But, Terrill dear, yu're such a kid. Yu don't know what bein' married means. We—things come aboot, yu know—happen to married people."

"I—I dare say," she replied, dubiously, leaning away to look at him.

"Yu cain't go on bein' a vaquero for-forever," he protested.

"No-o?"

"We'd want—yu know, yu cain't never tell—I shore love the idee—we—yu might ——"

"What under the sun are you talking aboot?"

Pecos knew he was not much on beating about the bush.

"Terrill, shore yu'd want a—a little Pecos ——"

She uttered a smothered shriek, and rolling away she bounded up to run like a deer. Halfway to the cabin she stopped to turn a crimson face.

"Pecos Smith, I'll be ready in a half-hour for anything."

By midday Pecos and Terrill rode into Eagle's Nest.

Pecos had scarcely stepped off his horse when he realized that this hamlet had changed in the interval since he had been there. Half a dozen Texas faces turned to him right in front of the new store, and one of them he recognized just the instant it broke its still repose to a warm smile. The owner of that face stepped out, a Texan of about Pecos' age, sunburnt, tow-headed, blue-eyed, a fine strapping fellow who yelped:

"Pecos Smith or I'm shore loco!" he ejaculated, and Pecos laughed to think what the Heald outfit would have thought of that.

"Howdy, Jerry Brice. I'm shore glad to see yore darned old skinny snoot."

"Been hidin' oot, you rascal," returned Brice, hanging on to Pecos' hand. "Heahed somethin' aboot you, though. Whar you goin'? What you doin'? Who's this heah boy with the big eyes?"

"Boy? Huh! Thet's no boy, Jerry. Thet's my girl, Terrill Lambeth. We're goin' to be married, an' by golly yu've got to see me through it. . . . Terrill, hop off an' meet a real shore Texas pard, one I'd be scared to have yu meet if it wasn't our weddin'-day."

Terrill came sliding off to slip to his side. Pecos ran his arm through hers and felt it tremble.

"Pecos, you amazin' dod-blasted lucky cuss!" ejaculated Brice.

"Terrill, this heah is Jerry Brice, an old friend. . . . An' Jerry, meet the sweetheart I was always gonna find some day—Terrill Lambeth."

"Wal, Miss Lambeth, this is more than a pleasure," said Brice, bareheaded before her, making her a stately bow. "I shore am happy to meet you."

"Thank you. I—I'm very glad to meet you," replied Terrill, flushed and shy.

Brice gave their horses into the charge of some one he knew and dragged them into a restaurant, where he divided his pleasure between compliments to Terrill and wonder at Pecos. They had dinner together, during which Brice told him of a new ranching venture he and his brother had undertaken in New Mexico, and which was going to be slow but sure. After that there followed an abundance of news. Pecos expressed surprise at the way sleepy little Eagle's Nest had come to life. At which Brice laughed and bade him wait till he saw something. Texas steers were on the move north. Dodge City and Abilene, the two ends of the great Chisholm Trail, were roaring towns. Rockport, the southern terminus, was full of trail drivers, cattlemen, ranchers, traveling settlers, gamblers, desperadoes, which was no news to Pecos. Stock prices were on the rise. Pecos asked innumerable questions, and finally got down to the most important thing for Terrill and him.

"How aboot this Judge Roy Bean?"

"Funny old codger. Shore is a law unto himself.

Justice of peace, magistrate, judge, saloon-keeper—
he's shore the whole show."

"Can he marry us?"

"Course he can. Good an' fast, too, so Miss Terrill
cain't get away from you."

"Thet's fine," retorted Pecos, with satisfaction.
"But all the same, Jerry, just to make *shore* I'll have
the weddin' service done over again when we get to
San Antonio."

They made merry over that while Terrill tried to
hide her blushes.

"Come on. Let's go an' get it over," drawled Pecos,
and so they went out together.

Pecos did not need to see all the new houses to
realize that Eagle's Nest had indeed grown. Even during the warm noon hour the streets were lined with
vehicles, saddle horses hitched, riders, trail drivers,
cattlemen, and idle sloe-eyed Mexicans. There were
ten Mexicans to every white man, so that altogether
there must have been a daily population at Eagle's
Nest in excess of two hundred. Pecos saw a couple of
familiar faces, the last of which dodged out of sight.
It would be natural, he thought, to gravitate toward
some incident calculated to be embarrassing on this
wedding-day.

Terrill did not have a lagging step. Her face
glowed and her eyes sparkled. When not directly
drawn into conversation or especially noticed she was
beginning to enjoy herself. She did not attract particular attention, though she clung to Pecos' arm.

"Say, Jerry, yu remember Don Felipe," said Pecos,

suddenly reminded of his former employer. "Heah anythin' aboot him?"

"Shore. He got run oot of Rockport. Down on his luck, Pecos. I reckon he's run his rope."

"Thet so. It ain't such awful bad news," returned Pecos, ponderingly.

"I met a trail driver named Lindsay. He has a ranch on the San Saba. Told me Felipe had an outfit half white an' half greaser, workin' the east brakes of the Pecos. Lindsay also said Felipe had a mix-up with Rangers in the Braseda last summer."

"Ahuh. Dog-gone! Things do happen." But straightway the momentary ominous regurgitation passed as they reached the court-house of Judge Roy Bean. Evidently something was going on, for there were a number of Mexicans on foot, and several mounted on burros.

"This is the back of his place," said Brice. "We'll have to go round in front, where I reckon he's holdin' court or servin' drinks."

The structure Bean called his court-house had been built of clapboards, and stood on posts high off the ground. A stove-pipe protruded from the roof. Presently the front of the building stood revealed—a rather wide porch upon which court was apparently in session.

"Thet's the judge settin' on the box at the table," said Brice, pointing. "The rest are greasers."

Pecos bent most interested eyes upon the judge. He appeared to be a short stout man, well along in years, with a long gray beard, cut round in a half circle. He was in his shirt sleeves, wore a huge light sombrero, and packed a gun at his hip. A Mexican peon stood bareheaded before him. There were three other Mexicans, all sitting in the background. A rifle leaned against the post nearest the judge. Behind him on the corner post was a board sign upon which had been painted one word—Saloon. Above the wide steps, at the edge of the porch roof, was another and much larger one bearing the legend in large letters—*Law West of the Pecos*. Above that hung a third shingle with the judge's name. Although Pecos and his companions were on the edge of the front yard, they could not distinguish what was said.

At this juncture two cowhands rode into the yard and dismounted at the steps. Red and lean of face, gun-belted and wearing shaggy *chaparejos*, they fetched a drawling remark from Pecos. "Folks, this heah is better'n a show."

"Howdy, Judge," called out the foremost rider as he doffed his sombrero. "Will you adjourn court long enough to save two hombres' lives a-dyin' of thirst?"

"Step right up, boys," boomed the judge, kicking his box seat back as he rose. "There ain't no law heah but me, an' we adjourn."

He waved the two tall cowmen into the courthouse, and stamped after them. The peon on trial stood there and waited. The other Mexicans peered in as if they would not have minded being invited to drink.

"Dog-gone me!" ejaculated Pecos. "If thet doesn't beat the Dutch!"

"Isn't he a funny old fellow?" whispered Terrill. "Fancy our being married by him! Pecos, it's all so like a story."

Presently the thirsty couple came out, followed by the judge, who was certainly wiping his lips. The cowhands strode down to their horses, led them aside a few steps, and proceeded to light cigarettes.

When the judge had reseated himself on his box he banged the table with a force and finality that presupposed he had imbibed instant decision while in the barroom.

"*Cinco pesos!*" he shouted.

One of the Mexicans jingled silver upon the table. Then all of them left the porch. The Judge closed his big book.

"Now's our chance," whispered Pecos, squeezing Terrill's arm. "Jerry, be shore to stick to us."

Terrill giggled, though laboring under suppressed excitement. Pecos whispered to her. "Honey, this shore is aboot all."

Pecos strode up on the porch, holding Terrill to his side. She dragged a little the last few steps. Brice hung back a trifle. Judge Bean looked up. He had hard, shrewd blue eyes and a good-natured, smug face. Pecos' instant angle was that this gentleman who constituted within himself all the law west of the Pecos might be eccentric, but he was no fool.

"Howdy, Judge," drawled Pecos.

"Howdy yourself. Who might you happen to be?" he replied, sharply, his gaze growing speculative.

"I shore got a lot of names, Judge, but my right one is James Smith."

"All right, James Smith. What you want heah in court?"

"Can you marry me?"

"*Can* I? Say, young feller, I can marry you, divorce you, an' hang you."

"Wal, I only want the first."

"Where's your woman? I'm tolerable busy today. Why you come bellyachin' aboot gettin' married, takin' up my time when you've no woman?"

"Heah she is, Judge," replied Pecos, who, despite his cool audacity and the poignancy of his errand, wanted to howl his mirth.

"Where?"

"Heah." And Pecos had to indicate the drooping Terrill.

"Hell! Are you drunk, man? This heah's a boy."

"Nope. Yu're mistaken, Judge," returned Pecos as he removed Terrill's broad-brimmed hat. "Hold up your haid, Terrill."

She did so, struggling with mingled emotions. And her face resembled a red poppy.

Judge Bean stared. He slammed both hands on the table. He was astounded. Suddenly his smug face beamed.

"Wal, I should smile you are a girl. Prettiest who ever stepped into this court. . . . What's your name?"

"Terrill Lambeth."

"Lambeth? I've heard that name somewhere."

"My father was Colonel Templeton Lambeth."

"How old are you, Terrill?"

"Nineteen."

Then the Judge turned to Pecos. "I'll marry you, Smith. What's it worth to get spliced to this pretty girl? It cain't be done nowhere else in this country."

Pecos saw through this old robber. "Wal, it's

shore worth aboot a million dollars to me," he drawled. "But I cain't afford much—no more'n say twenty."

"Fork it over," retorted the Judge, swiftly, extending one hand toward Pecos while with the other he felt for something in his desk.

Pecos was in an embarrassing position. He had forgotten to segregate a twenty dollar bill from the roll he had inside his vest. There was no help for it. When the Judge's eyes came up from a search for the little Bible in his hand and espied Pecos stripping a bill off that fat roll of greenbacks, they popped right out.

"Say, have you held up a bank?" he growled, snatching the bill Pecos dropped on the table.

"No. I been savin' up a long time for this heah occasion."

"I forgot to charge you for the certificate. That'll be ten more."

"Yeah. Make it twenty, Judge."

"All right, it's twenty," retorted Bean, and he took the second bill with alacrity. Then he opened the book and began to read a marriage service. He skipped some unimportant parts, but when he came to the vital points he was less hurried. The questions he put were loud and emphatic. But Pecos realized what was happening so fleetingly, and he choked over his "Yes," and heard Terrill's low reply.

"I pronounce you man and wife," finished the Judge. "Whom God has joined together let no man put asunder!"

Then he sat down at his desk to fumble in his drawer for the certificate which he soon filled out.

"Sign your names."

Pecos' hand was as steady as a rock, but Terrill's shook. Brice leaned over them and said, gayly: "Pecos, old boy, good luck an' long life! . . . Mrs. Smith, I wish you joy an' all ———"

A loud voice, slightly foreign, interrupted Brice.

"Señor Judge, stop da marriage!"

Brice exclaimed violently and wheeled to mark the intruder, a tall thin man in black sombrero. Pecos, who stood on the inside behind Terrill and his friend, froze in his tracks.

"What's eatin' you, Felipe?" boomed Bean, angrily. "A-rarin' into my court this way."

"I stop da marriage. Da Lambeth señorita ———"

"Hell, man! You'll stop nothin' heah, unless it's breathin'. . . . I've pronounced this young couple man an' wife."

"Oh, Pecos, it's Don Felipe," whispered Terrill.

"Jerry, take her aside," hissed Pecos, straightening up to push them toward the judge. Then in a single leap he landed in front of the steps.

His enemy, stalking swiftly, had reached the lower steps. His trim, small, decorated boot halted in mid-air, stiffened, slowly sank.

"Howdy, Don. The bridegroom happens to be Pecos Smith."

"Santa Maria!"

The half-breed's lean, small face, black almost as his stiff sombrero, underwent a hideous change that ended in a fixed yellow distortion. Fangs protruded from under his stretched lips. His slim frame vibrated under the thin black garments. And that vibration culminated in a spasmodic jerk for his gun. As it left the sheath Pecos fired to break his arm, but the heavy bullet struck the gun, spinning it away to the feet of the cowhands. Then a swifter and a different change transfixed the half-breed. He appeared to shrink, all except his beadlike eyes.

"Ump-umm, Don. Yu've got a bad memory," said Pecos, cold and sarcastic. "It's damn lucky for yu this is my weddin'-day."

Pecos aligned his gun a little higher, where it froze on a level, spurted red, and thundered. The bullet tore Felipe's stiff sombrero from his head and never touched a hair. Then Pecos aimed at the flowery silver-spurred boots.

"Dance, yu ——"

And he threw the gun down to fire again. This bullet cut more than leather. "Dance on my weddin'-day or I'll bore yore laig!"

Felipe made grotesque, almost pitiful dance steps until his will or flesh ceased to function.

"Wal, yu're as rotten a dancer as yu are a shot. . . . Stand still now ——! And heah me. I'm callin' yu before Judge Bean an' these cowmen, an' the rest of this outfit. . . . Yu're a low-down greaser-hirin' rustler. Yu hire pore ignorant vaqueros an' kill them to get out of payin' their wages. I rode for yu. I learned yore Braseda tricks. I know yu stole most of Colonel Lambeth's stock an' tried to steal his daughter. I chased yore new outfit across the river just a day or so ago. Brand-burnin' *my* stock. Watson caught yu an' got away, only to be shot by yore pard Breen Sawtell. An' before I killed Sawtell I got yore case from him."

Pecos spat as if to rid himself of the bitter restraint

he must hold this day. "An' now yu yellow-faced greaser dog! Get out! Get across the river! Hide in the brakes! . . . 'Cause if I ever lay eyes on yu again I'll—*kill* yu!"

Amid a stunned silence the half-breed lunged around, head down like a blinded bull, and spreading the crowd, he disappeared. Pecos stood motionless a moment, until suddenly he relaxed. He flipped his gun. It turned over in the air to alight in his palm. Sheathing it, he turned to face the fuming judge.

"Not on our marriage program, Judge," he said, with the old drawl edging into the ring of his voice.

"Hell, no! Not on my court proceedin's at all. . . . Pecos Smith, whoever yu are, yu have a high-handed way."

"Yes, an' yu better savvy this," retorted Pecos. "I've done yore little community a good turn. Thet man has been the bane of Eagle's Nest. Yu heahed why I couldn't kill him."

"Smith, I'm not rarin' aboot yore drivin' Felipe off. But it'd been a better job if yu'd bored him instead of shootin' fancy didos around him."

"Ahuh. Wal, what's eatin' yu, then?"

"It's agin the law, shootin' heah. Contempt of court. An' I'm compelled to fine yu, suh."

"What?" ejaculated Pecos, completely floored.

Terrill came hurriedly from the door to catch his arm and press it. "Oh—Pecos!" was all she could falter.

"I said 'contempt of court,'" repeated the judge, imperturbably. "I'm compelled to fine you."

"Leapin' bullfrogs! . . . How much, Judge Roy Bean, Law West of the Pecos, Justice of the Peace, Saloon-keeper, Bartender, an' Parson, an' Gawd only knows what else? How much?"

"I was aboot to say fifty dollars. But it's seventy-five."

"What'd it cost me if I'd plugged the breed?" inquired Pecos, sarcastically.

"I reckon my law on the case now reads one hundred dollars."

"Yu got Don Felipe skinned to death!" yelled Pecos.

"Upon reflection the fine imposed for more contempt of court will be one hundred twenty-five dollars—not pesos."

"Robber! Road agent!"

"One hundred fifty!" shouted Judge Bean, purple in the face.

Terrill gave Pecos a wrench that fetched his face round to hers.

"Pay him before he ruins us!" cried Terrill, and Pecos did not know whether she was bursting with mirth or alarm or both.

"Hullo, honey. Dog-gone! I forgot aboot yu. . . . Shore I'll pay it," he declared, whipping out the roll with magnificent gesture, and peeling off bills galore. . . . "Reckon I'm never goin' to be married again. . . . Heah, Judge, buy yoreself some lawbooks an' paint another big signboard in big letters: 'Shell out, stranger, or yu cain't get west of the Pecos!' "